Connor's New Wolf

Georgina Stancer

ISBN: 978-1-9160067-1-3

All characters and events in this book are fictitious. Any
similarity to real persons, living or dead, is coincidental and not
intended by the author.

Editing by Stacey Jaine McIntosh

Cover design by EmCat & Butterfly Designs

www.georginastancer.co.uk

This book is dedicated to my wonderful partner and children. Without their love and support, I wouldn't be where I am today.

CHAPTER ONE

Burning!

Pain consumed Anya along with the flames that covered her body.

She rolled around on the ground down a filthy alley in a desperate attempt to extinguish the fire. It was slowly melting away her skin right down to the bone.

The smell of singed hair and sizzling flesh filled her nose and mouth. She tried to fill her lungs with air so she could scream for help, but barely a sound made it past her parched lips.

"Help me!" She screamed as loud as she could, but nobody could hear her.

Nobody would come. Nobody else would be stupid enough to walk down an unlit alley, in the bad part of town, in the middle of the night. The only people who were likely to go down there were the homeless and less fortunate.

"Help me!"

Again, she struggled to force the words from her ravaged throat. Again, she failed.

Tears evaporated from her eyes before they even had a chance to reach her cheeks.

Scuffling sounds from the dark shadows surrounding her broke through the pain that racked her body, giving her a moment of hope before being quickly dashed.

Instead of the help she so desperately needed, she was met with a vicious snarl as an animal approached her. Undeterred by the flames consuming her, the animal pounced on her.

She could feel its breath against her face as it crushed her chest under its enormous weight. A second later, it sank its teeth into her neck, sending a shock wave of pain through her body.

Shit!

***

Anya bolted upright in bed. Her hands instantly flew to her throat, to where the animal had sunk its teeth into her. But there was nothing there.

There were no cuts or marks of any kind that she could feel. It was exactly the same as normal.

Her heart was racing as she leaned over to switch on the bedside lamp. Her hands were shaking so badly, it took her several tries before she was successful.

She blinked rapidly as her eyes adjust to the bright light. By the time she was able to see, the nightmare had begun to fade from her mind, but she still checked her neck and body for signs of blood or burn marks.

Her skin was hot to the touch, and she was covered

in sweat, but there were no signs she was ever on fire or bitten by a wild animal.

Exhaling with relief, she flopped back on the bed as she looked over at her alarm clock.

"3:27a.m. Perfect!"

Her alarm wasn't set to go off for another four hours.

"Stupid fucking nightmares," she grumbled as she kicked off the duvet and sat up again.

There was no way she would be able to get back to sleep after that nightmare, so she decided to she might as well get up for the day.

"On the upside, at least I'll be able to catch up on some housework before work."

As much as she didn't enjoy doing housework, it sounded like a lot better idea than lying in bed thinking about the nightmare for four hours. Which she knew would be the case.

She was already sat on the side of her bed thinking about the dream. That's when it occurred to her that she couldn't recall getting into bed. Nor how she got home from work.

The last thing she could remember, she was saying goodbye to her work colleagues as she headed towards the bus stop. Obviously, she made it home okay, but how? And why couldn't she remember?

It didn't matter how hard she tried to recall what happened after work, nothing came back to her. So, she gave up trying.

There was no point trying to force her mind to remember something. The more she tried to force the memory, the less chance she had of remembering.

Generally, when she stopped trying to think about something, it would come to her naturally.

Anya slid her feet into the fluffy slippers she kept at the side of the bed and then stood up. She stretched out her muscles before making her way to the bathroom, turning on all the lights along the way.

Normally, the dark didn't bother her. She knew the layout of her flat and could find her way around with her eyes closed, so she didn't need to have the place lit up like a Christmas tree all the time.

But tonight was different. The nightmare had scared the shit out of her so much that for the first time since she moved into the apartment five years ago, she didn't feel safe.

Once she was in the bathroom, she turned the shower on. It would take a few minutes to heat up, so she turned around and headed straight back to the bedroom to strip the bed while she waited.

It was times like this that Anya regretted not having more than one bedding set. Fighting with the sweat soaked duvet, she swore several times when it refused to do as she told it. She found herself tangled up in it more than once, and was completely out of breath by the time she was finished.

Huffing, she grabbed the pile of dirty bedding and took it to the kitchen. She threw it in the washing machine and switched it on before turning her attention to the coffee machine.

Steam billowed out of the shower by the time she returned to the bathroom. She quickly stripped out of her sweat soaked night clothes and stepped under the hot water.

Anya let out a sigh as the heat worked its magic and began to ease her tense muscles. After a few minutes soaking up the heat, she picked up the shampoo bottle and squirted a dollop on the palm of her hand. Massaging the suds into her scalp helped relieve the tension headache that was building.

She rinsed her hair before scrubbing her body twice. The remnants of the nightmare disappeared down the drain along with the soap bubbles.

When she was finished, she turned off the taps and stepped out of the shower. She wrapped a towel around her hair and then dried her body before wrapping another around her.

Before leaving the room, she stopped at the sink to brush her teeth.

Anya instantly regretted wiping the steam off the mirror above the sink. Dark circles surround her eyes. They were bad enough on their own, but coupled with paler than usual skin, and she looked like a panda.

"Ugh," she grunted as she pulled a face at her reflection.

Despite knowing it had been nothing but a nightmare, Anya couldn't stop her eyes from going to the spot where the animal had sunk its teeth into her.

As she expected, there wasn't a single mark on her. Not even a scratch or a faded bruise.

Anya could have sworn the circles around her eyes were getting darker by the second though.

Spitting out the toothpaste, she wiped her mouth. And with one last look at her reflection, she left the bathroom.

The coffee machine gurgled in the kitchen as she walked back through the open plan living area to the bedroom.

"Mmm."

There was nothing better than the smell of freshly brewed coffee first thing in the morning. The only thing that would make it better was if it was mingled with freshly baked pastries.

Admittedly, she would prefer not to smell either at that time of the morning, but what was she supposed to do? There was no way she could sleep again after the nightmare she'd had. Plus, she didn't have any clean bedding.

Even if she did manage to get back to sleep, she would just wake up in a bad mood later. And that would not go down well at work, so it was best not to bother.

She pulled on a pair of black yoga pants and a light grey vest top before drying her hair. She may be up, but it didn't mean she had to get ready for work just yet.

Anya grabbed her slippers from the bathroom before heading back into the kitchen to pour herself a large mug of coffee.

Deciding against doing the housework, she settled for watching the sun rise from her balcony. It was still pitch-black outside, but it wouldn't be long before the sky started to lighten and people began to emerge from their homes.

Anya didn't need to step outside to know it was

going to be cold. So, she grabbed her dressing gown from the bedroom first. As she walked past the sofa, she picked up the blanket hanging over the back of it for extra protection against the cold and then headed outside.

An icy blast hit her as soon as she opened the door. Anya shuddered as she pulled the dressing gown closed and tied the belt.

With a mug of coffee in hand, and a blanket chucked over her shoulder, she stepped out onto her balcony, closing the door behind her. It wasn't the largest of balconies, but it was plenty big enough for her.

A small table with two chairs were on one side, and a two-seater bench with a table in the middle were on the other. Potted plants lined the edges, turning it into her own little haven when they were in bloom.

Cocooned in her dressing gown and blanket, Anya sat on the bench and inhaled the crisp morning air. Letting the mug warm her freezing hands like a mini hot water bottle, she leaned back and relaxed as she waited for the sunrise.

***

The entire time Anya was out on her balcony, wrapped up in a blanket as she sat on the bench, he stood watching her from the street below.

Not once did she look down towards the street. If she had done, she might have noticed him watching her.

He probably could have stood in the middle of the road and she wouldn't have noticed. But it wasn't time for him to reveal himself to her yet, so he stayed partially hidden by the shadows.

It wasn't long before the sun rose and she went back inside, but he didn't leave even though he couldn't see her.

"Are you sure she won't remember?" he asked.

He didn't need to turn around to know a witch stood behind him. He picked up her scent the instant she appeared.

She was a beautiful woman, but he had no interest in her. The only thing he was interest in was her magic and what she could do with it.

Once she was no longer useful to him, he planned to kill her. But until that time came, he had to hide his abhorrence of her and her kind.

"I've already told you it will," she replied. "Trust me; you just have to give it time."

Even though he couldn't see her face, he knew she was rolling her eyes at him as she spoke.

He didn't trust her as far as he could throw her. For that matter, he didn't trust anyone. He'd made that mistake once before, he wasn't about to make it again. But for the time being, he had to keep her sweet while he needed her magic.

"I want you on call in case anything goes wrong."

"Nothing will…"

"I know nothing will," he interrupted. "Because you're going to make sure nothing does, or it will be your head I'm after."

"Don't threaten me," she ground out between clenched teeth. "I am not some weakling you can push around."

"That wasn't a threat," he told her. "It was a promise."

Without another word, she vanished just as quickly as she appeared.

CHAPTER TWO

Bang! Bang! Bang!

Anya groggily woke up to the sound of someone beating the shit out of her front door. Whoever it was, they had gone past the point of knocking politely and were being downright rude.

Realizing she had drifted off to sleep on the sofa, she rubbed her eyes and stretched as she sat up.

"Anya! I know you're in there." *Bang! Bang! Bang!* "Open the bloody door!" Sasha shouted as she continued to bang on the door.

"One sec," she shouted.

As soon as she realised who it was, Anya jumped up and raced to let her in. She quickly unlocked and swung open the door before Sasha could break the damn thing.

"What's wrong?" she asked, concerned that something bad had happened.

"What do you mean, 'what's wrong?'" she snapped. "I've been banging on this door for the last half hour!

Not to mention the amount of times me and the guys at work have tried calling you on the phone. Not once have you answered. Not once!"

Sasha was fuming as she entered the apartment and made a beeline for the coffee pot. Anya didn't have a clue what she was talking about. She hadn't heard her phone go off once while she'd been sleeping.

"You had us all worried that something bad had happened to you."

Pulling a face at the cold pot of coffee, Sasha tipped it out and began making a fresh pot. Anya sat at the breakfast bar and watched her move around in the kitchen.

"I haven't heard my phone ringing," she told her "It should have woken me because it's not on silent."

As usual, Sasha was impeccably dressed. Today she wore a light grey skirt suit that brushed the tops of her knees, paired with a light pink shirt and elegant six-inch black stilettos.

Her makeup was done to perfection, and not a strand of her long white hair was out of place from the intricate braid she had it in.

It must take her most of the morning just styling her hair.

Anya didn't know how Sasha had the patience to spend that amount of time on her hair and makeup in the morning.

Most of the time, Anya couldn't even be bothered to brush her hair, let alone doing intricate braids first thing in the morning. Putting it up into a ponytail was a lot quicker and easier.

Makeup was reserved for special occasions, like an odd night out on the town. It certainly wasn't something she was prepared to spend ages on as soon as she crawled out of bed.

"You didn't hear me beating the shit out of your door for the last half hour, either," Sasha pointed out as she switched the coffee machine on and set out two mugs on the counter.

"What do you expect at this time of the morning?" she asked. "Any sane person would still be asleep, not banging on other people's doors."

"Half past one in the afternoon is not early, Anya."

What the fuck?

That meant she hadn't just dozed on the sofa like she originally thought, but had slept solidly for hours.

"You're joking, right?"

Sasha scrutinized Anya as she shook her head and then tilted it with a concerned look on her face.

Well, at least I didn't have another nightmare.

That was something to be grateful for. She would rather not have a repeat of that nightmare.

Sasha's head was tilted to the side as she looked at Anya.

"What the fuck happened to you?" she asked.

"Nothing. Why?"

Anya ran her hands through her hair to try neatening it up, but it probably didn't make a difference. Bed head was always worse when she'd slept on the sofa for some reason.

"You look like shit," she said bluntly. "Are you feeling alright?"

"To be honest, I didn't have the best night's sleep," she admitted. "Do I really look that bad?"

"No, it just looks like you had a very… busy night," she said. "Did you have a late night visitor by any chance? Is that why you slept in so late today?"

"Sorry to burst your bubble, but no late night booty calls. Just a really, shitty, night's sleep," she reiterated.

"And here I was," Sasha said dramatically. "Hoping you finally had something juicy to tell me."

"Nope, sorry," Anya said. "Not unless you want to hear about my insomnia."

"I think I'll pass, thanks," she said. "But it is about time you found another man. You can't mope over what your ex did to you for the rest of your life."

Sasha was convinced the only way to get over a relationship, whether it was a bad break-up or not, was to jump straight into another one. Anya thought differently.

She wasn't interested in getting tangled up with another man. No, thank you. Her ex had been bad enough. She didn't need or want another man fucking up her life, not when she was finally happy and settled.

"Not interested."

"Oh, come on Anya. It's been how many years since you split from that asshole?"

Not only had her asshole of an ex treated her like shit, belittling her at every opportunity he got and making her feel inferior and that she deserved everything he did to her, but he also cheated on her with a multitude of women throughout their relationship.

Sasha was the one that told her about him cheating on her. Anya hadn't believed her at first. It wasn't until she'd witnessed it with her own eyes that she accepted what Sasha told her was the truth.

The first couple of days after she left him had been the hardest. With nowhere to turn, and no money to fall back on, she had no choice but to live in her car.

She had been asleep in her car when Sasha spotted her on her way into work early one morning. She swore to Anya that it would be the last time she'd have to sleep in her car, and it was.

Anya still didn't know how Sasha managed it, but by that evening Anya was moved into this amazing apartment with no bond and cheap rent. For the size of the apartment, and the area it was in, it should have been at least double what she was paying.

She owed Sasha big time for helping her out in her time of need, not to mention saving her from a shitty relationship.

"It doesn't matter, I'm still not interested," she said adamantly. "Now, can we please change the subject?"

It had taken her years to get over the humiliation, build her confidence back up, and mend her broken heart. Even though she was in a better place emotionally, she still wasn't ready for another man in her life.

"Okay, if you don't want to talk about men, how about a holiday instead?" Sasha asked with a cheesy grin.

"Now that, I'm happy to discuss," Anya replied,

with her own cheesy grin plastered on her face.

Whenever Sasha mentioned going on holiday, she always had something up her sleeve, and this time was no different.

"Before heading over here, I checked what days we both had left," she confessed. "We don't have many, but it's enough for a long weekend."

"Okay, so where are you taking me this time?"

Anya hadn't travelled much before they met. When Sasha found out she'd never been on a real holiday, she took it upon herself to rectify it. And in a matter of hours, she had their first of many holidays booked.

Anya had been sceptical at first. She wasn't sure it was a good idea to go on holiday with somebody she barely knew, but with a small amount of encouragement from Sasha, she finally gave in and was glad she did.

After that, Sasha became the sole holiday organizer, and Anya was more than happy to keep it that way. Sasha even managed to convince Anya to get a passport, so they could go abroad.

"Since it's just for the weekend," she said, dragging out the word 'weekend'. "I thought we could go to a swanky hotel and spa."

"Sign me up!" she said excitedly. "When do we leave? And where is it?"

Anya loved the idea of being pampered for a whole weekend.

She'd leave straight away if she could.

"This weekend, in Scotland."

Okay, that's somewhere we haven't been before,

Anya thought. *Might be a bit cold this time of year, but why the hell not? You only live once.*

They could easily wrap up in extra layers to keep themselves warm if they ventured outside. She would love to explore the rugged landscape, that's if the weather allowed it.

Anya had heard so many wonderful things about Scotland. She even had it on the list of places she wanted to visit, so she could finally tick it off. Plus, she could definitely do with being pampered.

"Yeah, I'm up for that."

"Brilliant!" Sasha shouted. "Have your bags packed ready to go Thursday morning."

Done with the conversation, Sasha turned around and continued pottering around in the kitchen. The coffee machine gurgled as she began searching the cupboards.

"Go get ready for work while I find something to eat," she said over her shoulder. "The guys need you in this afternoon. I tried getting you the rest of the day off, but they were having none of it, especially since we're now off for a long weekend."

"Okay," she said, sliding off the barstool and then walking towards the bathroom. "I won't be long."

Locking the door behind her, she switched the shower on before facing her reflection again.

Just as she suspected, running her hands through her hair had made absolutely no difference. She looked like she'd been dragged through a bush backwards, and sideways.

The dark circles around her eyes hadn't disappeared

any. They were still just as dark as they had been before she fell asleep.

For fuck's sake.

No wonder Sasha thought she was ill. She genuinely looked it. It was going to be one of those rare occasions when she needed makeup, if only to hide the dark circles and bring some colour back to her skin.

Anya quickly jumped in the shower before heading into her bedroom to get ready. It took her less time to pick out an outfit and get dressed, than it did to apply makeup. But at least she looked human again.

She slipped on some low heels to finish off her outfit, and then with one last look in the full-length mirror, she left the room.

By the time she emerged from her bedroom, Sasha had made her some toast and set it down at the dining table along with a large mug of coffee. Her stomach rumbled at the smell.

"You look more human now," Sasha said as she joined her at the table.

"Thanks."

"By the way, you need to seriously go shopping," she pointed out. "There is fuck all in the cupboards, and I just used the last of your milk."

"Yeah, I know," she said. "I'm going after work tonight."

She was meant to go on her way home from work the night before, but that obviously didn't happen. She still couldn't remember how she got home, so it was no surprise she hadn't gone shopping.

"Anyway," Sasha said. "Eat up and let's get going."

Anya suddenly lost her appetite. An uneasy feeling turned her stomach, but since Sasha had gone to the trouble of making it, she forced herself to eat at least half of it. Each bite was like eating a handful of sand.

When she couldn't force herself to take another bite, she quickly gulped down the coffee before taking the dirty dishes to the sink.

"Ready?" Sasha asked.

"Yeah, just let me grab my bag."

After a few minutes of searching, she finally found it on the floor in her bedroom. She usually hung it up with her coat, so she was surprised to find it on the far side of her bed.

Something was definitely off about the night before, and it was starting to worry her. It wasn't like her to completely forget even a small amount of time, let alone hours. Since she didn't drink or take drugs, she couldn't blame it on either of them.

"You okay?" Sasha asked.

Anya spun around at the sound of Sasha's voice behind her. She had been so engrossed in trying to recall what had happened, that she hadn't heard Sasha walk up behind her.

She swallowed down the lump in her throat before replying.

"Yeah, I'm good," she lied. "Let's go."

Sasha had a concerned look on her face, but she didn't pry, which Anya was grateful for. She didn't want to lie to her friend, but she didn't want to worry her over nothing either. So, it was best not to say anything.

Thankfully, Sasha changed the subject. She talked about all the spa treatments the hotel had to offer, and the order in which she was going to try them. She was still talking about it as they waited in line at the bakery around the corner from where they worked.

While waiting for their order, Anya got an unnerving feeling that she was being watched. She casually looked around the small bakery, but she couldn't see anyone that seemed to be paying her any attention.

By the time their order was called out, Anya was more than ready to leave the shop. But if she thought the feeling would go away, then she was sorely mistaken. It just intensified when she walked outside.

Her legs were shaking uncontrollably when they finally reached work. It took all of Anya's willpower not to let her hands shake as well.

CHAPTER THREE

Listening to his alarm going off in the early hours of the morning, Connor regretted offering to take the early shift, but he'd promised his friend.

Kellen needed the time off to deal with the trouble his little sister, Kayla, had gotten herself into. She was a typical teenage pup, always getting into mischief.

He groaned as he sat up and stretched. He shut off his alarm before heading into the bathroom for a quick shower.

After spending the entire night trying to save a female from being ripped apart repeatedly, he was more exhausted than before he'd gone to bed, and it wasn't the first night either.

Whoever the female was, she had picked the wrong place to visit if she expected to get out alive on her own. That's assuming she was real and not some fucked up figment of his imagination, which was a high possibility.

Every time he'd drifted off to sleep, he'd found himself in one of the Hell realms. He knew all about the other realms, it was something all shifters were taught when growing up, so he knew what to expect to see in each one.

Some realms were absolutely stunning. The Fae and Elf realms were prime examples, neither of which compared to the beauty of his home, though. Nothing could beat the beauty of the Shifter realm.

Some were harsh and unforgiving, where danger lurked in every shadow. The Hell and Demon realms were some of the deadliest. Connor avoided them as much as possible. There was too much death and destruction that ran rampant in those places.

He knew all too well of the creatures from that realm. They were what humans described as hell hounds. Dog-like creatures with mangled black fur and beady red eyes. Blood and saliva dripped from their gaping maws.

They were vile creatures that killed anything, and everything, they came across.

Each time the dream started the same. He would open his eyes at the sound of her screaming, and then he'd quickly leap up and search for her in the distance.

He would spot her nearly instantly, but she was never alone. The hell hounds were always catching up with her.

They weren't something he wanted to take on alone, whether in his wolf or human form. Their teeth were as sharp as knives, and once they had hold of someone, they weren't letting go without taking a chunk of flesh with them.

Even knowing they would rip him to shreds given

half the chance, he still tried to save the female. He couldn't stand by and watch an innocent person being torn to shreds, it wasn't in his nature.

Unable to shift in the dream, he tries in vain to catch up with her in human form before they do. His human form he was a lot stronger and faster than any normal human, but he still wasn't fast enough. They always caught up with her first, and began ripping her apart before he was anywhere near her.

The dream would suddenly end as they ripped into her. His heart raced every time he jolted up in bed, covered in sweat, and her screams still ringing in his ears.

After a quick shower, he dressed before making his way downstairs. Aidan was already waiting for him in the kitchen when he walked in.

"You're up late," Aidan said. "Are you still not sleeping?"

"I'm sleeping," Connor said honestly. "Just not very well."

"You look like shit," Aidan was blunt as usual.

"Cheers," he said sarcastically.

As one of his oldest and closest friends, Connor was used to Aidan's bluntness.

Growing up in the shifter realm together, along with their friend Kellen, had been nothing but fun. They had spent most of their childhood honing their hunting and fighting skills through play, much to their mother's displeasure. But it had been an integral part in preparing them to be active members of the wolf pack.

"Did you get any sleep last night?" Aidan asked.

Connor held a hand over his mouth to cover a yawn before he could reply. "Not much."

He poured a cup of coffee and then joined Aidan at the table, slumping in the chair opposite.

"You still dreaming about that female?" he asked as he leaned on the table.

"Yep."

"Any closer to figuring out who she is?"

If he knew who she was, he would be able to track her down and warn her about the danger she would be in if she travelled to the Hell realm. That's if she wasn't just a figment of his imagination.

Plus, if she was real, she might be able to tell him why he was dreaming of her in the first place. But unfortunately, the only thing he knew was that she had long strawberry blonde hair and pale skin.

Connor shook his head. "No, but I think she might be getting closer."

"What do you mean 'closer'?" he asked. "Did you manage to get a closer look at her this time?"

"No. I don't know." Connor couldn't hide the frustration in his voice. "I haven't been able to get closer to her in the dream. I just have this feeling that she's... physically... closer, if you know what I mean."

He would be amazed if Aidan understood what he meant. Especially since he didn't understand it himself.

"So, you still don't know what she looks like?"

"No," he sighed.

"What are you planning on doing about it?"

"There isn't anything I can do about it," he said.

"Until I know who she is, or what she looks like, there's nothing I can do."

"Have you told Rush about last night?"

"No, not yet," he admitted. "I was planning on telling him later today. But there isn't anything he can do either."

As Alpha of their pack, Rush needed to know what was going on, otherwise it would make his job a lot harder, and ultimately, their job as well. Connor had already informed Rush about the dreams, he just hadn't updated him on the latest one. Not that he could do anything about the dreams.

"Yeah, that's true," Aidan agreed.

"Anyway, we've got work to do," Connor said, changing the subject.

He didn't want to even think about the female anymore, let alone talk about her. It was frustrating the hell out of him that he couldn't get close enough in the dream to find out what she looked like.

He couldn't wait for the dreams to stop so he could have a decent night's sleep again, but he had a feeling that wasn't going to happen until he figured out who the female was and how to help her.

"How come you're working today?" Aidan asked. "I thought Kellen was supposed to be on patrol today?"

"Kayla's in trouble again," he said. "So, he's had to go and deal with that."

"What's she done this time?"

"I don't know, but I'm sure we'll find out soon

enough."

Connor pulled on his boots and then downed the last of his coffee before taking the cup over to the sink.

"I heard she's been hanging around the mountains, near some of the Dragon caves," Aidan said. "I wonder if that's where he's gone today."

"Where did you hear that?" Connor asked.

"From Caleb and Misti," he said.

It didn't surprise Connor that his younger siblings knew about Kayla hanging around in the mountains. Those three were as inseparable as Connor, Aidan, and Kellen had been when they were that age.

"It wouldn't surprise me if they're involved as well," he said honestly.

Generally, if one of them was involved in something, the other two were as well.

"You should ask them," Aidan told him.

"Oh, trust me," he said. "I will be asking them, and they best give me the right fucking answer."

One way or another, they were going to tell him everything they knew about what Kayla had been up to. And if it turned out they had anything to do with it, he would make sure they shared whatever punishment was dished out.

"Anyway," he said. "It's time to go."

"Yeah, I know."

They weren't the only hunters out on patrol today. There were always at least a dozen groups patrolling the boundary of their territory. Normally, it was small groups of two or three people, depending on who was on duty.

It wasn't that they were expecting to have problems with the other shifters in the realm, but they weren't the only ones with access to the realm either. There were plenty of other beings that could find their way to the shifter realm.

Some knew where to find the portals, and others had the ability to use magic to get them there.

Humans were not an issue. The portals in the human realm, no matter what realm they lead to, were concealed with magic. It was a protective barrier that prevented the humans from accidentally finding their way through to any of the other realms.

It was one of the reasons they had been able to stay hidden from the humans for so long, that they eventually turned into myths and legends. They were nothing more than stories told to entertain or frighten, which suited them just fine.

Every time a different species had shown themselves to the humans, they had been hunted down and brutally killed. Witches were prime examples. The witch hunts had been some of the most brutal in recent history.

Thankfully, the humans weren't able to kill them all. Some still lived among them, but most had left the realm in search of a safer place to live. Somewhere they didn't have to hide who and what they were.

He knew if they were ever exposed to the humans again, it would lead to another mass murder. Only next time, it would be the humans that would suffer the greatest loss.

Connor followed Aidan outside and closed the door

behind them. He didn't bother locking the door, there was no point. Anyone who wanted to get in would be able to, whether he locked it or not.

Plus, with his heightened senses he would know if anyone had entered his home while he was out, even if they didn't touch anything.

Once on the veranda, they both shifted. One second they stood on two legs in human form. In the next, they were on all fours, looking out at the world from a wolf's perspective.

Connor opened a telepathic link and asked, *"You ready?"*

"Yeah, let's go," Aidan replied before loping off the porch and running in the direction they were to patrol.

Being on patrol wasn't a bad way to spend the day. He enjoyed being in his wolf form surrounded by nature, so he didn't mind patrol duty.

They rarely came across any problems. The other shifter packs generally kept to themselves. It was mainly their own youngsters that caused trouble, and they were easily dealt with.

Occasionally, beings from other realms thought they could stir up trouble among the shifters, which was why they needed to be on constant patrol. There had even been the odd one or two that had tried to take over the realm, but none of them ever succeeded.

Shifters, no matter what species, always pulled together whenever something like that happened. They were always able to put a stop to the intruders before they could do any real damage.

Shifters protected what was theirs, to the death if

need be.

"What are your plans for this afternoon?" Aidan asked after a while.

"I need to update Rush on the dream from last night," he said. *"After that, I'm having dinner at my parents' house."*

"Are you going to ask Caleb and Misti what they know about Kayla?"

"Definitely." It was one of the first things he planned on doing when he goes to his parents' house. *"Because no doubt they have something to do with it. I'm not letting Kayla take all the heat if they're just as much to blame."*

"I don't blame you," Aidan said.

"How about you?"

"The same as usual," Aidan admitted. *"I'm just going to hang out at the club house for a bit. See if any of the females want company for the night, then go home."*

Aidan spent most of his time at the club house. It was where everyone in the pack went to socialize and have fun. The building was the size of a large warehouse, with multiple rooms inside.

Each room was completely different inside, so as to accommodate everyone in the pack. There was a bar in one of the rooms, and a nightclub in another. Another room was set aside for the elderly, so they had somewhere quieter to socialize if they wanted.

There was even a large soft indoor play area for the little ones in the pack. They could be dropped off to play safely while another member of the pack looked after them. It gave their mothers a break for a little while, so they could relax in one of the other rooms.

"I'm surprised you manage to get anyone to go back to your parents' house with you," Connor laughed. *"You know, you would probably have better luck if you had your own home."*

"You'd be surprised how many females are more than happy to share my bed, even though I still live with my parents," Aidan boasted. *"I definitely have more luck than you, and you've got your own place."*

It wasn't a case of luck. Connor wasn't interested in just sex. He wanted a long term relationship. He wanted to find his mate. But first, he wanted to get to the bottom of the dream so he could get them to stop.

CHAPTER FOUR

Sasha had definitely outdone herself. The accommodation was spectacular, and the location was even better.

The hotel and spa was in the middle of nowhere, surrounded by beautiful woodland and overlooked by mountains. The closest town was at least five miles away, if not further.

She had booked Anya into a large spacious double bedroom with en-suite bathroom. The bedroom was beautifully decorated in reds, browns, and golds.

The en-suite was just as spectacular. It had a huge fitted walk-in shower with a waterfall effect on one side, and a claw footed bath that overlooked the mountains.

Anya took full advantage of the views while she waited for dinner the first night. She lit candles all around the bathroom, added some bath salts and essential oils to the water, and relaxed with a glass of wine that she continually topped up.

She had lazily watched the sunset through the window. It was the perfect end to an incredibly long drive, one that was made even longer by Sasha constantly asking if they were there yet.

After dinner, she had snuggled down in bed dressed in the fluffy white bathrobe the hotel had supplied. It was so incredibly soft; she wanted to take one home with her.

She had left the curtains open before climbing into bed so she could look out at the stars. It had been nice watching the stars twinkle in the sky as she fell asleep, but waking up the next morning with the sun beaming in through the window was a different matter.

She wasn't much of a morning person at the best of times, but after another restless night's sleep, she was even more grouchy than normal.

Her hopes of having a nightmare free night had been dashed as soon as she drifted off. It didn't matter how hard she tried to steer the dream to something else, she was dragged straight to Hell to repeat the same nightmare over and over again.

Anya was sick and tired of the nightmare. All she wanted was a good night's sleep. So, to help wear her out, she decided to go for a hike up the mountain.

Determined to get a good night's sleep, she went for a quick swim before breakfast, and then got ready to go for a hike. She couldn't wait to explore the area.

She had heard so many wonderful things about the Scottish Highlands over the years, and she wanted to see if they were true. So far, she hadn't been disappointed.

Anya pulled on her coat and backpack before heading out. She had packed a few essentials to last her the day, along with a map and compass.

"Where are you going?"

Anya leapt at the sound of Sasha's voice behind her as she was locking the bedroom door ready to leave.

"Bloody hell, Sasha," she said, holding a hand over her heart. "You're going to give me a heart attack one of these days."

"Sorry," Sasha told her, looking anything but sorry as she tried to hide a grin behind her hand.

"Don't sneak up on me like that," she admonished.

"I didn't sneak," she said adamantly. "You just weren't paying any attention."

It was true; she hadn't been paying any attention to what was going on around her, which was unlike her. Normally, she noticed everything. But since the nightmares had started, she was struggling to concentrate on anything, let alone her surroundings.

Not only that, but every time she did pay attention to her surroundings, she would get the feeling of being watched. Anya didn't know what was worse, the nightmares or the feeling of being stalked.

"Shall we start again?" Sasha asked with a lopsided grin. "Good morning, Anya, how are you today."

"Good morning to you too," Anya couldn't help smiling back as she replied. "I'm fine, how are you?"

"Can't complain," Sasha said. "After all, we're in such a beautiful place, and I have a full day of pampering ahead of me."

Anya had to admit, it was a beautiful place, but she

didn't want to spend the entire time indoors.

"Now that we have the pleasantries out the way," she said, raising her eyebrows. "Where are you going?"

"I'm just going for a hike."

"What? At this time of the morning?" Sasha said dramatically.

She looked at Anya as if she was crazy, and maybe she was. Thinking about it, she must be mad going on a hike when she could be getting pampered all day, but that wasn't going to stop her. She was looking forward to a day out.

Anya smiled as she shook her head at Sasha's theatrics. "It's the best time to start if I want to get in a full day of hiking."

It was more of a guess than actual knowledge. She had never been on a hike before, so she didn't have a clue when the best time was to start one. And honestly, it would probably turn out to be more of a walk in the woods than an actual hike up the mountain.

"You're going to be out all day?" Sasha asked.

"That's the plan," she said. "I don't mind waiting for you if you want to come with me?"

She said the last part as more of a question, but she already knew what the answer would be.

"Nah, it's okay," Sasha said, confirming her suspicion. "It's not my type of thing. I'd rather just go down to the spa and be pampered all day. Have fun though."

Anya didn't know if it was her type of thing either, but she would soon find out. She had been itching to explore the area since before they had even arrived.

"Well, the offer is there if you change your mind," Anya told her.

"Yeah, I know," Sasha said. "I don't think I will change my mind, but thanks anyway. Are you going to be back in time for dinner tonight?"

"Yeah, I will be."

At least, she hoped so. As long as she didn't get lost along the way, she should make it back in time without a problem.

I best pay attention then, she thought to herself.

"Do you want to meet me in the restaurant for dinner at around seven?" Sasha asked. "Will you be back by then?"

"I should hope so, but that's as long as I don't get lost," Anya said jokingly.

The last thing she wanted to do was to get lost in the Highlands on her first day there.

"Please, don't get lost," Sasha pleaded. "I don't fancy calling mountain rescue to come and find you."

"All those hunky highlanders?" Anya asked. "Are you sure you don't want me getting lost?"

"Ooh," Sasha said dreamily. "On second thoughts, get lost. You never know, one of the rescuers could be the man of your dreams."

"More like the man of your dreams," Anya pointed out.

"Nah, I'm too picky," Sasha said, pulling a face at the thought. "Plus, knowing my luck, they would all be married, or old enough to be my dad."

Anya shook her head at Sasha. After all the times

Sasha had tried setting her up with different men, she hadn't once seen Sasha with a man of her own.

Anya didn't know what the deal was there, and she wasn't going to pry either, but it did make her wonder. Why was Sasha eager to set Anya up with someone, but not want to get into a relationship herself?

It was one of the many mysteries about Sasha that she would probably never get to the bottom of.

"I think I'll pass as well, thanks. As long as I stick to the pathways, I shouldn't get lost," Anya said, steering them back to a safer subject.

"Just to be on the safe side, show one of the reception staff the route you plan on taking," Sasha told her. "They know the area and will be able to direct the rescue team to your location if you do get lost."

"I'm not going to get lost," she assured her. "I promise."

"I know, but still tell someone," she insisted. "Otherwise, I'm going to worry."

"Okay, just for you," Anya relented.

She was happy to do it even if it was just to give Sasha some peace of mind.

"Thank you. Are you having breakfast before you go?"

"Already had some, got a packed lunch and snacks in my bag, and plenty of water to last the day," she said proudly.

"Sounds like you have everything you need. Just don't forget…"

"…tell them where I'm going," Anya interrupted.

"Don't worry, I'll tell them on my way out."

"Okay, good," she smiled. "I'll see you later. Have fun and stay safe."

"Yes, mum," Anya said as she turned and began walking away. "You have fun too."

Anya heard Sasha's bedroom door close as she reached the end of the corridor and headed downstairs. She made sure to stop at the reception desk to show them the route she was planning on taking.

She hadn't picked a strenuous route, where she might need a guild and climbing gear. It was a well-used one that was easy enough for anybody to do by themselves, so she was confident she wouldn't get lost.

Once that was taken care of, she finally stepped outside and took in the sight. The early morning sun bathed the mountains in golden light, inviting her to explore their wonders.

Anya stood still as she admired the scenery and breathed deeply, taking as much of the crisp clean air into her lungs as she could. She stayed like that for several minutes before setting off on foot for the start of the trail.

She wasn't in a rush, so she strolled leisurely up the mountain. It didn't take long for her to be fully engrossed in the beauty around her. The highland mountains were definitely a stunning place, and she was glad Sasha had brought her there.

Before long, Anya had completely lost track of time as she walked through open fields and enclosed woodlands. The only thing she kept an eye on was the trail as it led her further up the mountain.

She paused a few times along the way to take photos. It was a good job she had brought her camera with the memory card in it. Her phone would have run out of space in no time with the amount of photos she had taken.

She stopped for lunch in a small clearing. It had a well-placed rock that was large enough for her to sit on. The ground was still slightly damp from the morning dew and she didn't want to risk getting a wet bottom.

It would be just her luck that someone would see her with a wet ass and think that she'd pissed herself. So, she was over the moon to find a dry rock to perch on.

While she'd been sat eating her lunch, she spotted an eagle flying above her. Anya didn't know if it was a good sign or not, but she was going to take it as a good one.

Then, as she was packing away her rubbish ready to carry on walking, she spotted a family of deer nestled among the trees. The graceful creatures graze as they meandered through the foliage.

Anya was in awe of the wildlife she was seeing along the way. She was glad she had decided to go for a hike, and she couldn't wait to tell Sasha all about it at dinner.

Once the family of deer had moved on out of sight, she picked up her backpack and carried on up the mountain.

***

"Are you sure she's heading in that direction?" he demanded.

As soon as he realised where she was going with her friend, he had tasked one of the demons working for him to follow her and report back. It was a good job he had done; otherwise, he wouldn't have known that she was staying in a hotel close to the portal that led to the shifter realm.

That in itself wasn't a problem. The fact that she was heading dangerously close to the portal was the problem.

"Positive. What would you like me to do?" the demon asked.

He considered the pros and cons of her being found by one of the shifters before replying. There were many points for each, but he eventually decided not to intervene.

"Stay with her," he said. "But make sure you're not seen. If they come in contact with her, or she stumbles upon the portal, I want to know about it straight away."

"Do you want me to intervene if they do?"

"No," he snapped. "I don't want you to be seen, especially by them."

If they did come across her, they would just think that she was like any other human. But if they realized she was being followed by a demon, they were more likely to get involved.

He didn't know how long she planned to be away, but it didn't matter. Come the next full moon, whether he had to retrieve her from the shifter realm or not, she would be in his grasp.

CHAPTER FIVE

The morning had passed without incident, just as Connor knew it would. Thankfully, the time flew by.

After work, he headed straight over to Rush's house to speak to him about the dream. He'd explained as best he could about how she felt closer, but he couldn't elaborate on what that might mean.

Other than keeping Rush updated, there wasn't much either of them could say or do until they found out the identity of the female. Until then, he just had to carry on as usual, no matter how frustrating it was.

He couldn't stop the last dream from playing out over and over in his head. But it didn't matter how many times he replayed, he couldn't figure out what was different. As far as he could tell, it was exactly the same as ever other one, except for the feeling that she was closer.

Did it mean she was physically closer to him in real life? Or was there an entirely different meaning to it?

Connor pushed it to the back of his mind as he

walked into his parents' house. He found his mother, Amelia, cooking dinner and packing a picnic basket.

"Mm, something smells nice," he said as he walked up behind her.

He leaned over her shoulder to grab a warm bread roll that was fresh out the oven. He kissed her on the cheek at the same time as a distraction, but it didn't work. She slapped his hand away and tutted at him.

"Well, you can keep your grubby hands to yourself," she said, nudging him away with her elbow.

"Aww, come on Mum, just one little bread roll?" he pleaded in his sweetest voice.

"No! You can wait like everyone else," she told him as she shooed him out the kitchen. "They're all in the living room, so go see them while you wait."

"Okay, okay. I'm going," he said as he backed away from her with his hands held up in surrender.

Before leaving the room, he watched her for a moment as she added more food to the basket. As far as he was aware, everyone was supposed to be home for dinner. Not that they all lived there anymore.

Both he and Myra had moved out years ago. Only Caleb and Misti still lived at home because they were too young to move out yet.

So, if everyone was there for dinner, then what was with the picnic basket?

"Who's the basket for?" he asked.

"It's for Myra, she not staying for dinner." She didn't look up as she answered him.

"Why? Where's she going?"

"She's going over to help Kellen with Kayla," she

said.

"And you're sending her with food?"

"I thought it would be nice for the two of them to have a proper home cooked meal for once," she told him.

"You know," he said. "Kellen does know how to cook, and so does Kayla."

It wasn't the first time Connor told her, but it didn't make a blind bit of difference. Amelia was adamant that they needed a proper meal every so often.

Ever since Kellen's parents had died, Amelia had taken it upon herself to watch out for them. It was in her nature, and nothing was ever going to change that.

Connor knew it had been hard for them when they lost both parents close together, especially since Kayla was barely older than a toddler at the time. So, he had appreciated all the help he could get.

When shifters mated, it was for life. So, when one mate died it was only a matter of time before the other mate followed them into the afterlife. In Kellen's case, his mother had died of an illness and his father joined her a couple of days later, leaving Kellen and Kayla to fend for themselves.

Luckily, Kellen was old enough to take care of him and Kayla; otherwise another pack member would have taken them in until they were ready to live on their own.

"That may be so," she said, finally turning around to look at him. "But it doesn't hurt to have someone else do it for them every once in a while." She turned her back on him again as carried on packing the picnic basket. "That poor boy has his hands full just looking after Kayla; he could do with a break from cooking."

There was no point arguing with her, it wouldn't make any difference. Once she had her mind set on something, there was no changing it.

She was right about Kayla being a handful. Connor didn't envy the responsibility Kellen had in caring for her. She would probably be constantly locked in her room if it was left to him.

"So, I take it Myra isn't staying for dinner?"

"No, she's going to have dinner with them tonight," she said. "She'll be leaving as soon as I've finished packing everything in the basket."

"So, she's still here?"

"Yes, she's in the other room getting ready to leave."

"Who else is here?"

"What is this?" she said, sounding exasperated with him. "Question time or something? Go find out for yourself."

She shooed him towards the living room before turning back to what she was doing.

"Okay, I get the hint," he said as he turned to leave, adding under his breath, "Such motherly love."

But he wasn't quiet enough. Amelia heard him and launched a wooden spoon at him. It whacked him on the back of the head before landing on the floor with a clank.

"Ow!" he said, rubbing the back of his head. "What was that for?"

"Thought I'd show you some motherly love," she said sweetly.

Connor was still rubbing the back of his head as he walked into the living room. His father, Kai, sat in his favourite chair by the window, watching the world go by outside.

Both Caleb and Misti were sat quietly on the sofa facing the fire. He hadn't forgotten about them, he was still going to speak with them.

It was only fair that they share the punishment if they had anything to do with whatever Kayla was in trouble for. But they weren't going anywhere for the time being, whereas, Myra wasn't staying for long.

He wanted to know if she had any information about what happened before confronting the terrible twosome.

"Hi Dad, where's Myra?" He asked when he didn't see her.

"I'm out here!" she shouted from the hallway.

"There's your answer," Kai nodded.

Connor laughed. "And you didn't even have to open your month."

"I know," he grinned.

Myra sat on the stairs pulling her shoes on when he walked into the hallway.

"Mum said you're going over to Kellen's," he said, leaning against the wall opposite her.

"Yeah, we're having dinner and then I'm watching Kayla for a bit."

"Do you want me to come with you?"

"What, for babysitting duties?" She looked up at him with a raised eyebrow.

"Yeah, maybe not," he grimaced. "Where's Kellen

going?"

"He's still trying to come to some kind of arrangement with the Dragons."

"Whoa, what?"

"Didn't he tell you what she did?"

"No, I've not seen him," he told her. "Aidan said something about her hanging around near their caves, but I didn't think it had anything to do with them. What did she do?"

Myra took a deep breath and then said, "Kayla managed to get spray paint from somewhere and has sprayed graffiti in a couple of their caves, but mostly in Balzar's cave."

"Oh, shit. I bet they're not impressed, especially Balzar."

"That's an understatement. They are fuming, and he's demanding she clean it all off as soon as possible."

"I can imagine."

Dragons were the most peaceful species out of all the shifters, but they were also the most dangerous. Especially when it came to protecting what was theirs.

Piss them off and there would be hell to pay, so it was no surprise Kellen was still trying to come to some sort of arrangement with them. They certainly wouldn't make it easy on him.

As soon as Myra was ready, she picked up her coat and headed into the kitchen. Connor followed her back through the house.

"Were those two involved?" he asked her, indicating the two in the living room.

"Apparently, not this time they weren't," she said.

"You sound like you don't believe it."

Myra signed. "You know those three, they're always together. But this time Kayla is adamant she did it alone, and she was the only one caught by the Dragons."

"And don't you go interrogating them, either. Myra and Kai have already done enough of that," Amelia told him.

"I won't."

He had planned to, but he didn't want another spoon thrown at his head. He could still feel where the last one hit him.

For such a small woman, his mother had a lot of strength in her. She certainly knew how to throw kitchen utensils.

"Good," she nodded. "Now, get out my kitchen, the pair of you."

"Okay," they said in unison.

"I'm going now anyway, Mum. I'll see you tomorrow." Myra kissed Amelia on the cheek and then picked up the basket. "See you later, Connor."

"Yeah, bye Myra."

As soon as she was gone, Connor made a hasty retreat to the living room.

Caleb and Misti had made their own hasty retreat while he'd been in the kitchen. They were nowhere to be seen. Connor assumed they raced upstairs when the hallway was clear.

"Why were you rubbing the back of your head when you came in earlier?" Kai asked, as Connor sat on the sofa.

"Oh, that." Connor smiled. "Mum threw a spoon at me."

"Ah, what did you do this time?"

"I didn't do anything," he swore.

"Somehow, I don't believe you." Kai shook his head. "You do know, if I ask her, she'll tell me."

Connor held a hand over his heart. "I swear, she said it was her way of showing motherly love."

Kai burst out laughing. Connor tried to look hurt, but he couldn't keep up the pretence. Before long, he was sporting his own grin.

"Do you still want help with the basement conversion?" Kai asked when he finally stopped laughing.

"Yes, please."

When he had originally built his house, he made sure the basement was large enough to be turned into usable rooms. But until recently, he couldn't think what to do with the space.

"What are you doing in the basement?" Amelia asked, as she stood in the doorway.

"I'm turning it into three rooms," he told her. "There will be a laundry room, a store room, and a den down there. The den will be the largest room since it's going to be used like a second living room. Then the rest of the space will be divided equally between the laundry and store room."

"That sounds nice. It's about time you finally did something with the space," she said.

"When do you want to make a start?" Kai asked.

"Some point over the next couple of days, if that's okay?"

"Yes, that's fine. Is it just us?"

"No," Connor shook his head. "Aidan and Kellen are going to help as well, that's as long as Kellen can spare the time."

"I don't think the Dragons are going to be too hard on him," Amelia said. "After all, they know he's not to blame, and they know how hard he tries to keep Kayla under control."

"It's not as if their young don't get into trouble every now and then," Kai added.

"Every young shifter goes through a rebellious stage at some point or other," Amelia said.

"Do you remember when Connor went through it with Kellen and Aidan?" Kai asked her.

"Only too well." She shook her head. "Those three were a lot worse at times."

"Anyway," Connor cut in before they could start reminiscing about the antics he got up to when he was younger. "With more of us working on it, it shouldn't take us too long."

"Just don't invite too many people, otherwise we'll be getting under each other's feet all the time," Kai told him.

"Oooh, that means I won't have to do your laundry anymore," Amelia said happily.

"I can still bring my washing here if you want," he joked.

"Don't you dare," she said sternly. "I've done enough of your laundry over the years. It's about time you started doing it yourself."

"But I thought you enjoyed doing it for me," he said sweetly.

"Well, you can think again. It was bad enough having to do it while you were growing up, I didn't expect to still be doing it now that you've left home. At least Myra has been cleaning her own clothes since she moved out."

"That's because she's a girl, it's what they do," he stated jokingly.

If he wasn't careful, he was going to get a slap around the head and he knew it.

"Do you want a slap?" she asked him a moment later.

He could see Kai out of the corner of his eye. He was silently laughing as Amelia glared daggers at Connor.

"No, Mum. Sorry, Mum," he said, trying his hardest to hide his own grin.

"So, you should be," she scolded before turning on her heel and walking back into the kitchen.

As soon as she was out the room, both Connor and Kai burst out laughing.

CHAPTER SIX

It wasn't until the first fat raindrop landed on Anya's face that she realized the sky had gotten darker. She looked up through the trees to see dark rain clouds rolling across the sky.

She'd been so engrossed with taking photos that she hadn't notice the weather changing.

Anya quickly returned the camera to the backpack and zipped it safely in an inside pocket so it wouldn't get wet. Then she turned around and began heading back down the mountain.

Anya knew she didn't stand a chance in reaching the hotel before it started raining in earnest. She didn't mind a bit of rain, but after seeing how dark the clouds were getting, she had to call it a day and head back.

She hadn't gone far when the heavens finally opened. The rain came down in a deluge, soaking her nearly instantly.

As the wind picked up speed, she picked up the pace as best she could. But the wind and rain was making it increasingly harder for her to keep her balance and see where she was going.

Her feet slid uncontrollably in the wet mud. It didn't help that the pathway was narrow, with a steep slope on one side and outcropping of rock on the other.

Anya had heard the weather could change extremely fast up in the highlands, but she honestly didn't think it would change so quickly. Never before had she struggled so much just to see through the rain while walking. Driving yes, but not walking. She didn't know it was possible until then.

The ground suddenly gave way beneath her feet, making her scream in fear as she tumbled down the steep slope. She frantically tried to grab hold of anything to stop her fall, but nothing helped to slow her descent.

"Oomph."

Pain shot through Anya's side where it made impact with a tree. She hit it so hard that the air was knocked from her lungs and she was left gasping for breath.

When she finally got her breath back, she took stock of the situation. The tree had broken her fall, but she was nowhere near safe where she was. Somehow, she needed to find a way off the tree and then the rest of the way down the slope safely. Which was easier said than done.

With a little bit of searching with her feet, she found a root sticking out of the ground. Ignoring the throbbing pain in her side, she used the root as a ledge and managed to lift herself into an upright position.

Clinging desperately to the tree, she tried not to fall

any further as she adjusted her position so she could look around her. The heavy rain was still obscuring her vision.

"Fuck!" she said when she didn't spot a single path.

There was no easy way to get out of the predicament she found herself in. Anya could only see two options. One was to stay where she was and wait for help, which was probably the wisest option.

The second was to slide down the slope. The problem with that idea was she didn't know what awaited her at the bottom. It could be another pathway, or even a wide open field. But it could also end with a sheer drop and jagged rocks at the bottom, or a river.

After contemplating her options, she decided not to stay and wait for help. The weather was getting worse by the second, and it could be hours before somebody went looking for her. They might not even send out a search party straight away, which meant she could be there all night.

The thought of spending a night in the tree spurred her on. There was no delicate way of getting down, but she didn't care, she couldn't stay where she was.

Once she plucked up enough courage, she maneuvered into a sitting position next to the tree, and gingerly let go. Gravity took care of the rest.

She did her best to keep her descent slow by grabbing hold of anything she could, and prayed that she didn't go flying off a precipice at the end.

Thankfully, luck seemed to be on her side for once. She breathed a sigh of relief when her descent started to slow without her help. The ground soon levelled out, and she came to a stop.

Anya scanned her new surroundings. She still couldn't see another path, or even another way off the mountain, but she did spot an area where she could take shelter from the storm that was brewing.

A large rock jutted out from the ground. It was balanced on top of two smaller rocks, making a perfect place for her to wait out the storm.

Anya didn't waste any time. She crawled over to the rock, ignoring the throbbing pain that was now all over her body.

As she crawled closer to the rocks, she realized it wasn't just a small bit of shelter hidden beneath them, but the entrance to a cave. Anya didn't know if it was safe inside the cave, or if there were any occupants, but she decided to take her chances in there, anyway. As long as she was away from the unpredictable weather, she would be happy.

It was a bit of a squeeze getting past the main overhang of rock, but it was high enough inside for her to walk around without having to crouch. Not that she was in a fit state to attempt standing at that moment in time.

"Thank god!" She breathed a sigh of relief.

As soon as she was safely inside the cave, her arms gave out from underneath her and she collapsed to the floor.

Every part of her body hurt. She didn't think there would be a single inch of her that wasn't going to be covered with bruises by the morning. And to top it off, she had a feeling she had cracked a couple of ribs when she hit the tree. It really wouldn't surprise her, given the force of the impact.

Anya didn't know how long she laid there in agony. Her eyes were closed as she tried to suppress the pain. When she finally opened her eyes again, it was pitch black outside.

She pushed herself up until she was leaning against a wall, and then she carefully removed the backpack.

Thankfully, it was the type of bag that clipped together at the front, as well as going over her shoulders. Otherwise, she would have probably lost it on her way down.

She unzipped the bag and fished around inside it, blindly looking for the pocket containing her phone. When she found it, she pulled the phone out and pressed the button to check the time. The bright light momentarily blinded her. She blinked rapidly as her eyes adjusted.

"Well, shit."

Any hope she had in making it back to the hotel in time for dinner, was well and truly squashed. The time that she was meant to meet Sasha for dinner had come and gone hours ago.

Anya knew she should have paid more attention to the time and turned back earlier, but she had been too focused on taking photos and enjoying the natural beauty that was around her. Keeping track of the time had been the last thing on her mind.

She wondered if Sasha had already reported her missing. If she hadn't done so already, then it would only a matter of time before she does.

"Well, I guess I'm staying the night."

Which didn't seem like much fun, especially since her clothes were soaked through and caked in mud. She hadn't expected to need a clean set of clothes, so she hadn't packed any.

She didn't need to worry about food. She had packed plenty of energy bars to keep her going through the day, and she had hardly touched them.

Water was a different matter. She didn't know how long the water she had was going to last. At some point, she might have to look for more, but that depended on how long she was there.

The cave lit up as a bolt of lightning streaked through the sky, letting her know that she was going to be there for some time. A few seconds later, the loud rumble of thunder echoed in the cave.

Anya didn't need to count the seconds to know the lightening was right above her. She could already tell how close it was by the way it lit up the cave and by how loud the thunder was.

"Well," she said to the empty cavern. "It doesn't look like I'm going to get much sleep tonight, but I'm definitely staying here."

Rain was one thing, she didn't mind getting wet. But there was no way on earth she was traipsing down the mountain in the dark while a thunderstorm raged on.

Through a lot of grunts and groans, Anya managed to get to her feet. Using her phone as a torch, she explored the cave.

Her shoes made squelching sounds with each step

she took. She knew she shouldn't go any further into the cave without the proper equipment, but her curiosity got the better of her.

The cave was larger than it appeared. From what she could see, it looked like an oval shape. As she walked the perimeter, she found a passageway at the opposite end from the entrance.

Taking a deep breath, she carried on deeper into the mountain.

She hadn't gone more than a couple of steps before she regretted the decision. Her feet slid out from under her again, this time because of the slippery rock.

Anya hadn't thought it would be wet. Considering she was far from the entrance, she assumed it would be dry. The smooth, wet rock along with her muddy shoes meant she had no grip.

She threw her hands to the sides to try to stop the fall, but there was absolutely nothing to grab hold of. Just even more smooth rock.

It wouldn't have been too much of a problem if she had just landed on her ass. She would have climbed to her feet again and headed back the way she'd come. But instead, she slid down what seemed to be a giant slide, gaining speed as she went.

Anya was beginning to think it would never come to an end when it finally did. With the speed she had built up, and with nothing to grab onto to help slow her down, there was nothing she could do to avoid hitting the wall at the end.

She didn't have a chance to brace herself as she slid across the ground and collided with the wall. Her head hit the rock with such force, it knocked her out.

When Anya finally came to, she was in a heap against the wall, and lying in a puddle.

Pain radiated throughout her body, and she shivered uncontrollably. Her head felt like it was going to explode. So much so, that she wished for the sweet oblivion of nothingness again.

After what felt like an eternity, she tried to push herself into a sitting position, and almost threw up. The movement sent sharp shooting pains through her body and increased the pain in her head.

She had no choice but to give up when tiny white dots appear in her vision, and she started going dizzy. Anya knew she couldn't stay where she was, so after a couple of minutes, she tried again, and kept on trying until she finally succeeded.

However, sitting was as far as she could get. Every time she attempted to stand, the pain in her head would become too intense, and she had to give up. It was either that, or she was going to pass out again.

Since she didn't want to pass out again, she decided to give up trying to stand. Instead, she looked around for a way out that didn't require her to be on two feet.

Anya couldn't see a thing. There was absolutely no light coming from any direction. She felt around on the floor, hoping to find her phone so she could use the torch to find her way, but there was no sign of it.

All she could feel was solid rock and puddles of water under her hands. Thankfully, she also found what appeared to be another passageway.

Well, I can't just stay here and hope somebody finds

me.

After all, why would anyone think to look for her in a cave? And if they did, how would they know to look for her in the one she was in? For all she knew, there could be hundreds of caves dotted around the area. They certainly wouldn't come across her by chance, either.

No, Anya needed to find her way out of the cave on her own. She just hoped she didn't come across any more problems on her way back to the entrance.

Anya ignored the pain as she maneuvered onto her hands and knees, but that was as far as she could get before the pain became too severe. So, sticking to her hands and knees, she explored the area.

She carefully tested the ground to make sure it was solid before putting her weight on any spot. She didn't want to fall again and cause more injuries to herself. Twice in one day was more than enough.

Anya wasn't normally a clumsy person, but she had more than made up for it since going on the hike. She was glad she hadn't taken a harder route up the mountain.

There seems to be a pattern happening here, she thought as she was left with another decision to make.

She couldn't stay where she was, so she was left with two choices. Either attempt to go back the way she'd come, or try to find another way out.

It was highly unlikely that she would make it back up the rock slide in the state she was in, but at least she knew where the entrance was. It would probably be the wisest choice.

Her only other option was to see where the new passageway took her. It could lead to a way out, or she could find herself in an even worse situation than she was currently in.

Anya decided to trust her instincts, and it was telling her to choose the passage, but she was going to be extra vigilant.

Staying on her hands and knees, mainly because her head wouldn't have it any other way, she carried on feeling around on the floor as she slowly made her way along the passage.

A few minutes after she set off, she came to a section that was covered in spider webs. It took all her willpower not to turn back screaming as it attached to her face.

She tried clearing the web from in front of her, but no matter what she did, it didn't seem to make any difference. Thankfully, she made it through without coming into contact with any spiders, otherwise she really would have screamed.

Once Anya was through the web, she could feel a breeze coming from ahead of her. Hoping and praying she had found a way out, she crawled as fast as she could while still being careful.

It didn't take her long to find the entrance. It wasn't the same one she had entered, but she didn't care. It was a way out, and that's all that mattered to her.

When Anya reached the entrance, she looked outside. It was still dark, which meant she couldn't have been unconscious for too long. She also noted that it had stopped raining.

It didn't look like dawn was arriving anytime soon, so she crawled over to the side of the cave and laid down. She tried to get as comfortable as she could on the hard rock, but it wasn't easy.

She closed her eyes and tried to block out the pain radiating through her head and body. She needed to get as much rest as she could get, ready for her trek back to the hotel.

CHAPTER SEVEN

Rush called an emergency meeting early the next morning. All the Hunters were required to be there, but he wouldn't tell them why.

By the time Connor arrived at Rush's house, everyone else was already there. Since there wasn't enough space for everyone in Rush's office, they were gathered in the spacious living room instead.

Rush stood in front of the large fireplace. He waited patiently for everyone to arrive and get settled, but Connor could tell he was growing impatient.

Every seat in the room was spoken for, which left the majority of the Hunters standing. Connor found an empty space at the back of the room. He leaned against the wall and waited for the meeting to start.

Aidan and Kellen spotted him as soon as he entered the room. They quickly headed over to join him.

"Do you know what this is all about?" Aidan asked him.

Connor shook his head. "I've no idea."

Before they could say more, Rush spoke.

"Thank you for coming," he began. "I know you're all wondering why I've gathered you here."

A few people nodded their heads, but nobody spoke.

"Well, last night a human female was found in one of the caves leading to our realm."

There was an audible gasp in the room at the news, but nobody interrupted him. The majority of the people in the room were genuinely shocked, but there were a handful of people that didn't appear surprised.

Connor was among those that were shocked. It was the last thing he thought Rush would say. He assumed the few that weren't surprised were the ones to find her, and Rush confirmed his suspicions a moment later.

"While on patrol last night, Tanya and Krystal came across her at the entrance to the cave." He indicated the two female Hunters that were sat close to the front. "She was unconscious when they found her, and in a really bad state. They called Dominic and Ryder to search the area for any sign that more humans had come through. Thankfully, there was no evidence to indicate that she wasn't alone. They informed me what was happening as they were taking her to the medical centre. She's now being cared for by the Healers." He paused for a brief moment to let it sink in before he continued. "For the time being, I want at least two Hunters stationed at the entrance to the cave at all times. At least, until we can be sure no others come through after her."

When Rush stopped talking and looked around the

room, a barrage of questions were thrown at him.

"One at a time," he told them.

"Is the female going to be okay?" the first person asked.

"As far as we can tell, she will be fine," he said. "Apart from a couple of cracked ribs, she only has a few minor cuts and bruises. Other than that, she's physically fine. She's still unconscious at the moment, so we'll know more when she comes round, which we're hoping will be soon."

"What's going to happen when she wakes up?" another person asked.

"For the time being, she's staying in medical," he said. "At least until she's awake and moving around. After that, I don't know. We'll have to wait and see what happens when she wakes up."

"So, she's not being sent back as soon as she wakes up?" somebody else asked.

"Not straight away. It'll be a couple of days before she's in any fit state to travel. Until then, she will be closely supervised. The less she knows of our kind and where she is, the better."

"Do you know how she got through the portal?"

"No, but trust me, we're going to find out."

"How did she find the portal?"

"I don't know the answer to that yet either."

Connor stopped paying much attention after that. The same questions were being asked over and over, just in a slightly different way. Rush still answered every question that was thrown at him even though he'd already supplied the answer.

"Can you believe it?" Aidan said. "How the hell did she find her way through?"

"As much as we like to think it's impossible for a human to find the cave, it isn't," Kellen told him. "There could be any number of reasons for how she found her way here. For all we know, she could have just stumbled upon the entrance."

"Well, it should be," Aidan said. "The last thing we need is more of them making their way here. What's the point in hiding the portals if they can still find their way here?"

Connor had to agree with Aidan. The spells that were in place to hide the portals from the humans should do just that. If that wasn't the case, they needed to find some other way of keeping the humans out.

They had done enough damage to their own realm, tearing up the ground and polluting the air and water, they didn't need another realm to destroy. Not only that, but last time the humans found out about another species living among them, they nearly wiped them all out of existence.

Connor still remembered the witch hunts as if it only happened yesterday. He didn't have a problem with humans, but the last thing they needed was for the humans to find out about them and then go on another killing spree.

"Any more questions?" Rush asked finally.

When no one replied, he dismissed them all.

Connor started to leave with everyone else, but stopped when he heard Rush call his name.

He walked over to Rush and asked, "What's up?"

Rush waited until the last person left and they were finally alone before answering. "I want you to come with me and tell me if you recognize this female."

"Why would I recognize her?"

"I want to know if she looks anything like the female from your dream."

Connor didn't know why he would be dreaming of a human, it was more likely to be another shifter, but it wouldn't hurt to have a look.

"Okay, I'll have a look," he said. "But I doubt it will be her. Plus, I still don't have a clue what the female in my dreams looks like, I haven't been able to get close enough to find out."

It was frustrating the hell out of him, but no matter what he did, he couldn't get close enough to her to get a good look.

"From the description you've given me," Rush said. "I have a feeling you'll know straight away if it's the same person or not."

It was a long shot at best, but if it turned out to be the same person, then hopefully the dreams would finally come to an end. She might even have some insight as to why he was dreaming of her in the first place.

Connor was looking forward to having a decent night's sleep again. He'd tried everything to prevent himself from dreaming, but nothing worked. Not even running in wolf form until he was ready to drop from exhaustion.

When he'd left his parents' house the previous night, he had gone for a long run, hoping it would wear him out so he could sleep peacefully. He even stopped off for a swim in the river near his home on the way back there. But none of it worked.

The dream still bombarded him as soon as he drifted off to sleep.

Intrigued about the mysterious female, Connor followed Rush to the medical centre.

It didn't take long to reach the medical centre from Rush's house. He preferred to live near the main compound, so he was within easy reach in an emergency.

There were a couple of people milling around the reception desk when they arrived. Rush walked over to where they were gathered and spoke to one of the Healers.

"Has she woken yet?" he asked Candi.

"No. Not even a twitch when we cleaned her cuts with antiseptic."

"Okay. Is she still in the same room?"

"No, we moved her to a more secure room down the hall. We didn't want to risk her seeing something that would need an explanation."

"Good idea," Rush told her. "Is somebody still guarding her?"

"Yes. Dominic took over about half an hour ago."

"Good. Show me which room she's in."

Candi nodded before leading them through the building, to the furthest room from the reception area. As soon as they turned the last corner, Connor could see Dominic sitting on a chair opposite the room.

Connor knew the room they were keeping her in. It

was mostly used as a store room because it was easy to restrict access. The window was a small slit high up in the wall, and the door could be locked from the outside.

Dominic didn't bother getting up when they reached him.

"I haven't heard any movement," he told them from where he slouched.

"I have a feeling it'll be some time before she wakes up," Candi told them.

"That's okay," Rush said.

Candi unlocked and opened the door, and then stepped out of the way for them to enter. Rush walked into the room first, with Connor following close behind.

Once they were in the room, Rush moved to the side, so Connor had a clear view of the bed. He stopped dead in his tracks when he caught sight of the female.

What the hell?

Connor couldn't believe his eyes. As soon as he looked at her prone form lying on the bed, he knew without a doubt it was the female from his dream. Even without getting close enough in the dream to see her facial features, he knew it was the same female.

He understood now why Rush thought he might recognize her; her hair was a dead giveaway. There was no mistaking the long strawberry blonde hair and pale skin, no matter how much the dirt and bruises tried to hide the colour of both.

"I take it from the look on your face that this is the same female," Rush said.

Connor didn't know how it was possible, but… "It's her."

He didn't realize he'd spoken aloud until Rush said, "I thought as much."

Now that she was right in front of him, he was finding it hard to tear his eyes away from her. He could hear Rush talking with the others in the corridor, but he didn't care what they were saying. The female in front of him held all of his attention.

A faint spattering of freckles covered the bridge of her pert little nose. Dark lashes stood out against her porcelain skin, hiding the worst of the dark circles under her eyes.

The strawberry blonde hair that had haunted his dreams, framed her beautiful features perfectly. Cuts and bruises covered every inch of skin he could see, but it didn't retract from her beauty.

"I'm going now," Rush announced a moment later.

Connor could see Rush standing next to him out of the corner of his eye, but he didn't look away from the bed. He couldn't.

"I'm staying." The words were out before he could think better of it, but he didn't want to take them back. He added, "I want to be here when she wakes up."

"I thought you might," Rush admitted. "I've told Dominic that you're taking over watch. Let me know when she wakes up."

Connor nodded in agreement, but he didn't take his eyes off the female. Rush didn't hang around after that. He turned and walked out the room, closing the door behind him.

Seeing her lying there, all bandaged up, covered in cuts and bruises, affected him more than he was willing to admit. He didn't know what it was about her, but he felt even more drawn to her now that she was right in front of him. It was a hell of a lot more intense than it had been in the dream.

When he'd been dreaming of her, he'd felt compelled to save her. But now, his feelings for her ran deeper, and it confused him. He wanted to protect her and keep her safe for as long as he lived.

He didn't know how long he stood there watching her sleep. He was so fixated on her; he hadn't noticed it had gone dark outside until someone opened the door, letting light in from the corridor.

One of the Healers walked in carrying a chair for him to sit on. He was finally able to drag his eyes off the sleeping form on the bed when someone tapped him on the shoulder.

He turned his head to see Candi standing next to him with a soft smile on her face.

"You've been standing for hours," she told him. "Sit down and rest for a while. She isn't going anywhere."

"Thank you," he whispered.

She smiled before walking back out the room, leaving him alone once again. He sat on the chair before turning his gaze back on the bed.

He was mesmerized by the rise and fall of her chest. She looked so peaceful lying there. He was torn between wanting her to wake up so he could speak with her, and wanting her to stay asleep so she could recover quicker. Not that he would wake her up, anyway.

No, there would be plenty of time to speak with her after she'd woken, so he would leave her be. No doubt Rush would have plenty of questions for her, and Connor had a few questions of his own. But for the time being, he was just content to watch her sleep.

***

"What do you mean, she's disappeared?" he shouted at the demon.

It would never have happened if the witch was still following her. But apparently, she had a pressing matter that needed to be dealt with. He didn't believe her for one second, but there wasn't much he could do. He needed her help for the moment.

He was tempted to just kill her and find another witch because she was turning out to be more trouble than she was worth. Unfortunately, it would take time to find a suitable candidate to replace her, time that he didn't have to spare.

The demon tried to explain what had happened when he lost sight of her, but he was too pissed off to pay any attention.

Instead of listening to the demon babble on, he demanded, "Find her!" and then hung up the phone.

Everything would have run smoothly if she hadn't decided to take an unexpected trip away. She was a crucial part of the plan, but she wasn't irreplaceable. It would be a setback if it came to that, though.

He had a feeling he knew exactly where she was. It

wasn't impossible to get to her, but it would take a bit of finesse.

He smiled as a plan started to formulate in his mind.

CHAPTER EIGHT

Sasha had known something was wrong when Anya hadn't returned to the hotel in time for dinner, but she didn't report her as a missing person. She could find her a hell of a lot faster than any human on the planet could, so she didn't need to report her as missing.

Even though she insisted that Anya told the reception staff at the hotel where she was heading, she needn't have bothered. Sasha knew exactly where she was, she just didn't know how she found her way there.

The only reason Sasha had mentioned it at all was because it was something a normal human would say. And since she was trying to blend in with the humans, she had to say and act the same way as them.

It hadn't taken long for her to figure out where she had disappeared to. Knowing there was a portal to the shifter realm on the same mountain Anya had gone to explore, it made sense that she had somehow found her way there.

The only other possible explanation for her disappearance was that someone with the ability to teleport had kidnapped her. But thankfully, that wasn't the case.

It was a good job Sasha wasn't human. If she had been, then she wouldn't have known where Anya had gone. She would have thought she'd vanished off the face of the planet. When in reality, she had travelled to a different realm.

She knew where all the portals were located, and which realms they led to. Every Fae was taught about them when they were young, but more so for her.

For the last few days, Sasha had kept an eye on Anya. If not physically, then with the aid of magic. So she knew the moment Anya had left the human realm.

Something was off about Anya, and had been since the day she was late for work. Sasha couldn't put her finger on what it was, but there was something different about her. Which was why she had been keeping track of her.

The first clue had been her not turning in to work on time. In all the years they had worked together, Anya hadn't once been late. Even when she was sick, she'd always called in before she was due to be there.

The second was her aura. It had completely changed colour, which was normally impossible to do, especially to the extent hers had changed.

The fact she managed to find the portal was another glaring sign that she wasn't the same. Either on purpose or by accident, she shouldn't have been able to find the portal. It was heavily concealed by strong magic.

The magic wasn't as strong as hers, but it should still have been strong enough to hide the portal from humans.

Sasha used her magic to veil herself as she navigated her way through the shifter realm. She didn't stop until she came to the home she was looking for.

With the portal being in his territory, if anyone knew where Anya was, it would be Rush.

The moment she reached his house, she knew she was in the right place. His house was full to bursting with wolf shifters. No doubt they were all gathered there because of Anya.

Sneaking inside, Sasha stood at the back of the room so nobody could accidentally bump into her, and waited for the meeting to begin. It didn't take long for Rush to confirm her suspicions.

After hearing him talk about the state Anya was in when they found her, she was eager to check on her. But first, she wanted to know what they planned to do with her.

Unfortunately, Rush didn't divulge what he planned to do with her when she woke up. After informing everyone in the room about her arrival and answering their many questions, he discussed upping the patrols before dismissing them. All except for Connor.

Sasha was going to leave the house with everyone else, but something held her back, and she was glad it did. If she had left, she wouldn't have known about Connor's connection with Anya.

She had to admit, she was surprised when Rush mentioned that Anya might be the female Connor had been dreaming about. Intrigued, she had listened intently for more details of the dream in question, but she was disappointed when neither of them elaborated.

Staying veiled, she had followed them to where Anya was being held.

Even after hearing Rush talk about the state Anya was in, she still hadn't been prepared for seeing her friend in such a bad way. Covered in cuts and bruises, she was lying unconscious on the bed.

From the look on Connor's face, Anya was definitely the female from his dreams.

Why would a wolf be dreaming of a human? she wondered.

Did the dreams have anything to do with what was happening with Anya? If so, she might be able to get to the bottom of what was going on with her sooner rather than later.

Unfortunately, they didn't mention anything else to do with the dream. Instead, Rush left Connor to stare at Anya's sleeping form.

Still keeping the veil in place, Sasha followed Rush back to his house. When he was seated behind his desk in his office, she finally dropped the veil.

"Hello, Rush." Sasha couldn't stop the smile on her face as he jumped at the sound of her voice.

Even with the pissed off look on his face, he was an incredibly handsome man.

"Who the fuck are you?" he demanded. "And what are you doing in my home?"

"I'm Sasha, and I'm here because of my friend."

Sasha could see the wheels turning in his head

before he asked, "Who's your friend?"

He knew exactly who she was talking about, but if he wanted to act as if he didn't, then so be it.

"The lovely mystery lady you just left sleeping in a store cupboard," she told him.

"And who might that be?"

"She would be Anya."

"So, that's what her name is."

"What happened to her?" she demanded.

"We would like to know the same thing."

"When I last saw her, she wasn't covered in cuts and bruises. If I find out you had anything to do with her injuries, there will be hell to pay."

Sasha didn't have many friends. In fact, Anya was her only friend. So, if someone hurt her, Sasha would make that person's life a living hell. She didn't care who it was.

"She was found in that state," he said adamantly.

"Where was she found?"

"Why?"

"Don't worry, little wolf, my interest is solely in Anya." She could see that her nickname for him did not amuse him, but his reaction to it did amuse her, so it was all good.

"Fine," he relented after a moment's hesitation. "She was found in the cave by the portal."

"Do you know how she managed to find her way through?"

"No," he confessed. "But I would certainly like to know the answer."

So would she like to know. "I'll be back soon."

"Where are you going?"

"Keep her safe," she told him instead of answering his question.

If she was going to find the answers she was searching for, then she couldn't stand around chatting to Rush.

Before he could say another word, she teleported out of his office.

CHAPTER NINE

No matter how hard she tried to fight it, she couldn't prevent herself from waking up. But with consciousness, came pain, and lots of it.

The pain she had felt before drifting off to sleep in the cave came rushing back with a vengeance. It woke her up better than any alarm clock ever could.

Every inch of her body hurt. It was even painful to breathe too deeply, which she found out the hard way. So, in an attempt to avoid the pain, she kept her breathing as shallow as she could.

Her head felt like it was about to explode. She tentatively reached up and touched her head where it had hit the wall. But instead of touching her hair, her hand came into contact with a bandage. It was in that moment that she realised she was no longer in the cave.

The cold, hard rock of the cave she had fallen asleep on, had been replaced with a soft, warm mattress. Her shoes had been removed, and her soaking wet clothes had been swapped with a thin nightshirt and blanket.

Anya froze as she listened for the slightest sound to indicate that she wasn't alone. She was about to sigh in relief when she heard a rustling noise coming from close by.

Slowly, she lowered her arm and cracked open her eyelids a tiny bit. She definitely wasn't in the cave anymore. Now she was in a room, a very white room from the look of it. And she definitely was not alone.

Even without being able to see clearly, she could make out a large dark form moving in the corner opposite the bed.

"You can open your eyes, I know you're awake." A deep male voice said, confirming her suspicions.

Since he knew she was awake, there was no point in trying to deny it, so she opened her eyes and looked at him. Anya would have thought she was still dreaming if it hadn't been for the pain. The man was drop dead gorgeous.

The light blue eyes that stared back at her were framed by dark lashes. A shiver raced down her spine at the flash of lust she spotted, but it disappeared just as quickly as it appeared.

Her eyes took on a life of their own as they drank in the sight of him.

His full lips, perfect for kissing or biting, softened his strong jawline. The five o'clock shadow gave him a rugged look, but if the dark circles under his eyes were any indication, then it wasn't intentional.

Shaggy brown hair, the perfect length for grabbing when in the height of passion, framed his face nicely.

My god! He's fucking gorgeous! And huge!

Even sitting there was no mistaking the size of him. He must be at least a foot taller than her, and he was incredibly well built. The way he slouched in the chair didn't make him appear any smaller, but it gave her a great view of his powerful body.

His broad shoulders and muscular chest were barely being contained by the dark t-shirt he wore. Her fingers itched to slip under his t-shirt so she could run her hands over his muscles.

Her gaze continued down his body to where his t-shirt tucked neatly into faded blue jeans.

She followed his shirt down to where it tucked into faded blue jeans that hugged large, strong thighs.

Anya couldn't stop her eyes from going to his crotch. It was like a magnet, drawing her attention.

Anya could feel her eyes widen. If the bulge beneath his jeans was anything to go by, then he was huge everywhere.

Fuck me!

She wouldn't have been surprised if her mouth was wide open and she was drooling a little. Her mouth was definitely watering at the indecent imagines that were flashing through her mind.

Anya jumped when he cleared his throat. Her eyes shot straight back up to his face and clash with his.

Her face was on fire with embarrassment. She didn't need a mirror to show her how red her face was, she could feel it burning up. Even if her mouth was closed and there was no drool, she still couldn't deny what her eyes had been focused on.

If she thought looking at his face would clear her

mind of images of them tangled together, then she was sorely mistaken. It was just as hard to keep her mind out the gutter when looking at his face either.

"Um…where am I?" she asked, hoping to break the uncomfortable silence.

He didn't answer. He just sat there watching her silently, as if he didn't have a care in the world, and as far as she knew, he didn't.

Just then, the door opened. Anya finally managed to drag her gaze away from the piercing blue eyes that held her captive, just as a petite young woman with brown hair peeked her head around the door. When she saw Anya was awake, she smiled.

"I thought I heard talking," she said to Anya before turning her attention to the man. "Does Rush know she's awake?"

A curt "Yes" was his reply

"That's good," the woman said as she walked into the room.

Anya resisted the urge to look at him again, barely. Instead, she took the opportunity to survey her surroundings.

There wasn't much to look at in the room. Apart from the bed she was lying on, and the chair where the man sat, there were a couple of empty shelves and nothing else.

The walls were an off white colour and looked like they could do with a fresh coat of paint. The bed frame was metal and had seen better days as well, but thankfully, the mattress was in better condition.

There was one door in the room, and only a small

window close to the ceiling behind the bed. From the angle she was seeing it from, it wasn't big enough for her to fit through.

Anya hoped there wouldn't be a fire blocking the door, otherwise she would be screwed.

"Do you want some help sitting up?" She was carrying a couple of pillows as she walked over to the bed.

She gently put them down on the end of the bed before holding her hands out to Anya.

"No, it's okay." Anya smiled at the woman. "Thank you for the offer, but I can manage it on my own."

She soon regretted her decision. After several failed attempts to sit up like she normally would, she tried rolling on to her side and pushing up with her hands, but she failed at that as well. The pain in her chest made it impossible to sit up unaided.

She hated feeling like a burden, but she hated lying down while surrounded by a bunch of strangers even more. She couldn't stand feeling vulnerable, but there wasn't much she could do about it. So, after a moment's hesitation, she reluctantly accepted the help.

The woman had a warm smile on her face as she introduced herself. "Hi, I'm Candi."

Anya couldn't help smiling back as she said, "I'm Anya."

It might not have been the best idea to give them her real name, especially since she didn't know them from Adam, but it slipped out before she could think, and now she couldn't take it back.

Candi slid her hands under Anya's arms until they

were beneath her shoulder blades. Then, without any effort, she lifted her into a sitting position.

Anya wasn't a large person by any means, but it should have taken Candi a little more effort to move her than it did. It was as if Candi was helping a baby sit up and not a full grown adult.

"You okay?" Candi asked before letting go of her.

"Yes."

"Good. Just hold there a sec."

Grabbing the pillows from the end of the bed, she rearranged them behind Anya and then helped her move back until she was leaning against them.

"Where am I?" she asked again, hoping Candi would tell her.

She certainly wasn't getting an answer from the drop dead gorgeous man sitting in the corner of the room. It hadn't escaped her notice that his eyes had been on her the entire time. Not only could she see him watching her out of the corner of her eye, but she could feel the heat of his gaze.

"You're in medical," Candi said as if it should answer her question, which it didn't.

There were hundreds, if not thousands, of medical centres across the country, but Anya didn't think she wasn't in any of them. If she was, then why wouldn't they just tell her?

Yes, it had all the right smells associated with medical centres and hospitals. It even had the nasty off-white washed walls. But she couldn't shake the feeling she wasn't in a normal medical facility.

"Which medical centre?" Anya persisted when

Candi didn't elaborate.

Instead of answering her, she smile at Anya as she said, "Rush will be here soon."

Anya quickly realized that neither of them had a Scottish accent. Everyone she had met since arriving in the Highlands had at least a slight accent. So why didn't they have one?

"Are you comfortable?" Candi asked her. "Is there anything I can get you?"

"Could I have some water, please?"

Anya couldn't remember the last time she drank anything. Her throat was so dry; she was amazed she was able to speak.

The only reason her mouth wasn't as dry as her throat was because of the hunk watching her like a hawk. Just the thought of his incredible body made her mouth water. Not to mention other body parts of her.

Anya could feel her cheeks begin to heat as Candi left her alone in the room with him again. Thankfully, she returned a moment later with a glass of water.

"Thank you," Anya said, as Candi handed the glass to her.

She took a couple of small, tentative sips before gulping down the entire glass. When she was finished, Candi took the glass and placed it on one of the empty shelves.

A man with short black hair and obsidian eyes had followed Candi into the room. He stood to one side of the room and waited patiently for her to have a drink before stepping toward the bed. He wore black trousers and a white button down shirt. He left the top couple of buttons undone.

He was just as handsome as the other man in the room, but he didn't set butterflies off in her stomach when he looked at her like the other man did. There was an air about him that said he was the one in charge. If that was the case, then hopefully he would be able to tell her where she was.

"Hello, Anya. My name is Rush," he introduced himself as he held a hand out to her. Not wanting to appear rude, she shook his hand. "You've already met Candi and Connor."

So that's his name. Anya thought, as she finally let her gaze flick to him.

She couldn't look at him for too long without imagining his sweat-soaked body above hers as he brought them both to climax.

Anya mentally shook her head before turning her attention back on Rush.

"It's nice to meet you," she said, smiling. "Can you tell me where I am?"

Rush shook his head. "I'm sorry, but for the time being, all I can tell you is that you're in medical."

"Why can't you tell me more?"

"To be honest, I am not prepared to disclose our location to someone we don't know. We don't know who you are or if you can be trusted with that information. Until we can be sure of your intentions here, it will stay that way."

Intentions? Anya didn't have any intentions other than to go home. She didn't even care where she was, she just wanted to go back to her apartment. She wasn't interested in anything else, not even going back to the hotel.

Her weekend of rest and relaxation was well and truly ruined.

"The same could be said of you." She stated. "I don't know any of you either, yet you are basically asking me to trust you. Trust goes both ways. If you're not willing to trust me, then why should I trust you? As far as I know, you could be a bunch of murders and rapist."

She didn't think that was the case, but you could never be too careful. The nicest person in the world could turn out to be an evil son of a bitch. She learnt that growing up in children's homes and foster care.

"Yes, I understand that, but you are only one person. I have to think about all the people I am protecting by not telling you. There are a lot of families here that I have to take into consideration. I'm not keeping our location from you to be malicious. I'm doing it to make certain that the people who rely on me to keep them safe, stay that way."

Anya had no idea what to say after that. She had absolutely no intention of causing harm to anyone.

"Well, can I at least use a phone to let my friend know I'm okay?"

Sasha must have gone out of her mind with worry when Anya hadn't returned to the hotel in time for dinner. Or even later that night. She wouldn't be surprised if there was a search party out looking for her.

"I'm sorry, but there are no phones here."

Of course, there weren't. It was beginning to feel like she was being held prisoner, and she didn't like it one bit.

"If you don't mind," he said. "I have a couple of questions for you."

Well, it wasn't like she could go anywhere any time soon, so why the hell not have question time instead.

"Shoot. What do you want to know?" she asked.

If it meant she could go home sooner, or back to the hotel as the case may be, then she would answer as many questions as it took.

"How did you find your way into the cave where you were found?"

"I was hiking when I got caught out in the rain," she admitted. "I fell down a steep slope, and when I reached the bottom, I came across the cave entrance. I decided it was safer to take shelter there than to risk falling again."

"Why didn't you stay by the entrance?"

How did he know she hadn't stayed by the entrance? After all, they would have found her by *an* entrance. Yes, technically it was a different entrance than the one she first used, but they shouldn't have known that.

Anya decided honesty was the best policy, so she told them the truth.

"I didn't know how long I was going to be there. I had plenty of food to last me until today if I rationed, but I only had a small amount of water. So, I went in search of an underground stream or something."

"Do you have a habit of carrying a weeks' worth of food and only a days' worth of water when you go on hikes?" Connor asked as he sat forward, leaning his elbows on his muscular thighs.

"What? No," she said, confused by his question. "I had enough food and water to last the day. I hadn't eaten all the lunch the hotel packed for me, plus I had some energy bars as well, so I had more than enough on me until I got back. Why would I carry a weeks' worth of food for a day trip?"

Nobody in their right minds would carry that much food and water for a day trip.

"Well, then," he said, raising an eyebrow. "You didn't have enough food to last until today."

"Why not?" she asked him.

"Because, you've been here for five days."

"What?"

Anya looked between Connor, Rush, and Candi, hopefully that it was all a lie. But from the pity she could see on Candi's face, she knew he was telling the truth.

CHAPTER TEN

Connor couldn't help but feel sorry for her.

He could tell by the look on her face she was shocked by the news. But who wouldn't be shocked when they found out they'd been unconscious for nearly a week? And she had certainly been unconscious. There was no way she'd just been asleep.

None of the healers were quiet when they had gone in to check on her. Not to mention, they rolled her this way and that, checking on the progress of her wounds. Even with all of that going on, she hadn't stirred.

The entire time she was unconscious, he watched over her. He'd barely left the room since she arrived. On the rare occasion he did, somebody else took his place.

Connor had wanted to be there when she woke up. It was bound to be hard enough being in a strange place; he didn't want to add to her stress by her being alone as well.

There were plenty of other people who would have stayed with her, but Connor found he didn't like the idea of anyone else watching her. He didn't want anyone else near her while she was so vulnerable.

It wasn't only for her benefit that somebody watched her the entire time. It was also for the safety of everyone in the pack, as well as everybody in the realm. The last thing they needed was for a human to be wandering around the realm unattended. That would cause nothing but problems for them. He was more than happy to take up the post.

Ever since the dreams had started plaguing him, he had felt an undeniable pull towards the female. Even without seeing her face, his protective instincts had kicked in, and he'd wanted to do anything in his power to keep her safe.

Now that she was in front of him, those feelings were a hundred times stronger.

He didn't know what it was about her, but he couldn't bring himself to leave her for more than a few minutes at a time. A quick shower here and there, and the odd trip outside for fresh air was what the last five days had consisted of for him.

The healers had regularly brought him food and drinks. If they hadn't, he probably wouldn't have eaten for days because he hadn't wanted to leave her side long enough to get himself something. What little sleep he managed to get while sitting in the god-awful chair one of the healers brought in for him was intermittent at best, but it was better than nothing.

The only saving grace was the dream had finally changed. Now, instead of being in one of the hell realms, he was in the human realm. She was still in danger, but thankfully, she wasn't being ripped apart right in front of him anymore.

Connor didn't think he could have coped with those dreams for much longer without going insane.

He couldn't pinpoint where the danger was coming from, but it was there, hovering in the background. At least he could see her clearly now, not that it would have made any difference. He still knew it was her.

"Please tell me you're joking," she said after a couple of minutes.

"I'm sorry," Rush told her. "I wish we could."

Anya suddenly threw the blanket off and attempted to get up, uncaring that she only wore a nightgown. "I have to go."

"Whoa, hold on a sec." Candi said, as she rushed over to stop her.

"I can't. My friend is probably going out of her mind with worry. We should have been back home by now."

"I'm sorry, Anya, but I can't let you leave yet," Rush told her.

"Why the fuck not!" she snapped.

"For one thing, you're in no fit state to be travelling that far."

"Where have you taken me?" she demanded. "Because I wasn't that far from the hotel, all I had to do was walk down the bloody mountain."

When none of them replied, she shook her head and said, "Just call me a taxi or something then, and I'll make my own way back."

"It's not as easy as that."

"Why not? Don't tell me, you don't have taxi's here

either," she said sarcastically.

"That's correct," Rush confirmed. "The only way to get back to where you're from is to go back the way you came, which means going through the cave again, and as I said, you're not up to that at the moment."

Anya was becoming more and more pissed off, and Connor couldn't blame her.

He understood her frustration, and sympathized with the situation she was in, but things like phones were irrelevant, since they could communicate telepathically. And it wasn't that they didn't have cars, they just didn't have taxi's.

Most of the time, they preferred to travel by foot. Whether they were in animal or human form, it didn't matter. Even if they did have taxi's, she still wouldn't be able to get one to take her where she wanted to go.

The only way to leave the realm was to either have the ability to teleport, or to walk through one of the portals leading to the other realms, most of which were not easily traversed.

"Well, point me in the direction of the cave and I'll find my own way back," she said.

He could see the determination in her eyes and the way she held herself. If they let her, she would be gone within minutes. But Rush was right, she wouldn't make it far in the state she was in. She couldn't even sit up on her own.

Not only that, they still needed to get to the bottom of the dreams. And before she went anywhere, he wanted to find out what the danger was that he felt stalking her in the dreams. He would never forgive himself if she went back to the human realm and something happened to her. Especially if he could prevent it.

"As I said before," Rush told her. "You're not in any condition to make the journey. The pain you feel in your chest is from three cracked ribs and one broken, which is why you're struggling to move or breathe. You also had a nasty bump on your head that could have caused a concussion. Not to mention, you've been unconscious for days. So, yes, we would like you to rest and recover before going anywhere. When *we* are sure you are well enough to make the journey, then we will gladly take you home. But until then, it is in your best interest to stay here."

"Don't tell me," she said, rolling her eyes. "I've got to stay in this room until then?"

"No, I will arrange suitable accommodation where you can stay until you have recovered enough to make the journey back," Rush assured her.

Connor thought she was going to argue, but she surprised him when she climbed back on the bed with help from Candi.

"Fine," she relented. "But as soon as I'm well enough, I want to go home."

"You have my word." Rush bowed his head slightly to her before turning to him. "Connor, I would like a word."

Connor nodded, and followed him out into the hallway.

Rush didn't speak until the door was closed, and he was sure Anya couldn't overhear them. Not that they needed to bother leaving the room.

"I want her to stay with you."

That was the last thing he expected Rush to say. He was so surprised, his mind went blank as he tried to think of a response.

"What?"

"I want her to stay with you until she's recovered."

"Don't you think it would be better if she stayed with one of the female hunters?" he asked. "I can ask Myra if she could stay with her. I don't think she would mind having a visitor for a few days."

"No." Rush shook his head. "For some reason, you're the one being plagued with dreams of her. I think if we're going to get to the bottom of the dreams, we need to know more about her. Hopefully, we'll find out how she found her way here at the same time. Since you're the one having the dreams, you're the person for the job, and it will be easier to do if she's staying with you."

He understood Rush's reasoning, but he still didn't think it was a good idea. The only reason he'd kept his hands to himself over the last few days was because she was unconscious. But that wasn't going to be the case if she was staying with him. She would be very much awake for the majority of the time.

Just the thought of them being alone together in his home had his blood heating as images of all the things he'd like to do to her incredible body flashed through his mind. Yep, it definitely wasn't a good idea.

"I still think she would be better off with one of the females." Connor tried again to get out of it.

"You have a guest room in your house, don't you?"

"Yes, but—"

"Well, that's settled then," Rush interrupted. "She can stay with you. Get close to her, find out as much as you can, then we'll figure out where to go from there. You never know, she might know why you're dreaming of her, or she might have some insight as to what the danger is that you've been sensing around her."

Connor didn't want to get to know her. There was something about her that drew him in, demanded his attention, and he didn't like it one bit. He was concerned if he got to know her better, the attraction he felt for her would intensify to the point of no return.

Since she wasn't a wolf shifter, there could never be anything between them. It had only been a few days, and he already didn't want to leave her side. What was it going to be like once he got to know her?

Connor didn't want to find out the answer to that question.

The sooner they found out what danger she was in, and why he was dreaming of her, the sooner they could deal with the problem and she could go back to where she belongs.

"Fine," he gave in.

It still didn't seem like a good idea, but he held back from voicing his concern.

Even if he did agree with Rush's logic, it didn't make it any easier. It was going to be pure torture having her so close. Hopefully, she'll make a swift recovery, and they could get to the cause of the dreams quickly, then she could return to the human realm and things could go back to normal for him.

At the end of the day, there was no point refusing his Alpha. It would cause more trouble than it was worth.

"Good," Rush said with a smirk on his face. "I'll let you break the good news to her."

"Thanks."

His Alpha could be a right pain in the arse at times, and this was definitely one of those times.

"Good luck." Rush said as a parting gift.

Connor was definitely going to need luck on his side. If he wasn't happy about the sleeping arrangements, then Anya certainly wasn't going to be happy about them either. Not that either of them had much choice.

He stood alone in the corridor for a few minutes after Rush left, wondering how the hell he was going to break the news to Anya.

Candi would have heard every word he and Rush spoke in the corridor. If he had any hope that she would tell Anya the good news so he didn't have to, it was dashed the moment he stepped back in the room.

From the look on her face, she found it all amusing.

"Is everything okay?" Candi asked sweetly.

Anya was silent as she looked between him and Candi, waiting patiently for him to speak. But he was still struggling with how to break it to her delicately. With no other option, he decided to just get it over with.

"You're going to be staying at my house for a while," he blurted.

The look on Anya's face would have been comical if

it hadn't involved him. But as it was, he didn't find any of it funny. Candi, however, was trying her hardest not to burst out laughing. Luckily enough, Anya couldn't see Candi's face because he could tell she didn't find it amusing, either.

"You can't be serious," Anya said incredulously.

"Afraid so."

"Great." She dragged the word out as she slumped back against the pillows and looked toward the ceiling.

"It's not so bad, Anya," Candi assured her when she finally had herself under control again. "It's only for a few days, and Connor will make sure you're well look after. He has a lovely house and lives alone, so you'll have plenty of space to get some peace and quiet while you rest and recover. Before you know it, you'll be going home."

Anya didn't look convinced, but she didn't argue or refuse to go with him, which was a step in the right direction. Now, if he could only assure himself that everything would be okay, then they would be on to a winner.

"Fine," she sighed. "When do we leave?"

"As soon as you're ready, we can leave," he told her. "I don't live too far from here, so you should be able to walk there fine."

"Just let me get dressed and then we can go." Anya looked around the room, no doubt looking for her clothes.

"They've been washed for you," he told her. "When you arrived, you were soaking wet and covered in muck."

"You're not going anywhere until you've eaten something," Candi said sternly. "You haven't eaten anything in days, and you've barely drank anything either. I know it isn't far to Connor's house, but you still need to eat something first."

Anya's stomach took that moment to growl. It was so loud; Connor wouldn't be surprised if everyone in the building heard it.

"Food sounds good," Anya smiled. "A shower would be nice as well."

As soon as she mentioned having a shower, Connor was inundated with indecent images of them in the shower together. He mentally slapped himself and quickly cleared his mind before his body could give away how he was feeling.

"That can be arranged," Candi said, snapping his attention out the gutter and back into the room. "Would you rather have a shower before you leave, or do you want to wait until you get to Connor's?"

Please say here. Please say here. He repeated like a mantra in his mind.

He knew she would eventually use his shower since she would be staying with him, but hopefully by then he would have better control over his body and mind.

"I think sooner would be better," Anya said as she pulled a face.

"There's a shower room across the hall," Candi told her. "I'll get you some towels and you can have a wash while I get you something to eat."

"Sounds good to me," Anya said, as she started to climb of the bed.

"I'll be in reception," he informed them before turning around and leaving them alone in the room.

Standing on the other side of the bathroom door sounded like a really bad idea. He was already finding it difficult to keep his distance from her. It would be ten times worse if he stood listening to her shower, knowing she was completely naked on the other side of the door.

No, it was better to put some distance between them before he did something stupid. Like joining her.

CHAPTER ELEVEN

Even though Connor and Candi had assured her it wasn't far to Connor's house, it still wasn't close enough for Anya. She was trying not to show how much pain she was in, but it was becoming increasingly harder with each step she took.

Taking a shower had zapped all the energy out of her. She didn't think it was possible to be so tired, especially after the amount of sleep she'd had. But between the shower and the walk, she was exhausted and couldn't wait to go back to bed.

Now she appreciated Connor's offer of giving her a place to stay for a few days until she was better. She wouldn't admit it to Rush, partly because she didn't know him, but he had been right. She wouldn't have made it very far through the cave, let alone back down the mountain on the other side as well.

It didn't help that she had no idea how far she was from the entrance on this side mountain. For all she knew, she could be miles away from the cave.

It would help if she knew where she was to begin

with, but since nobody was prepared to tell her, she would have to wait until they were ready to show her the way back. After all, she didn't want to get lost in a strange place. And she certainly didn't want to have any more accidents, either.

As much as she hated being in pain, she was enjoying being outside. She took a deep breath, ignoring the pain as she filled her lungs with fresh air as she took in the scenery.

When they first left the medical centre, they had walked through an open field, but that soon gave way to woodland.

There were a handful of small buildings clustered together by the medical centre, and one incredibly large building that sat in the middle of them all. A few people milled around, but none of them seemed to pay her or Connor any attention as they left medical and headed for the woods.

As soon as they disappeared from view, Anya felt her muscles loosen. She hadn't known how tense she was until that moment. Listening to the birds singing while being surrounded by nature had always helped her to relax in the past. She was glad that sense of peace hadn't left her after everything she'd been through.

The sights, the smells, and the sounds all rolled together. It soaked into her skin and burrowed into her bones, soothing her. Anya was amazed how much she always felt at home when she was among nature. Even though she lived in the city, her heart would always feel more at home among the towering trees of a woodland or forest.

It was her dream to one day have a place of her own in the middle of nowhere. As much as she loved her apartment, it wasn't hers at the end of the day. It would always belong to somebody else.

Renting was all well and good, but she didn't want to live in someone else's house for the rest of her life. Never knowing if she would be evicted from one minute to the next wasn't an ideal way to live.

She wanted more security than that. And she wanted the freedom to decorate however she liked, without having to ask for permission first. Anya didn't think it was too much to ask for.

It would take some getting used to, mainly because of the constantly changing weather, but Scotland was by far the best place she had seen. Even in her current situation, she felt like she could happily settle down in the area. Maybe not where she was at the moment, wherever that was, but she could definitely see herself living somewhere in the highlands.

She could have sworn the season were all screwy though. One minute it was the start of autumn, and in the next it was the middle spring. Even after witnessing how quickly the weather could change, she hadn't thought it was possible for the seasons to change so drastically as well.

Anya had been so caught up in admiring the stunning display of colours nature had to offer, and hoping to catch sight of the birds that were singing so beautifully, that she hadn't noticed the large house hiding among the trees. It wasn't until they came into the clearing where it stood that she finally noticed it.

"Wow." She breathed.

The house was stunning. The beautifully crafted log cabin was as large as a two story family home. The way it nestled among the trees and plants made it almost disappear as it blended in with its surroundings. She didn't know if it was planned that way, or a happy accident, but it worked well.

"This way."

Anya jumped when Connor spoke. It seemed to be turning into a habit where he was concerned.

It wasn't that she forgot he was with her... it wasn't possible to forget that a man like him was near... she just never expected him to speak to her. Guys like him didn't normally look in her direction, let alone speak to her.

"It's just 'round here," he said as continued walking.

Anya realised she'd stopped to gawk at the house. But who wouldn't stop to take in the beautiful architecture? The way plants climbed up, hugging the building, made it appear as if Mother Nature herself accepted it as hers. And the smell was heavenly.

"I take it you like the look of my house," he said as she caught up with him at the back of the property.

"It's beautiful," she said in awe. "Did you build it yourself?"

It hadn't escaped her notice how he seemed pleased by her response. The ghost of a smile on his face sent butterflies off in her stomach.

"Yes, I had some help from friends and family, but I did most of the work myself. It's all my own design, though."

"I bet it took ages to build."

With the amount of work that must have gone into it, she wouldn't be surprised if it had taken years, and that was just the workmanship she could see on the outside. She had yet to walk in and see what he had done inside.

If the outside was anything to go by, then the inside was bound to be just as spectacular. Anya couldn't wait to step inside and find out if she was right.

"It didn't take too long," he told her.

"How long did it take?" Anya couldn't help asking.

"There are still a couple of bits that need finishing…"

"Ha! See, it's taken you that long, you still haven't finished."

Connor smiled and said, "It's just the basement that needs finishing. I wasn't sure what to do with it until recently. But it took about six months all in all, and then I was moved in."

Oh. My. God!

He was even more devastatingly handsome when he smiled. For the second time that day, Anya had to check that her mouth wasn't wide open.

"That fast?" she said, recovering quickly from the unexpected smile.

Anya would have to be on guard while around him; otherwise she might end up embarrassing herself. The last thing she wanted was for him to see her lusting after him.

"We don't hang around," he said, holding the door

open for her to enter. "If something needs doing, then we get it done as quickly as possible."

"Impressive."

If Anya had been expecting to walk into an unfinished house, then she was sorely mistaken. Just like he said, it was completely finished and fully lived in. The interior was done to the same exceptionally high standard as the exterior, if not better.

She walked straight into a large open plan kitchen and dining room. The cupboards looked as if they had been specially made out of solid oak to fit the room. All the latest mod cons were there as well. A large range cooker, American style fridge-freezer, dishwasher, were all in black to match the granite worktops and floor.

A large solid oak dining table, more suited to a family than a single man living alone, stood proudly on the opposite side of the room from the kitchen. Eight chairs were placed neatly around it, but it could easily seat twelve without a problem.

"This way," he said, leading her through to a grand hallway.

Along one wall stood a sideboard, with a large canvas hanging above it. A beautifully carved staircase stood proudly to the other side of the entrance hall. Stained glass added a delicate touch to the solid oak door, casting fascinating colours on the oak floor.

Anya automatically stopped when she came alongside the canvas.

"Wow, that's stunning."

Painted on the canvas was a family of wolves in a woodland setting. The proud parents stood in the centre along with two other family members on either side, while two young pups ran around playfully.

"Whoever painted this is a fantastic artist."

"I'll let him know you said that next time I see him, which will probably be some point over the next couple of days."

"Your friend painted this?"

"Yes," he said, looking up at the painting briefly before turning back to her. "I'm sure you will meet him while you're here, so you can tell him yourself, if you like."

"Does he sell any of his work?"

"No."

"Would he consider selling any?"

"I don't know. You would have to ask him. Your room is this way," he said, changing the subject.

Before she could ask any more questions, Connor carried on towards the stairs. With one last look at the painting, she followed him upstairs.

Anya got the hint. She wouldn't bring up the subject again. It seemed such a waste that he wasn't selling his art. With paintings like that one, he could be making a decent wage.

There were even more paintings of wolves hanging on the walls, along the stairs and on the landing. Occasionally, she would spot another family portrait hanging among them, but with the pups at different ages. It was lovely seeing them grow into adults through the pictures.

"You must really love wolves," she said absentmindedly as she gazed at another picture.

"I do," he said, looking fondly at the pictures.

"I've never seen one before."

"You haven't?" he asked, sounding surprised.

"No, but I would love to," she admitted. "I refuse to go and see them in zoos. I would rather not see an animal, than see it in a cage. It doesn't matter what they call enclosures, or how much space they have, it's still a cage."

Connor nodded his head in agreement, but didn't say anything on the subject. He stopped outside a room and opened the door for her to enter.

"This is your room. The bathroom is across the hall, and my room is on the left next to the stairs."

"Okay, thank you."

"Candi's going to pick up some clothes for you. She'll drop them off later."

"Oh, okay, thank you," she said as she walked into the bedroom.

It hadn't even occurred to her what she was going to do about clothing. Thank god someone had thought about it, otherwise she would have ended up wearing the same clothes every day. She didn't even want to think about what she would have done when they needed cleaning.

"Do you need anything?" he asked from the doorway.

"No, I'm good, thank you."

"You don't need to keep thanking me, Anya."

The way her name rolled off his tongue, mixed with

the devilish smile on his face, was like melted chocolate… delicious, but ultimately bad for her.

"Um… I think…" Anya stuttered as she tried to remember what they were talking about, but no nothing came back to her. "I'm… um… going to rest for a bit… if that's okay?"

Yeah, that was smooth, Anya. Real smooth.

What the hell was wrong with her? It was like she was a school girl faced with her first crush or something.

"That's okay. I'll be downstairs if you need anything."

"Um… Okay… thank you."

Anya could have kicked herself at that moment in time, and she would have if he hadn't been watching her.

Connor smiled at her before he turned and walked away, leaving her alone to berate herself.

Seriously, she needed to pull herself together before she spent any more time around him. If not, it was only a matter of time before she made a complete fool of herself. That's if she hadn't already.

CHAPTER TWELVE

Connor took pride in his home and was always pleased when someone showed appreciation for what he designed and built. But knowing Anya liked his home affected him differently.

It shouldn't matter to him whether she liked it or not, but for some reason it did. It mattered a lot.

He knew what she must have thought when she saw the size of his dining table. And his home for that matter. It may be a bit big for just himself, but he'd built it in preparation for making it a family home for his future mate and pups. Not that Anya needed to know that.

When she stopped to look at the pictures he'd commissioned Kellen to paint, he'd waited with bated breath for her reaction. He couldn't tell her it was a portrait of his family in their wolf forms, so he let her assume it was just an ordinary painting of a wolf family.

He loved that she admired the artwork, but he hadn't been expecting her to speak so passionately about animal welfare. He whole heartedly agreed with her, no animal deserved to live out their lives in a cage. Especially for the sole purpose as entertainment for others. The whole idea was barbaric.

Connor walked into the kitchen and grabbed something to eat before heading downstairs to make a start on the basement renovation. Thankfully, his mother had stopped by earlier in the day and restocked his fridge and cupboards; otherwise there would be nothing in to eat.

Since he was going to be at home for the next few days, he might as well get as much work done on the basement as he could. Hoping it would take his mind off the sleeping beauty upstairs, he threw himself into clearing out the space, ready for dividing it up and turning it into separate usable rooms.

Hours passed as he laboured away. Once the room was clear, he moved onto the next stage in the development, and before he knew it, the space was starting to take shape.

Satisfied with the progress he'd made so far, Connor packed up his tools and headed upstairs to the bathroom. He needed to clean the dirt and grime off before starting dinner.

He stripped off his dirt covered clothes before turning on the shower. Without waiting for the water to heat up, he stepped in and began washing.

He'd never been one to spend hours in the bath or shower, and now wasn't any different. He made quick work of washing his hair and body.

When he was finished rinsing away the bubbles, he

switched off the shower and climbed out. He wrapped a towel around his waist and made his way to his bedroom.

He couldn't stop his eyes from going to Anya's room. When he didn't hear any sound coming from inside, he assumed she was still asleep.

Sleep was the best thing for her. Her body should naturally begin to heal itself as she slept. If she was a shifter, she would heal a lot quicker. But since she was a human, it would take her body time to recover from all the damage that was done to it.

Before he could do something stupid, like going in to her room to check on her, he went into his bedroom and threw on a loose fitting pair of trousers and a t-shirt.

With one last look at her bedroom door, he made his way down to the kitchen.

He was just about to put a pot of coffee on when the back door was flung open and Myra walked in with Candi.

"Hey big bro, how's it going having a female living under the same roof as you?" Myra said.

"She's not living with me," he said adamantly. "She's just staying here until she's well enough to go home."

Candi was carrying a bag of clothes for Anya, as promised. She placed the bag on the dining table before turning to him. "Hi, Connor. How is Anya doing?"

"She's resting," he told her.

"Isn't she the one you've been dreaming of?" Myra

asked.

"Who told you that?"

"Aidan."

"Of course, he did."

Connor should have known Aidan would tell Myra. He always did like to gossip, just like some of the females in the pack. In fact, sometimes he was worse than the females.

"What's that?" Candi asked.

"Connor's been dreaming of the female that was found in the cave," Myra informed her.

"I heard Rush say something about him dreaming of her when they were at medical earlier," Candi confessed. "But I thought I was hearing things."

"No, you heard right," Myra said, grinning from ear to ear.

"Wow," Candi said as she looked at him. "How long has that been going on?"

"It's been about two weeks now," Myra answered for him.

"So even before she arrived?"

"Yep."

Connor disliked how they spoke about him, as if he wasn't even in the room. They seemed to forget whose house they were in.

"I'm right here," he pointed out, but they carried on as if he hadn't said a word.

"Oh, wow, what do you think it means?" Candi asked.

"I think it means she's his mate."

He noticed Candi's mouth drop open as he spun his

head to glare at Myra. He wasn't sure who was more surprised by Myra's comment, Candi or himself.

"Really? What about Rush? Has he said anything?" Candi asked excitedly.

"She's not my mate," he stated. Not that they were listening.

"Apparently he doesn't know."

"Do you mind?" he demanded.

"What?" they asked in unison.

"You're talking about me as if I'm not here. It's my bloody house!"

"Yeah, we know, we've been here a while now and you still haven't offered us anything to drink. Mum would be ashamed of your skills as a host." Myra shook her head. "Is this the way you've treated Anya? Or did you at least ask her if she wanted a drink when she got here?"

"I asked if she wanted anything after I showed her to her room."

"So, you took her straight upstairs?" Myra raised an eyebrow as she glared at him.

"Yes, I was showing her where she was staying."

"You dickhead." Myra shook her head at him. "She probably thought you didn't want her down here."

"She said she needed to rest, which she does."

"That's because you took her straight to her room." Myra shook her head at him and then stormed out of the room. "I'm going to see if she's okay."

"Really, Connor?" Candi said, as she grabbed the bag of clothes and followed Myra out of the room.

"What have I done?" he shouted after them, but they

didn't reply.

Connor didn't have a clue what just happened. He stared at the ceiling as he tried to figure it out, running over everything that had happened since he'd brought Anya to his home, but nothing jumped out at him. As far as he was concerned, he hadn't done anything wrong.

No matter how many years he lived, he would never understand females.

***

Anya woke to a gentle tapping on a door. It wasn't coming from her front door because the sound was too close.

It took her a moment to remember where she was, and then it all came flooding back. She wasn't at home in her own bed, nor was she back in the hotel bedroom. She was in Connor's home.

The tapping came again, along with muffled talking on the other side of the door.

"One sec!" She shouted to whoever was on the other side of the door.

Anya sat up quickly and instantly regretted it. Her chest revolted at the sudden movement, reminding her that she needed to take it easy.

"Fuck. That hurt." She mumbled to herself.

"You okay in there?" Candi shouted through the door.

"Yeah, I'm good," she lied. "Just give me a minute."

She winced as more pain shot through her as she slid

her legs over the side of the bed. She slowly inhaled and exhaled a couple of times before pushing to a standing position.

The pain was nowhere near as bad as it had been when she first woke in the medical centre, but it was still strong enough to take her breath away. It probably wouldn't have been so bad if she hadn't moved so fast when she sat up moments ago.

The only thing Anya had removed before climbing into bed was her shoes. She was grateful she hadn't taken anything else off as she made her way over to the door. She certainly wouldn't have been able to dress without a few curse words slipping out.

Anya was half expecting Connor to be stood with Candi, but she was with a woman instead. Both women were smiling at Anya as she opened the door.

"Hi, Anya. This is Myra, Connor's sister," she introduced the woman with her.

Other than having the same hair and eye colour, Myra looked nothing like her brother. But just like her brother, and everyone else she'd met so far, she was stunningly beautiful.

"Hi, Anya," Myra said cheerfully. "It's nice to meet you."

"It's nice to meet you too."

Candi held up a bag for Anya. "I've brought some clothes for you. They should fit fine."

"Thank you." Anya took the bag from Candi and carried it over to the bed.

"You can keep them for as long as you need," Candi told her.

Both women had followed her into the bedroom. They stood on either side of the doorway when she turned around.

"Are you sure?"

"Yeah, the person I borrowed them from has loads of clothes, and I mean a massive collection, she can't even wear that many in a year." She winked at Anya.

"Hey! I don't have that many clothes." Myra glared at Candi before turning to Anya with a smile on her face. "But Candi's right, keep them as long as you need."

Her and Myra were about the same height, but Anya would have said Myra was slimmer. Still, she accepted the clothes with a smile.

"Thank you."

"You're welcome," Myra smiled back.

"Yes, you do," Candi said. "You have more clothes than anything else in your house."

"What can I say?" Myra grinned. "I like clothes."

Candi was grinning as well. "Are you hungry? Thirsty?"

Anya's stomach grumbled at the mention of food.

"I take that as a yes," Myra said, her pale blue eyes glinting with laughter.

"Yes, please." Anya smiled sheepishly.

"Okay, come downstairs and we'll get you something to eat," Myra said. "My brother is a really good cook."

"I can vouch for that," Candi told her.

Anya didn't say a word as she followed them downstairs. She pulled her hair back into a messy pony tail and wrapped a scrunchy round it as they reached the bottom of the stairs.

"Tell me if he doesn't take care of you properly," Myra said before they walked into the kitchen. "I'll set my mum on him."

Connor was leaning against the counter with a cup in his hand as they walked in. His eyes instantly latched on to hers.

Anya had to force herself to look away from his captivating eyes. She made the mistake of looking down at the wrong time and nearly bumped into Myra as she suddenly stopped.

"There's coffee in the pot if you want any." The sound of Connor's deep voice sent shivers racing down her spine.

"Ooh, yes, please." Candi made a beeline for the pot. "Do you two want one?"

"You know I do," Myra said.

"Yes, please," Anya said.

"Take a seat, Anya, and I'll bring it over," Candi offered.

"Thank you."

"Hey, what about mine?" Myra asked.

"You're fit and healthy, you can get your own," Candi laughed.

"So unfair," Myra pouted.

Anya couldn't help but smile. She could easily see herself being friends with the two women.

Thinking about friends brought up thoughts of Sasha. She must be going out of her mind with worry, and there was absolutely nothing Anya could do to alleviate those worries. She vowed to make it up to Sasha when she finally got home, whenever that would be.

"Here you go, Anya," Candi said as she handed her a mug.

"Thank you."

"What would you like to eat?" Myra asked her.

"Just some toast, please."

"You need to eat properly if you're going to get better," Candi told her.

"I'm already feeling better," Anya confessed.

As much as the sudden movement had hurt when she first woke up, she wasn't in as much pain as she should be.

Candi didn't look convinced, but she didn't question her about it. Anya couldn't quite believe it herself, so she wouldn't know where to start explaining it to them.

"Okay, toast it is," Myra said.

Anya was quiet as she watched the way Candi, Connor, and Myra interacted. She could tell there was a strong bond between the three of them. But even though Connor and Candi weren't related, he seemed to treat her like his sister.

She didn't think it was sexual between them, but she could be wrong. It wouldn't be the first time she'd made that mistake.

Anya didn't want to look into why she suddenly became jealous of their friendship. Or why she didn't like the idea of something more going on between Connor and Candi.

"Here you go," Myra said, placing a plate of toast on the table in front of her.

"Thank you," Anya said as she picked up a piece.

Myra smile as she took a seat on the opposite side of the table with Candi. "You're welcome."

Anya jumped when she felt Connor pull out the chair next to her. If any of them noticed, thankfully, they didn't say anything.

As soon as Connor sat next to her, she was surrounded by his scent. She had always loved the smell of sandalwood, but it was even better coming from Connor.

She could feel the heat coming off his body and seeping into her where they sat so close together. The mixture of his heat and scent surrounding her and filling her lungs was a heady experience.

Anya was finding it incredibly hard to concentrate on eating, or the conversation going on around her, with him sitting right next to her. Her mouth was so dry; she had to swig her coffee just to be able to swallow each bite.

"Is everything okay?" Candi asked.

Connor turned in his chair, brushing up against Anya in the process. Her mind instantly went blank and all she could do was nod at Candi.

"You look tired," Myra said.

"I am." She wasn't, but thank God Myra had given her a way out.

"Don't worry, we won't stop for long," Candi said.

"It's okay," she told them. "Don't leave on my account."

"You need to rest so your body has a chance to recover." Candi smiled softly as she spoke. "We can always come back to visit you another time."

"That would be nice, thank you."

"You are more than welcome," Candi said.

"Plus," Myra added. "I'll be stopping by to make sure Connor is taking good care of you."

"Don't drop by too often." Connor's deep voice sent shivers through her.

"I'll stop by as often as I like," Myra told him. "And if you're not looking after Anya, I'm going to tell mum."

"I'm sure Connor will take good care of her," Candi said to Myra before turning to Connor. "Won't you, Connor?"

"She'll be fine."

Myra and Candi glared at Connor, but they didn't say a word. Anya didn't have to look at Connor to know he was glaring at them as well.

Something was going on between the three of them, she just didn't know what.

"Well," Candi said, breaking the silence. "We better get going. If there's anything you want or need, Anya, just let us know and we'll sort it out for you."

"Thank you," she said. "For everything."

"Nothing to thank us for," Myra said. "We'd do the same for anyone."

"Yep, we would," Candi agreed. "But you're more than welcome."

Anya was grateful for the offer, but the only thing she wanted was to go home.

Liar! Her subconscious was right, she was a liar.

Going home wasn't the only thing she wanted. There was another thing she really wanted, but there was no way she was going to admit it, especially not out loud.

Candi and Myra stood up at the same time. They picked up their empty coffee cups and carried them over to the sink.

"Right, we'll leave you two to it," Candi said.

"Just remember what we told you, Anya," Myra added. "If there's anything you need or want, don't hesitate to ask."

"I will, thank you," Anya said, as she stood as well.

With Candi and Myra leaving, Anya didn't want to stay downstairs with Connor on her own. Not because she didn't trust him, but because she didn't trust herself.

It had been torture sitting so close to him. The gentle brushes against her as he shifted in his seat, sent shivers racing through her every time. Every. Single. Time.

It was like he had ants in his pants or something with the amount he kept fidgeting. Either that, or he knew exactly what effect he was having on her.

If the knowing look on Connor's face was anything to go by, then it was the latter.

Anya was ready to run and hide as soon as she was alone with Connor. Not once in her life had she been so turned on by such innocent touches.

Connor looked relaxed as he sprawled in the chair. She could feel his eyes boring into her as she said goodbye to Candi and Myra.

It was dark outside by the time they left, but neither of them seemed bothered about walking through the woods alone at night. Anya wasn't sure she would be so confident, but she might feel differently if she knew the area like they did.

As soon as the door closed behind Candi and Myra, Anya became all too aware she was alone with Connor. She knew without turning around that he was still watching her, waiting to see what she would do.

Before she could make a fool of herself by throwing herself at him, she said 'goodnight' and made a hasty retreat back to her bedroom.

CHAPTER THIRTEEN

Anya shot up in bed. Her heart was racing, and she was breathing erratically, but it had absolutely nothing to do with the nightmares that had plagued her dreams.

No, the culprit this time was none other than the man she was staying with, Connor. Even in her dreams, he was irresistible.

The dream was so vivid; it was as if she was actually experiencing what he was doing to her body. He'd played her body to perfection, and she'd relished in every second of it.

My. God. Did I ever.

She could still remember how his rough hands had run over her body, and how it felt to run her hands over his. His broad shoulders, hard pecks, and washboard abs were burned into her mind. His scent was all around her, even now that she was wide awake.

Not once had she ever been so turned on by a dream. Especially not to the extent that she'd nearly had an orgasm.

Fuck me, I had been so close.

If she hadn't woke up when she had, he would have tipped her over the edge. It would have been the most intense orgasm of her life, and it hadn't even been real.

Needing to take her mind off Connor and the erotic dream, she decided to take a shower. She should probably take a cold shower, but she didn't think even that would cool her heated body.

As she climbed out of bed, she glanced out of the window. It was still dark outside, but it had started to rain while she'd been asleep.

Her mind instantly conjured images of dark winter nights in front of a fire with Connor by her side. Anya shook her head to clear her mind as she turned away from the window.

After a little investigating, she found where Connor stored the towels. She grabbed two before making her way into the bathroom.

She eyed the bathtub for a moment, but decided against it because she didn't want to hang around waiting for it to fill. So, she switched on the shower instead.

Anya stripped off her clothes and dumped them in a pile on the floor. As soon as she was ready, she stepped under the water.

As it continued to heat up, she grabbed the shampoo and began massaging the suds into her scalp. By the time she was ready to rinse her hair, the water was at the perfect temperature.

She quickly washed and rinsed her body before

switching off the shower and stepping out. She dried off before wrapping a towel around her hair and another around her body. When she was finished, she gathered up her dirty clothes and headed back to her bedroom.

Anya rushed out of the bathroom and collided with something hard and warm. Strong hands grabbed hold of her arms, steading her before she could topple over.

At the same time, Anya put her hand out in front of her to help regain her balance. Her pulse quickened as her hand came in contact with firm, warm skin.

Anya looked up, her eyes clashing with Connor's piercing blue eyes as he stared down at her with a smile on his face.

She hadn't expected to see him standing outside the bathroom door. In her haste to get to the bedroom, she had nearly lost the towel as well as her balance in the process.

An uncontrollable urge to run her hands over his body swept through her like wildfire. Luckily enough, he moved back slightly before she could do anything stupid.

"I'm sorry; I wasn't expecting you to be up." Anya could feel her cheeks heating with embarrassment.

"That's okay, I wasn't expecting to be up either," he grinned as he released her arms. "How come you're up so late?"

"I couldn't sleep. You?"

"Yeah, same."

All too aware she was still only covered with a towel, and not a very large one at that, Anya scrambled for something to say.

"Well... um... I'm just gonna go get some clothes on," she stuttered.

As soon as the words left her mouth, Anya wished she could take them back. Up until that moment, Connor had kept his eyes at face level, but pointing out her lack of attire made his focus shift to lower down.

From the lust that flashed in his eyes as he looked down at the towel, he didn't mind her lack of clothing.

"Can I just..." she pointed to the hallway.

"Yes, of course," he said, stepping out of the way for her.

"Thank you." Anya looked down as she hurried past.

Not looking back, she raced into the bedroom and quickly shut the door behind her.

She leaned against the closed door and waited for her heart to stop racing. It felt like it was about to explode, it was beating so fast.

Why did the man have to be so god damn handsome? And shirtless?

Anya had not missed that part. The feel of his skin beneath her palm was exactly the same as what it had been in her dream.

Connor had on a pair of jeans, but that only seemed to make her hotter for him. Her fingers itched to undo his jeans and slowly slide them down his legs, revealing the rest of his perfectly sculpted body.

She nearly leapt out of her skin when Connor knocked on the door.

"Anya?" he called.

"Yes?" She was amazed her voice didn't shake when she replied.

"I'm going downstairs for a drink, I was wondering if you would like anything?"

"Yes, please."

"What would you like? Tea? Coffee? Or maybe something a bit stronger?"

"Do you have any hot chocolate?"

"I think you might be in luck. I'm sure Myra left some here for when she visits. Do you want me to bring it up?"

"Um… no, its okay, I'll be down in a minute."

She couldn't hide in the bedroom the entire time, even if it did seem like the safest bet. Connor was kind enough to let her stay, the least she could do was show she appreciated it by spending time downstairs.

"Okay," he said. "See you downstairs in a minute."

Anya grabbed the bag of clothes Candi and Myra had dropped off and carried it over to the bed. She emptied the contents onto the bed and then rummaged through it for something to wear.

Unfortunately, the only nightwear Anya could see, were sexy lace and silk numbers that showed more than they covered. They definitely didn't leave much to the imagination.

Anya owned a couple of chemises that she loved wearing, but she wouldn't wear them as a nightie in somebody else's house. They certainly wouldn't be as revealing as the ones on the bed.

Deciding against the sexy lingerie, she carried on looking until she came across yoga pants and a loose-fitting t-shirt.

Not bothering with underwear, she quickly dressed and then made her way downstairs.

Connor stood with his back to her as she walked into the kitchen. Still only clad in a pair of jeans, she watched the play of muscles on his back as he moved around making hot chocolate.

Anya was quiet as she admired the view, but she didn't have long to take it all in before Connor looked over his shoulder at her. Yet again, she'd been caught staring at him.

"Mm, that smells nice," she said when he smiled at her.

"If you say so. It's a bit sweet for my liking."

"So why are you having one, then?" She pointed at the two mugs on the counter next to him.

Connor shot her a mischievous grin. "Who says I'm having hot chocolate in mine?"

He had her there. Just because there were two cups on the side, didn't mean they were both for the chocolate.

"Sorry," she said, feeling stupid. "I just assumed."

"That's okay."

Anya walked further into the room and leaned against the counter opposite him. She crossed her arms in front of her chest to stop herself from reaching out to touch him.

"So, what are you having instead of hot chocolate?"

"I'm having a whiskey." As he poured the hot chocolate into one of the mugs, he stepped aside slightly so she could see the half empty bottle of whiskey on the counter. "I can add some to your hot chocolate if you want?"

"No, thank you." She grimaced at the thought of mixing the two. "I think I'll pass."

"Suit yourself." Connor grinned as he handed her the mug.

"Thank you."

"You're welcome."

They fell into an awkward silence. Anya was all too aware of the virile man opposite her as she blew on the hot liquid.

She'd never had such a strong attraction to man before. It was jarring how much he affected her just by being in the same room.

Anya took a sip of hot chocolate. She savoured the sweet taste in her mouth before swallowing.

As the silence dragged out between them, other noises became more noticeable. The patter of rain as it hit the window, the rustling of leaves blowing in the wind, even the steady beat of her heart was magnified in the silence.

Connor seemed to be watching her like a hawk. She tried not to look at him, but time and again, she failed. Like a moth to a flame, her eyes kept going back to him.

"You and Myra seem close," she said when she couldn't take the silence anymore.

"We are," he told her. "My whole family is close, to be honest. We see each other most days."

"That sounds nice. Do you have a large family?"

Connor shook his head. "I have two sisters and one

brother. Myra, who you've already met, and then there's Misti and Caleb. Those two are troublemakers."

"Are they younger than you?"

"Yes, I'm the oldest out of the four of us. Myra's two years younger than me. Caleb and Misti are teenagers. How about you? Do you have any brothers or sisters?"

"No, it's just me."

"That must have been cool," he said. "Growing up as an only child, I bet your parents doted on you."

"I wish that was the case," she said without thinking.

Anya didn't normally talk about her own upbringing because it was usually followed by pitying looks, so she was surprised she'd mentioned anything at all.

"What do you mean?"

"I don't have any parents," she admitted.

"Oh, I'm sorry for your loss."

"They didn't die. Well, at least as far as I know, they didn't."

"I don't understand."

"I was abandoned as a baby. I grew up in children's homes and foster care."

"I'm sorry."

Thankfully, there was no pity in his eyes as he spoke.

"Don't be," she told him. "It wasn't all bad. Some of the foster homes were really nice, and I got a lot of opportunities that I might not have had otherwise."

Anya didn't know why, but she found it really easy to open up to him. She didn't feel the need to hide her past like she did with most people. It helped that he didn't seem to judge her because of it, which a lot of people did when they found out she grew up in care, especially men.

"Do you have a man waiting for you back home?" he asked out of the blue.

Anya wanted to think he was asking because he was attracted to her like she was with him. But he was probably just being polite by making a conversation rather than stand in silence like they had done.

"Nope. There's no man waiting for me at home."

"Really? I can't believe an attractive woman like yourself doesn't have a man in your life."

Hearing him say she was attractive, even if he didn't mean it, sent butterflies off in her stomach and she could feel herself blushing again.

"How about you?" she asked nervously. "Do you have a special woman in your life?"

"Nope, just like you, I'm free and single," he said, slouching against the counter as he downed the last of his drink.

"I'm surprised you don't have women lining up to be with you." Anya could have kicked herself as soon as the words slipped out of her mouth.

"Why's that?"

Of course he would ask her that. Anya didn't know what to say that wouldn't give away how she felt about him.

"Because…"

"Go on, because what?" he pushed when she stalled.

"Because look at you. You're every woman's wet

dream rolled into one," she blurted out.

Connor's lips curved in a devilishly handsome smile as he looked at her hungrily. Anya could feel moister building between her legs when his eyes darkened with desire.

"Are you hungry?"

Oh, fuck, yeah!

She didn't need to be a mind reader to know what he meant. The sinful look in Connor's eyes spoke volumes about what he had in mind, and it had nothing to do with food.

Anya quickly put the mug on the counter before Connor could see her hand shaking. She wasn't scared. She was excited and nervous all at the same time.

Connor took two large steps forward, which brought him toe to toe with her. With him so close, she could feel the heat radiating from his bare chest.

If she leaned forward an inch, she would be able to lick said chest. Instead, she looked up at his face.

Desire darkened his eyes. The way he looked at her with such hunger made her pulse quicken as moister pooled between her legs. Anya noticed his nostrils flare as he inhaled deeply.

Without a word, he lowered his head and tentatively brushed his lips against hers. When she didn't push him away, he wrapped one arm around her waist and pulled her close as he deepened the kiss.

Anya placed her hands on his bare chest. Delicious tingles raced through her as the last remnants of pain disappeared and was replaced by pleasure.

Licking the seam of her lips, he waited until they parted before sliding his tongue inside. Anya could taste the whiskey on his tongue as it tangled with hers. The mix of whiskey and chocolate was addictive.

Anya gave in to the temptation to run her hands over his sculpted body. Learning every dip and curve of muscle as Connor's hands roamed her body.

She sucked in a breath when his fingers brushed against her nipples through the fabric. They instantly responded to his touch.

She pushed out her chest, inviting him to touch her breasts some more. Connor took her up on the offer. He cupped her breasts and gently brushed his thumbs against the sensitive peaks.

Anya moaned into his mouth as pleasure shot through her. She wanted... needed... more.

Cupping the bulge in his jeans elicited a moan from Connor. Even through his jeans, she could feel how hard he was. She rubbed her hand up and down, feeling the size of his cock.

Before she could do more, he grabbed her hips and lifted her effortlessly onto the kitchen counter. She opened her legs so he could nestle between them.

Connor ran his hands through her hair and tilted her head to the side. Her toes curled and her heart picked up speed as he deepened the kiss further.

Anya didn't know how she got into this situation, but she sure as hell didn't want to get out of it.

Releasing his hold on her hair, he slowly slid his hands down her body. He lightly brushed her nipple through the fabric as he passed her breasts. Already heightened, each touch sent tingles racing through her straight to her core, but his hands didn't stop there.

The first touch of his fingers against her bare skin as he slid his hands under the hem of her top, sent shivers racing down her spin. As his hands glided back up her sides, he took her top with him.

They broke the kiss long enough to remove her top, and then his mouth was on her again. He trailed kisses down her neck as he gently leaned her back.

Anya automatically lifted her legs. She wrapped them around his waist, hooking her ankles behind him.

She gasped as Connor lowered her the rest of the way down to the worktop. The mixture of hot and cold coming from him and the worktop was a shock to the senses, but it wasn't as unpleasant as she thought it would be.

Instead of bringing her back to her senses so she could put a stop to what they were doing, it had the opposite effect. In that moment in time, Anya needed him more than she needed to breathe.

It scared and exhilarated her all at the same time.

CHAPTER FOURTEEN

Connor's heart raced as he carried Anya upstairs to his bedroom.

From the moment he first laid eyes on her, he'd wanted nothing more than to have her in his arms. And now that she was, the only thing that could stop him from sampling Anya, was her.

He wouldn't force her to do something she didn't want to do. As much as it would pain him to walk away, he would do exactly that if she wanted to stop.

He kicked his bedroom door shut before lowering Anya to her feet. Reluctantly, he let go of her waist and stepped back.

Anya held his gaze as she hooked her thumbs into the top of her trousers. She hesitated for only a second before sliding them over her hips and down her shapely legs to the floor.

Connor swallowed when he realised she wasn't wearing any underwear. He knew she wasn't wearing a bra, but he'd thought she would have panties on at least. It was a nice surprise to find out she wasn't.

Anya stood back up and stepped out of the trousers, kicking them off to the side. No matter how hard she tried to hide it, he could tell she was nervous. But she was also excited and aroused.

He didn't need to see the moister between her legs to know she was wet for him. He could smell her arousal.

The intoxicating scent had been driving him insane all afternoon and evening. Several times he'd had to fight the urge to pull her into his arms and claim her mouth with his.

Connor thought he was going to lose the fight when she ran into him after she'd been in the shower. He had to admit; he secretly hoped her towel would slip from her fingers and reveal her body to him.

He bit back a groan as he looked at her incredible body as she stood naked in front of him. His cock twitched, eager to slide inside her.

Anya's light blue eyes roamed his body. Her long strawberry blonde hair, still damp from her shower, framed her oval face. It hung in waves down to her waist, partially covering her breasts.

"You're so fucking beautiful."

Connor couldn't wait any longer. He needed to have Anya in his arms again.

He pulled her into his arms and lowered his head to hers. Anya instantly reached up and wrapped her arms around the back of his neck. Her lips parted of a sigh.

Connor intended for it to be a slow and passionate kiss, but the moment his lips touched hers, he was lost. He couldn't stop his hands from roaming her body as their tongues duelled.

He slowly backed her up to the bed. When she felt it behind her, she broke the kiss and turned around.

Connor groaned when she crawled across the bed on all fours. It took all of his willpower not to climb on after her and slide his cock between her legs.

She gave him a knowing look over her shoulder before turning around and reclining against the pillows. Anya lifted her knees up so her feet were flat on the bed.

She crooked her finger, beckoning him. Connor didn't need to be asked twice. He was on the bed in a flash.

He didn't dare remove his trousers. If he did, he wouldn't be able to stop himself from sliding his cock inside her.

As soon as he joined her on the bed, he covered her body with his and claimed her mouth again.

Anya moaned into his mouth as his hand snaked down her body to cup her sex. She gasped when he moved his fingers against her sensitive skin, breaking the kiss as her head fell back on the pillows. She was wet, just like he knew she would be.

Connor trailed kisses down her neck and chest as his fingers glided through her moist folds. When he reached her breasts, he swirled his tongue around one of the tips before sucking it into his mouth.

Anya ran her hands through his hair as he paid each breast the attention it deserved before moving on.

He continued the trail of kisses down her abdomen to the patch of strawberry blonde curls at the junction of her thighs. His cock twitched at the scent of her arousal.

Connor spread her open with his fingers. He took in the sight of her before leaning in for a taste.

If he was a feline shifter, he was positive he would have been purring. She tasted like the sweetest ambrosia, and he was addicted from the first lick.

Anya squirmed beneath him as he devoured her with his mouth. She gasped when he pushed one finger inside her.

She tried moving her hips in time with his finger, but he held her down using his free hand and arm.

He pumped his finger in and out of her several times before adding a second finger. He licked and sucked her clit as he built up speed with his fingers.

He knew when she was getting close, so he doubled his efforts. Her back arched off the bed, and her walls tightened around his fingers as she tipped over the edge.

When her walls finally stopped squeezing him, he removed his fingers and crawled back up the bed until he was leaning over her.

"Are you sure you want this?"

Even though they had already done plenty, and it would kill him to stop now, if she wanted to end things there, he would respect her wishes.

"Yes," she nodded. "I want this."

Connor felt exactly the same way, but he couldn't bring himself to admit it out loud.

Taking her mouth in a searing kiss, he lined up his cock with her entrance and slowly pushed the tip inside her.

Anya gasped as he breached her slick walls. She was so hot and tight, it took all of his willpower not to slam home.

Once he was fully seated, he held still for a moment to give her time to adjust to his size. As soon as she began to relax, he began to move.

He pulled out of her until only the tip of him remained inside her and then he pushed back in to the hilt. Connor moved slowly at first, watching her face for signs of what she liked and didn't like. It didn't take long for him to get into a rhythm they both enjoyed.

Anya lifted her legs. Wrapping them around his waist, she hooked her ankles together behind him. Her nails dug into his back as she held on to him.

He loved the flushed look on her face as she let go, completely giving in to the pleasure. Her eyes were closed and her head was tilted back as a light sheen of sweat coated her skin.

Connor could feel her walls tightening around his cock, signalling that she was close to climax. He shifted position slightly and tilted her hips to get a better angle.

Before long, Anya's mouth opened on a silent scream as she tipped over the edge. Connor bit his lower lip to stop himself from following her. He wasn't ready for it to end just yet.

Slowing his pace, he waited for her to stop pulsing around his cock. As soon as she did, he pulled out of her and spun her around so she was on all fours in front of him.

Anya didn't get the chance to protest the new position before he was entering her again. Her gasp at the sudden movement quickly turned into a moan when his cock slid all the way inside her.

Connor couldn't stop the groan from escaping his lips at the tight grip she had on his cock. The new position not only gave him a great view of her arse, it also meant he could go deeper.

He ran a hand up her back and gently pushed down between her shoulders. She instantly did as he wanted and rested her head on the mattress.

"Are you okay like that?" his voice sounded strained to his own ears as he did his best to hold still.

He didn't want her to feel any discomfort or pain, only pleasure.

"Yes," she breathed.

To prove her point, she rocked her hips against him.

"Good," he groaned.

Grabbing her hips, he pulled her back slightly before he began moving again. There was no slow build up this time. Even if he wanted to take it slow, his body had taken over control.

Sweat soaked their skin as he quickly picked up speed. Before he knew it, Anya was already on the verge of another orgasm. He reached around her waist with one hand until he found the bundle of nerves at the apex of her thighs.

He rubbed his fingers over and around her clit as he pounded in and out of her. Anya met him thrust for thrust. Her pleasure filled groans was music to his ears.

An overwhelming urge to mark her as his hit him so suddenly, he almost did exactly that. He fought the urge to lean over her and wrap his lips around her neck before sinking his teeth into the soft flesh there.

He bit his bottom lip instead. The taste of his own blood filled his mouth.

His balls tightened as he climbed closer to his own orgasm, but he wanted to feel her walls tighten around him before he let himself go to the bliss that awaited him. Connor rolled her clit between his finger and thumb before gently squeezing. That's all it took to send her screaming over the edge.

Her slick walls clamped down tight around his cock, sending him over the edge as well. He shouted her name as her hot pussy milked every last drop from him.

When they were both sated, he pulled out of her before rolling them both onto their sides. He wrapped an arm around her waist and pulled her towards him so her back was against his chest.

Anya instantly relaxed, and within minutes, her breathing evened out as sleep took hold of her. Connor wished he could fall asleep so easily, but his mind kept going over everything.

He still didn't know what the dreams meant, or how Anya was tied to them. Nor how she found her way into the shifter realm. She was human, so she shouldn't have been able to see the cave entrance, let alone be able to locate the portal once inside the cave.

But what was even more worrying was how strong the urge to mark her as his had hit him during sex.

He'd never felt the urge to mark anybody during sex before, and he'd had plenty of past lovers. So, what was so different about Anya?

Connor had a feeling he would find out the answer to that when he found the answers to all the other questions floating around in his mind. He just hoped he got the answers sooner rather than later.

Until then, he needed to keep his distance from her. Because if he gave into the desire again, he might not be able to resist the urge to sink his teeth into her for a second time.

***

"Get here, NOW!" he shouted down the phone.

He was sick and tired of waiting for an update on Anya's location in the shifter realm. Until he knew where she was being held, he couldn't move on to the next stage of his plan.

He was by no means a patient man. He expected things to be done his way, and in a timely manner. When that wasn't the case, people around him had a tendency to die. Mainly by his hand, but occasionally, he would pass the job onto another.

The witch didn't seem to understand that yet, but she would if she continued to ignore him. Three days had passed since he last had word from Kassadi, and that wasn't acceptable in the slightest.

Within minutes of him screaming down the phone, Kassadi finally appeared in front of him.

"I've located her," she said. "But getting to her isn't

going to be easy."

"Why not?" he demanded.

"Because she hasn't been left on her own since they found her," she told him. "They have her under constant guard at all times. It's as if they don't trust her. Either that, or they're expecting somebody to come for her."

"Interesting." Was it possible they didn't know about her yet? If so, then that could work in his favour. He just hoped it wasn't the latter, because that would make it more difficult to get to her.

"So, what do you want me to do about it?" she asked.

"I'm sure you'll come up with something," he told her. "Now go, and don't come back until you have her."

CHAPTER FIFTEEN

Anya couldn't believe she'd let things go as far as they had with Connor. Normally, she liked to at least get to know the guy before jumping in bed with him. She certainly didn't normally jump in bed with them on the first night.

In fact, she usually held out until she was in a committed relationship before going all the way. But she didn't regret any of it. How could she after he'd shown her such pleasure.

She was lucky to have one orgasm with her past lovers, but with Connor… all she could say was 'wow'. The man knew exactly what to do and when to do it, and she had happily handed over the reins.

Connor had shown her a different side of himself, one that was tender and affectionate.

As much as she tried to prevent it, she couldn't stop scenes of their night together from playing out in her mind. That mouth of his was magic, and so were his fingers.

The way he touched her, the way he made her feel like she was the only woman in the world, the desire she saw shinning back at her from his eyes. It all rolled into one amazing night that she would never forget.

No, Anya didn't regret what they did, but it appeared as though Connor did. He'd given her the cold shoulder the entire day.

Thankfully, Anya got the message loud and clear before she did something stupid, like offer herself up on a platter. Well, for a second time anyway.

She had never felt so uncomfortable after a night of passion with someone before. It was like the night never happened. Connor was back to treating her like an unwelcome house guest, and she was doing her best to stay out of his way.

Anya couldn't lie, the way he was acting hurt. But she was a big girl. If she could get over what her ex did to her - the lying, cheating son-of-a-bitch - then she could get over Connor as well.

If things had been different between them afterward, she would have eagerly gone back for more.

They stayed out of each other's way as best as they could, which wasn't easy when stuck in the same house together. Every time one of them entered a room, the one already in there left.

Mostly it was her that left the room. She thought it was only right, since it was his home.

It felt petty doing it, but she didn't know what else to do. It wasn't like she could just go home. As much as she wanted to go home, she had to wait until somebody showed her the way back to some form of civilization. Or at least, pointed her in the right direction.

She was more than happy to find her own way home; she just needed to know which way to go.

Anya spent most of the day in the living room. She sat looking out of the window, watching the day go by while trying to forget about their time together.

Connor, on the other hand, spent most of the day banging around downstairs in the basement. She didn't have a clue what he was doing down there, but from the sound of it, he was demolishing the place.

Anya was curled up on the sofa in the living room, watching the sun setting through the trees, when she heard movement behind her. She was surprised to find two men standing by the kitchen when she turned around. Both men sported grins as they stared at her in silence.

She assumed Connor was expecting them, since he joined them a moment later. Anya sat quietly as she watched Connor interacting with his friends.

They spoke in soft tones, so she couldn't hear what they were talking about, but she had a feeling it had something to do with her. And if the quick glances they kept throwing her way were any indication, then she was right.

After a couple of minutes, Connor and his friends finally turned to face her. For the first time that day, he spoke more than two words to her.

"Anya, these are my friends, Kellen and Aidan." He pointed at each man as he introduced them.

"It's a pleasure to meet you, Anya," Kellen said.

"Hi, Anya," Aidan said.

"It's nice to meet you," she said politely.

There must be something in the water, she thought.

Everyone she had met since waking up in the medical centre had been incredibly attractive. Myra and Candi were stunningly beautiful women, both inside and out. But the men, well, they were all pantie-melting hunks.

"How are you enjoying your stay?" Kellen asked as he took a seat in the chair closest to her.

Aidan sat at the other end of the sofa. He slouched back into the cushion and put his feet up on the coffee table, but Connor quickly pushed them off again.

Connor was the last to take a seat. He glared daggers at Aidan as he sat in the armchair furthest away from her.

Anya didn't know what was going on between the two men, but from where she was sitting, it looked as if Connor despised Aidan. Why then would he allow Aidan into his home?

She didn't know and didn't care. Whatever it was, it had nothing to do with her. Or at least, she hoped it didn't.

"It's okay, so far," she admitted.

She would have said it was peaceful, but with all the banging Connor had been doing, it was far from it.

"How's Connor treating you?" Aidan asked.

Anya glanced at Connor as she turned to look at Aidan. He was still staring daggers at Aidan.

"He's treating me well," she told him.

Which was true to an extent. There were times when he made her feel like the most important person in the world, and then there were other times where he made her feel like an unwelcome house guest.

It was either hot or cold with Connor. There was no middle ground with him, and it confused the hell out of her, but she couldn't say any of that to his friends.

"Has he shown you around much of the area?" Kellen asked.

"No, I haven't left the house since I arrived," she confessed.

Anya would love to explore the area. It looked beautiful and inviting out the window, but with the mood Connor had been in, she hadn't dared asked if they could go out.

"Really? Why not?"

Aidan was looking at Connor when he asked, but Anya answered anyway. "Because Connor's been busy."

"Busy doing what?" Aidan asked, still looking at Connor.

Anya couldn't answer this time, since she didn't actually know what he had been doing in the basement. So, she kept quiet, intrigued to know the answer as well.

"I've been sorting out the basement," he told them. "You know, the one you two were supposed to be helping me with."

"We didn't think you were starting it yet," Aidan said.

"Why not?"

"Because you have a house guest," Kellen told him.

"Well, I've got the time off work," Connor said. "And since I have nothing else planned, I might as well get as much done as I can."

Anya agreed with Connor. She would probably do the same thing if she was in his situation. Not that she was preventing him from going to work, but she didn't expect him to sit around all day just because she was there.

"If you've got time off, why don't you show Anya around?" Aidan asked. "I'm sure she would appreciate a bit of fresh air."

"It's okay, I really don't mind," Anya said.

She didn't want Connor to feel as if he had to take her anywhere. She knew how difficult it was getting free time to get things done at home; it took her months just to decorate her small apartment.

If looks could kill, then Aidan would be as dead as a door nail from the look Connor gave him. They didn't say a word to each other, but something passed between them.

"What do you do for work, Anya?" Kellen asked.

She knew what he was doing. He was trying to break the tension that was building between Connor and Aidan by talking about something else. Anya was thankful for the change in subject. She didn't want to cause problems for anyone, least of all Connor.

"I work in a law firm as a receptionist."

"That sounds interesting," Kellen said.

"I promise you," Anya said. "It's not interesting."

"Do you enjoy your work?" he asked.

"I like that it pays the bills, does that count?"

Kellen laughed. "I suppose that counts, yes."

"Well then, yes, I enjoy my job," Anya smiled.

Tension was still coming off Connor in waves, but she knew the second he stopped glaring at Aidan and turned his attention on her.

"Do you have a boyfriend, or husband, waiting for you back home?" Kellen asked her.

"No, neither."

And thank goodness she didn't, otherwise she would be the worst girlfriend or wife in the world. She would never forgive herself for cheating if she had a partner.

"Really?" Aidan said, dragging out the word. "So, you're free and single?"

"Free, no." She shook her head as she turned to look at him. "Single, yes, and planning on staying that way."

"Ahh, that's a shame. Are you sure I can't change your mind?" Aidan flirted.

Anya laughed. "I'm sure, thanks anyway."

She didn't mind a bit of playful flirting, and that's exactly what it was, but she wasn't going to flirt back. Especially with Connor sitting there watching her. She didn't want to give them the impression she was easy.

Too late for that, her subconscious reminded her.

"Never say never," Aidan said as he winked at her.

Anya smiled as she shook her head. Aidan was definitely the ladies' man out of the three of them, there was no doubt about it.

"She said she's not interested, Aidan. Now change the fucking record," Connor snapped.

"Someone got up on the wrong side of the bed this morning," Aidan taunted.

Anya heard a low, rumbling sound which seemed to be coming from Connor. The sound was so animalistic that it surprised her.

"Ignore Connor, all work and no play has his knickers in a twist," Aidan said.

"Please, ignore both of them," Kellen told her. "I do apologise for their behaviour. Aidan is a natural wind-up merchant, and Connor obviously hasn't had enough sleep." He glared at Connor a moment before turning back to her. "He tends to get a little grouchy when he's tired, and working on the basement all day would definitely knacker him out."

Anya was partly to blame for him being tired, since they spent most of the night having sex. Not that she was going to let Kellen or Aidan know that.

"No need to apologise," Anya said.

"There is," Kellen said. "But, I know what will chill both of them out."

"What's that?" Anya asked, intrigued.

"Whiskey," Kellen smiled. "It always does the job."

"That's a great idea." Aidan slapped his leg, making Anya jump. "Connor, break out your whiskey."

Anya watched as Connor silently got to his feet and walked over to the wall unit. He opened one of the cupboards and pulled out four tumblers and a half full bottle of whiskey.

He placed the tumblers on the table and poured equal amounts of amber liquid in each. Before taking a seat, he picked up two glasses and held one out to her.

"Thank you," she said, taking the glass from him.

He nodded curtly before returning to his seat.

"How's it coming along in the basement?" Kellen asked him.

"It's getting there slowly. It would go a lot faster if you two helped out like you said you were going to."

"We didn't think you would be starting that while Anya was staying with you, otherwise we would have been here."

Anya wasn't much of a drinker. She would have a glass of wine or two occasionally, but she normally stayed well away from spirits. A bad experience when she was younger had put her off the stuff for life, but she didn't want to seem rude, so she took a tentative sip.

It's not that bad actually, she thought as the flavour filled her mouth.

It wasn't until Anya swallowed that she experienced a burning sensation that it left in its wake. As much as she tried not to, her eyes watered as she began to cough.

She quickly placed the glass on the table and covered her mouth with her hand.

"You okay, Anya?" Aidan asked her, concern lacing his words.

"I'm... good..." she managed to get out between coughs.

"Would you like some water?" Kellen asked.

"Yes... please."

Even though Kellen was the one to ask, it was Connor who went to fetch her some. He returned a moment later with a tall glass of water with ice cubes.

"Thank you." She took the glass and instantly raised it to her lips.

The water cooled some of the heat from the whiskey, enough for her to stop coughing and be able to speak again, but she could still feel the remnants in the back of her throat.

Anya placed the glass of water on the table next to the tumbler. Then she wiped the tears from her eyes before sitting back again.

"Maybe you shouldn't drink whiskey," Connor said.

"Sorry, I don't normally drink, and it's the first time I've tried whiskey," she confessed. "I wasn't expecting it to be so strong."

"Even more reason for you not to drink it."

"Don't be such a dick, Connor," Aidan said.

"I'm just being honest. If she doesn't drink, then she isn't going to handle any spirits, let alone whiskey."

"You still don't need to be a dick about it," Kellen told him.

"No, it's okay," Anya told them. "He's right, I shouldn't be drinking whiskey."

"You can do what you want, Anya," Aidan told her. "Don't let Connor dictate what you can or can't do."

"I agree, Anya," Kellen told her. "If you want to have a drink, then you can."

"To be honest, I would rather just go to bed, if you don't mind."

She'd had enough of putting on a brave face for one day. She wished a black hole would open up and swallow her whole, but since that was unlikely to happen, she just wanted to run upstairs and cry into her pillow.

Anya could put up with a lot of things, like being ignored all day, but she couldn't put up with being made to feel like a child in front of others. And that is exactly how she felt right then.

"Of course, we don't mind," Kellen assured her. "If you're tired, then go and rest by all means."

"Don't think that you have to stay down here because we're here," Aidan added. "We will be leaving soon, anyway."

"Yes, I have my sister to get back to, and Aidan has curfew coming up soon," Kellen said, trying to lighten the mood again, but Anya was nearly at the point of no return.

She was already fighting back the tears. She didn't know why Connor was acting the way he was, but she couldn't take much more without bursting into tears in front of everyone.

"Just because I still live with my parents, doesn't mean I have a curfew," Aidan said, sounding offended.

"Yeah, okay," Kellen rolled his eyes dramatically.

"Anyway," Anya said. "It was nice meeting you both."

She plastered her best fake smile on her face as she stood up to leave.

"Likewise," Kellen said.

"Goodnight, Anya," Aidan said as he bowed his head. "I hope to see you again soon."

"Night," Connor said curtly.

"Goodnight, Anya. It was a pleasure to meet you," Kellen said.

"It was nice to meet you, too. Goodnight," she said as she made a swift exit.

Once she was safely tucked away in the bedroom, Anya leaned against the closed door and let the tears fall freely.

She didn't know what she'd done to piss Connor off so much, but it must have been pretty bad to warrant such hostility from him. Maybe he regretted their night together? But even if that was the case, she didn't deserve to be treated like that.

Anya didn't bother to change. She kicked off her shoes and climbed into bed. She wanted nothing more than to go home, but she was stuck there until at least morning.

Burying her face in the pillows, she cried until she couldn't cry anymore, and then she finally fell asleep.

CHAPTER SIXTEEN

Connor was grateful Anya had gone to bed when she had. Otherwise, Aidan was likely to get a fist in his face.

He hadn't liked the way Aidan had been flirting with her. He was certain Aidan was doing it to see if he could get a rise out of him. But no matter how hard he tried, Connor couldn't prevent the growl from escaping.

His hackles raised the moment Aidan sat down on the sofa next to Anya, and they didn't go down until she walked out the room. Only then could he relax around his friends.

Connor knew he was being ridiculous. She wasn't his, so he had no right to be possessive of her, but he couldn't stop himself.

He'd avoided her for most of the day, which made it easy to keep himself under control. But the second he walked into the front room and saw Aidan and Kellen standing there, a wave of possessiveness washed over him.

None of them spoke until they were sure Anya was out of ear shot.

"What the hell is wrong with you?" Kellen demanded.

"Nothing," he snapped.

"Yeah, it really sounds like nothing," Kellen said. "You've been acting like a dick since we arrived."

"I know what's wrong with him," Aidan said cheerfully.

Kellen raised an eyebrow as he looked at Aidan. "Well, would you like to share with the rest of the class?"

"He has the hots for Anya," Aidan smirked.

Connor was surprised Aidan had noticed anything other than Anya. Obviously, he had been watching Connor more closely than he originally thought.

"Really?" Kellen asked, dragging out the word.

"No, I don't," Connor lied.

"Oh, yes," Kellen said after staring intently at Connor for a moment. "I see it now."

"You don't see fuck all," Connor told him. "Because there's fuck all to see."

They were right, but he wasn't going to let them know it. And he certainly wasn't going to tell them what had happened between him and Anya. It was none of their business for starters, but also because they would want to know more than he was willing or able to share.

He knew one of the questions would be how he felt about her, and he couldn't answer that question because he honestly didn't know. He still wasn't sure what came over him in the first place.

"Keep telling yourself that, Connor," Kellen said.

"It still doesn't make it true."

"You should have heard what he said to me when I was flirting with Anya," Aidan said.

"When?" Kellen asked. "You were flirting with her the entire time she was down here."

"I just told you to stay the fuck away from her," Connor pointed out.

"See?" Aidan said. "He wouldn't do that unless he had the hots for her himself."

Connor didn't know why they were pushing the subject; it wasn't as if any of them were going to have a long-term relationship with her. She was human, so none of them could mate with her. Sex, yes. But there could never be anything more between them.

"Anyway, what's been happening with Kayla?" Connor asked, moving the conversation away from him and Anya.

"Don't get me started on her," Kellen sighed. "She's causing nothing but trouble at the moment."

If it put a stop to them probing into what was happening between him and Anya, then start he would.

"I hear she's gotten herself into trouble with the dragons again," Connor said.

"What?" Aidan's eyes widened in surprise as Kellen grimaced.

"Yeah, Myra told me she started a rock slide that blocked some of the entrance to Balzar's cave." Connor shook his head. "I feel sorry for Balzar. First the spray paint, and now this."

"Oh, wow," Aidan said. "That's seriously messed up."

"Tell me about it," Kellen groaned. "It's worse than having a two-year-old. In fact, I think I would prefer a room full of two year olds instead of dealing with the shit Kayla's causing at the moment."

"I bet." Connor wouldn't want to deal with either, but Kellen didn't have a choice. He was the only family his sister had, so he felt responsible for her behaviour.

"How did she manage it?" Aidan asked. "She must have had help from someone. I can't see her being able to pull something like that off on her own."

"It wouldn't surprise me if Caleb and Misti had something to do with it. Those three are always together." Connor still wasn't sure they weren't involved in the last incident, but all three were sticking to their story.

Kellen shook his head. "No, she's adamant she did it alone."

Connor downed the last bit of whiskey before refilling his glass. He held the bottle out, asking without words if the other two wanted a refill as well.

"That would be a big, fat, yes from me," Aidan said as he handed his glass over.

"I should probably be getting back," Kellen said, looking at the clock. "Kayla's at home by herself."

"So, one for the road?" Connor asked.

"Go on then," Kellen said. "Just don't pour as much in my glass as you did yours."

"Well, I don't have a temperamental teenager at home," Aidan said. "So, fill mine up."

"I wish she would hurry up and get past this rebellious stage," Kellen said. "It's driving me fucking insane."

"Well, it can't last forever," Connor said. "She's bound to grow up sooner or later."

"I'd rather it be sooner," Kellen said. "But knowing my luck, it's going to be later. Much, much later."

Connor didn't envy Kellen's responsibilities. He wouldn't know where to start with Kayla. Any child, or teenager as the case may be, was a handful at the best of times. But it was far from the best of times for Kayla.

Connor knew it would be different bringing up his own pups, but after seeing all the stress and worry Kellen went through with Kayla, he wasn't eager to have his own either.

"You're not going to believe it," Kellen said with an exasperated sigh.

"What?" Connor and Aidan asked in unison.

"He's outside now," Kellen said. "He's circling the house from the air."

"You're joking," Connor asked, not quite believing it.

Everyone in the realm had been informed of the human staying at his house. They were all told to stay away unless they were in human form. It certainly wouldn't be good for Anya to see a dragon flying around.

"Nope, I'm not joking," Kellen said. "He says he's

not going anywhere until I go outside and speak with him."

"He knows who's here, doesn't he?" Aidan asked.

"Yep, I've told him to keep his distance, so he isn't seen," Kellen told them. "But he isn't listening to me."

"You need to go out there and make sure he goes away," Connor told him. "Rush doesn't want her seeing anything that she shouldn't. And a dragon the size of a house is definitely something he doesn't want her to see."

"He's too angry to listen to reason," Kellen said. "Whatever Kayla has done this time, she has well and truly pissed him off."

Without another word, Kellen downed the last of his drink and then stood up and walked outside through the kitchen.

Connor hoped Anya was fast asleep already. The last thing they needed was to explain why there was a large dragon flying around his house.

"What do you think she's been up to this time?" Aidan asked him.

"I don't know, but it can't be good."

"Should I go up and check on Anya?" Aidan asked.

"Stay the fuck away from her," Connor growled.

Aidan held his hands up in front of him. "Okay, calm down. I'm only messing with you."

"Well, stop," Connor demanded. "I'm not in the mood."

"Yeah, I can tell," Aidan said. "Is she your mate?"

Connor had asked himself that same question, but it always came back to the fact she was human. So, it wasn't possible for her to be his mate.

"No, she isn't my mate."

"It would explain why you're behaving this way around her," Aidan said.

"She is not my mate," he reiterated.

"What makes you so certain?"

"Other than the fact she's human?" Connor asked. Before Aidan could say anything, he added: "I just am. Can you drop it now?"

Connor didn't want to think about the possibility of Anya being his mate, so he followed Kellen outside to see if he could help calm Balzar down instead.

Just as he stepped out of the back door and into the garden, Balzar landed in front of Kellen. Right under Anya's bedroom window.

For fuck sake. Connor was relieved when he looked up at her window and saw no movement.

He opened a link with Balzar and Kellen. While Balzar was in dragon form, it was the only way to have a conversation with him.

"What the fuck are you doing Balzar?" he demanded. *"You know I have a human staying here."*

"I don't give a damn about any humans," he raged. *"Something needs to be done about his sister."* Smoke billowed out of his nostrils as his large head swung towards Kellen. *"I will not put up with her destroying my home."*

Connor couldn't blame him for being pissed off. If Kayla had done that to his home, he would be just as angry. But it still didn't change the fact that there was a human sleeping in the bedroom right above them.

If she looked out the window, the first thing she would see was a dragon. As far as her kind was concerned, they didn't exist. It had been so long since a dragon was seen in her realm; they had turned into myths and legends.

"Rush will not be happy if she sees you and we have to explain your existence to her," Kellen pointed out.

"Why should I care if he's happy or not?" Balzar asked. *"He isn't my Alpha, so I don't have to answer to him."*

"Because even your king has agreed to stay hidden until she has gone back to her own realm," Connor informed him. *"So please, shift into your human form, or go away."*

"Fine."

In the blink of an eye, the dragon was gone and Balzar stood before them in human form. But Connor could tell he wasn't happy about it.

"Now, what is going on? Why have you come here at this time of night?" Connor demanded.

"His sister has done it again," Balzar shouted.

"Keep your voice down," Connor growled.

Balzar huffed, but nodded his head in agreement.

"What has she done now?" Kellen asked.

Balzar spun around to face Kellen. "She's caused another fucking rock slide, that's what."

"Whose home was it this time?" Connor asked.

"Mine again." Balzar hit his chest to emphasize his words. "And this time, she's completely blocked the entrance."

"Was anyone injured?" Connor asked.

"No, but that isn't the point," Balzar said. "If she does it again, then she might not be so lucky next time."

"I agree," Connor said. "But, that still doesn't mean you should be coming here in dragon form while there is a human here."

"I want something done about her," he demanded.

"What do you want me to do with her?" Kellen asked. "Seriously, I'm open to suggestions."

"I want you to make her clear away all the rocks and boulders from the entrance to my cave," he said.

"You want a young female pup to move rocks and boulders?" Kellen asked.

"Are you going deaf, wolf?" Balzar sneered. "Yes, I want her to move all of them. She put them there, she can move them."

"You're a dragon, for fuck sake," Kellen said. "It would be quicker and easier to clear them yourself."

"That's not the point," Balzar said. "I shouldn't have to clear them. She should be made to do it as punishment for causing the rock slide in the first place. Hopefully, she might learn not to do it again."

"Fine," Kellen relented. "But it's too late for her to start it tonight. Do you have somewhere you can stay for the time being?"

"Thank you." Balzar bowed his head. "Yes, I can stay elsewhere for the night, but I want to be able to go home and sleep in my own bed tomorrow night."

"You might have to give her more time than that," Kellen told him. "She's still only a pup."

"No, I want it cleared by dusk tomorrow." With that,

he shifted back into a dragon, and flew off.

"That was rude," Aidan said from the back door.

"How the hell does he think she's going to clear all that by tomorrow night?" Kellen asked. "Have you seen the size of the entrance to his cave? It's fucking massive!"

"It would have to be, just to fit him through the door," Aidan laughed.

"It's not funny," Kellen growled. "It'll take her a week to move it all by herself."

"Get Misti and Caleb to help," Connor told him. "It'll keep them busy for a few hours. And drag Aidan with you, as well. I'm sure his parents could do with a break from him for a while."

"True," Kellen said at the same time Aidan said, "Hey!"

"What? It's true," Connor said. "They deserve a break from you, and it's only right one of us helps Kellen with those three. I can't because I've got to stay here and babysit Anya, otherwise I would be there helping as well."

"Yeah, I suppose he could do with some help dealing with those three," Aidan agreed. "But my parents don't need a break from me; they hardly see me as it is."

"There you go," Connor said. "Now there are five of you moving it all. You'll get it done in no time."

"Are you sure your parents with be okay with Misti and Caleb helping?" Kellen asked.

"I don't see why not," Connor said. "But I'll speak to them first thing in the morning and explain the situation."

"Thank you." Kellen let out a sigh of relief. "Let me know what they say."

"I will do. Where do you want them to meet you? And what time?"

"We'll all meet at my house and make our way there together," Kellen said. "Eight am should do nicely."

"What time do you want me to meet you?" Aidan asked.

"Same time, same place," Kellen told him.

"Why can't I meet you there?" Aidan sulked.

"Because if I've got to deal with them three first thing in the morning, then so do you."

"Yeah, you can't leave poor Kellen alone with them three, they'll end up running circles around him," Connor laughed.

"I best get going," Kellen said a moment later. "I don't trust Kayla alone for too long at the moment."

"I don't blame you."

"I'm going to go as well," Aidan said. "Since I've been roped into helping."

"Alright, I'll see you both later," Connor said as he headed back inside. "Good luck for tomorrow."

"Thanks, we're going to need it," Kellen said as he and Aidan walked off together.

He really did feel sorry for Kellen at times. He was doing his best to bring up his sister and keep her safe, yet all she did was cause him nothing but problems.

Connor switched off all the lights as he made his way upstairs to bed. Before going into his bedroom, he listened outside Anya's door for a moment. He breathed a sigh of relief when he didn't hear anything out of the ordinary coming from her room.

Hopefully, she had slept through the entire time Balzar was there. If not, then they would have a lot of explaining to do.

CHAPTER SEVENTEEN

Anya jolted upright in bed as a shudder went through the house. Her first thought was that it was an earthquake, but she quickly rejected the idea when nothing else happened.

It was still dark outside, but that didn't deter Anya from climbing out of bed. She was curious to know what had caused the building to shake.

She got to her feet and tiptoed as quietly as she could towards the window. She didn't even make it halfway there before it became clear what had caused the shake.

Stood in the middle of Connor's back garden was a massive dragon. Deep red scales covered what she could see of its large body. It was mostly hidden behind wings that appeared to be leather, like a bat's wing.

"What the fuck?" she whispered.

Unsure she was seeing clearly, she rubbed her eyes, but the dragon was still there. Then, she pinched herself to make sure she wasn't dreaming, but nope. She was awake alright, and the dragon was still there.

Anya gulped as she tiptoed the rest of the way so she could get a better look. Her heart raced and her palms became sweaty the closer she got to the window, but no matter how scared she was, she couldn't stop her feet from carrying her forward.

Eyes the colour of rubies seemed to glow in the moonlight, giving it a savage appearance. A row of spikes trailed from the top of its large head all the way down its back to the tip of its tail. They gradually got smaller in size until they disappeared, only to be replaced by a long spike at the end of its tail that looked more like the blade of a scythe.

A smaller row of horns ran down the bridge of its long nose, ending between two large nostrils that blew out puffs of smoke.

Each one of the creature's legs was thicker than any of the trees surrounding the house. Sharp talons the colour of obsidian dug deep gouges into the earth as it moved around.

At the tips of its massive leathery wings, there were even more scythe like spikes. There was no mistaking that the creature was built for anything other than violence.

A shudder raced through her at the thought of what the dragon would be used for if it was even found and caught by the wrong people. The death and destruction it could cause would be devastating. And if myths and legends were anything to go by, then the creature could also breathe fire.

Anya didn't know what would be a worse way to die. Get eaten alive, ripped apart by sharp talons, impaled by the scythe like spikes, or get doused in dragon fire. She certainly didn't plan on hanging around to find out.

She was about to back away from the window when she realised the dragon kept looking at something on the ground. She followed its line of sight and found Connor and Kellen stood outside, looking up at it. Neither man spoke as they stared at the dragon, but they also didn't appear to be shocked that a dragon was casually stood in the middle of the garden either.

Anya rubbed her eyes, unsure she was seeing things right. But when she opened her eyes again, the dragon was gone. She quickly scanned the area, even checking the sky, but there was no sign of the dragon.

Instead of the dragon, there was a man stood with Connor and Kellen when she next looked down.

Whatever the three men were talking about, it seemed to be getting heated. Anya could hear their muffled voices at times, but she couldn't make out what they were saying.

She watched them talking for a couple of minutes, but just as she was about to turn away and go back to bed, the newcomer suddenly turned into the dragon. It happened so fast, that if she had blinked, she would have missed it.

Anya rubbed her eyes again, positive she was seeing things. But she wasn't. There it was, large as life, right in front of her.

What the hell?

Were they drugging her? Was that why she was seeing a dragon? It couldn't have been the whiskey because she'd barely had a sip, but that didn't mean the food and drinks she'd consumed so far hadn't been laced with something.

It was the only explanation she could come up with that made an ounce of sense. Dragons weren't real, and people certainly didn't turn into them.

Well, obviously they do because you've just witnessed it with your own eyes, her subconscious pointed out.

She didn't have a chance to take it all in before the dragon took off. With a couple of beats of its massive wings, the dragon was in the air and flying off over the trees. It disappeared from view a couple of seconds later.

Connor and Kellen continued talking for a moment before Aidan came into view. Not long after that, Kellen and Aidan walked off together, and Connor returned to the house.

Anya quickly climbed back into bed as quietly as she could. She didn't want Connor to know that she had seen anything, so just in case he decided to check on her, she pretended to be asleep.

As much as she wanted to run away screaming, she knew that would do no good. In fact, it would probably cause more problems for her.

If she was going to stand any chance in getting away from there, she needed to be smart about it. So, as much as she didn't want to stay a second longer, she had to wait until Connor was asleep. Otherwise, she might as well just come straight out with it and confess that she'd seen the dragon and then the man turning into the dragon.

Anya wasn't naive enough to think she was free to leave whenever she wanted, but they were even less likely to let her go home if they found out what she'd seen. She had a feeling Rush was keeping her there for a reason, she just didn't know what that reason was.

It felt like an eternity before the house was quiet enough for her to make a move, but she didn't leave straight away. She waited for as long as she could to make sure Connor was asleep. Anya couldn't take the wait anymore, it was now or never.

As she climbed out of bed, she slid her feet into her shoes. She'd left them off just in case Connor had come in to check on her before going to bed. It was easier to pretend to be asleep if she didn't have bulky shoes on under the blanket. Thankfully, she hadn't needed to bother.

She crept over to the door and listened for the slightest sound. When she didn't hear any movement, she opened the door an inch. Luckily for her, the door didn't squeak, but she still paused so she could listen again.

All she could hear was the beating of her heart. It was pounding so loudly in her ears; she would be surprised if she heard anything over it.

Taking a deep breath, Anya left the room and tiptoed as quietly as she could along the hall. She held her breath as she passed Connor's room, and didn't release it until she was at the bottom of the stairs.

She made it all the way to the kitchen without making a sound, but as soon as her shoes hit the kitchen floor, they began to squeak. She quickly slipped them off and carried them until she was out the back door.

Once they were securely on her feet again, she didn't waste any more time. She took off running in the opposite direction from where she had seen the dragon go. Well, at least she hoped it was the opposite direction. Knowing her luck, it was more likely to be the same way. But at that moment in time, she was willing to risk it.

Anya ran as fast as she could, ignoring the twigs and branches that whipped her as she passed. Trying to keep her footing wasn't easy, but at least she didn't have to contend with the pain in her chest anymore. She didn't know how it was possible, but she had completely healed from her injuries.

That wasn't the only thing Anya was amazed by either. For some reason, she could see in the dark nearly as well as she could in the day. By rights, she shouldn't be able to see where she was going, especially with the limited amount of light from the moon that managed to penetrate the canopy from the dense woodland.

Even with her enhanced eyesight, she still managed to tip over a handful of times.

Anya hadn't made it far before she heard a female voice.

"I can help you get home."

Anya jumped. She quickly spun around, scanning

the area for the source of the voice, but there was nobody there. Shaking it off as her imagination playing tricks on her, she carried on at a slower pace than before.

"You're going in the wrong direction." The voice came again, and again Anya looked around, but saw nobody.

"Who are you?" Anya whispered.

"Someone who can help you escape this place, but only if you do as I say."

"Why would you help me? You don't know me."

"Look, we don't have time for twenty questions. It won't be long before they notice you've gone. So, do you want my help or not?"

If it meant getting away from Connor and the dragon, then she would take all the help she could get.

"Yes, I want help," she confessed.

"Good."

"Where are you?" she asked quietly.

Try as she might, she couldn't figure out where the voice was coming from. It sounded like it was coming from all directions.

"I'm near the cave."

"How the fuck can I hear you, then?"

Anya wasn't anywhere near the cave, she knew that for certain. So, it shouldn't be possible for her to hear the woman.

"I'm speaking in your head," the woman made it sound as if it should have been blatantly obvious. All that was missing was the 'duh' at the end of the sentence.

Anya imagined she was rolling her eyes as well.

"That's not possible."

"If it wasn't possible, then how am I speaking to you this way?"

"How the fuck do I know, why don't you tell me."

"Well, I can either spend valuable time explaining the many ways it is possible," she said. *"Or, I can give you the directions to get out of here. But I don't have the time, or patience, to do both. So, pick one, and be quick about it."*

Anya had to admit, she was intrigued to know how the woman could speak telepathically, but more than anything, she wanted to go home. So, the decision was easy.

"Tell me which way to go."

"Okay dokey, let's get going. First of all, you're going in the wrong direction."

"Yeah, you already said that. Which way should I be going?"

"Turn clockwise ninety degrees. Then keep walking in a straight line until you come to a stream."

Anya didn't know if she could trust the woman, but after witnessing a man turn into a dragon, she didn't really have much choice.

"Why are you helping me?"

"Why not?"

"For one, you don't know me."

"And that's a reason not to help someone?"

"I suppose not, but if you don't know me, how did you know I needed help?"

The woman was quiet for so long, Anya didn't think

she would answer.

"Someone I know asked me to help you," she finally said.

"So, that person knows me as well?"

"Yes."

Anya wondered who the mutual friend could be, but the only person that came to mind, was Sasha. She was the only person who would care enough about her to send someone to help her. But if she knew where Anya was, then why hadn't she come herself?

Maybe she had done. Maybe she was waiting by the cave with the woman. But that just brought up even more questions, like how did she know the mysterious woman that could talk telepathically?

Before she could ask the woman if it was Sasha that sent her, and if so, how did they know each other, she picked up the sound of running water.

"I can hear the stream. Which way do I go when I get there?"

"You need to follow it to the left. About two hundred yards along, there is a small crossing. Cross over and then continue until you reach the base of the mountain."

"Okay."

She pushed the questions floating around in her mind aside as she followed the directions. It wasn't long before she came to the base of a mountain. She just hoped it was the right one.

"Now where?"

"Halfway up the mountain there's an outcropping. You should be able to see it from where you are."

Easier said than done, Anya thought. But as she looked up, she could clearly see the outcropping of rocks.

"Okay, I see it."

"I'm just inside the entrance."

"Okay, I'll be there soon."

Anya didn't hang around. She quickly made her way up the mountain and to the cave entrance. It was a steeper climb than it had been on the other side of the mountain, but thankfully, it wasn't as far up.

When Anya finally reached the cave entrance, she was greeted by the mysterious woman.

"Hi Anya," the woman smiled and held out her hand.

"Hi," Anya said as she shook the woman's hand.

"You can call me Kass."

"It's nice to meet you, Kass," Anya said. "And thank you for helping me."

"No problem," Kass smiled. "You ready to get going again? Or do you need to rest first?"

"No, I'm good to go." And surprisingly, she was ready to go.

Normally, Anya would need a rest after the distance she'd just covered, and that was on even ground with no incline, which was the complete opposite of what she'd just navigated.

Kass nodded as she flicked on a torch. "Okay then, lets go."

The ground wasn't as wet and slippery as it was the last time Anya went through the cave, so she was able to keep her footing as she followed Kass.

"I can't wait to get home," Anya sighed.

Her nice relaxing weekend away had been anything but nice and relaxing. Next time Sasha booked them a weekend at a spa hotel, Anya was going to stay in the hotel the entire time. Or if she did decide to go on another hike, she was going to take somebody that knew the area with her.

"Do you know if Sasha's still here?" she asked, hopeful that Sasha had waited for her. "Or has she gone home already?"

"I honestly don't know," Kass said.

"That's okay, the hotel isn't far away," Anya told her. "I'll stop in there on my way to the station."

It would only be a slight detour on the way to the station, and she needed to collect her belongings from the hotel first. Plus, she didn't want to leave Sasha waiting at the hotel if she was still there.

Anya wanted to jump for joy when she walked out of the cave on the other side of the mountain. And she might have done, if given the chance. But just as she was taking a deep breath, Kass stepped in front of her and blew a cloud of dust into her face. Before she could react, her vision went black, and her body gave out on her.

An image of Connor's face was the last thing that went through her mind as she crumpled to the floor and lost all consciousness.

***

Kassadi didn't feel guilty for lying to Anya about being there to help her, she couldn't. At the end of the day, Anya meant nothing to her. There were more important people in her life that needed her far more than an insignificant human ever would.

Well, technically, Anya was no longer just a human, but still, she wasn't Kassadi's priority.

That didn't stop her from feeling bad about what she had done to Anya in London. No one deserved to have their lives altered so drastically without permission, and certainly not without knowing about it.

Kassadi didn't enjoy what she'd done to Anya, and was still doing. If she had any other choice, she wouldn't have done any of it. But she didn't.

Unfortunately, she had no choice but to do whatever he wanted her to do because he had something that she needed. So, until he gave it to her, Kassadi would do anything he asked, even if it meant ruining somebody else's life.

If Anya managed to live through everything he had planned for her, then her life was going to be completely different.

Kassadi secretly hoped Anya did survive. She also hoped the wolf shifters were able to catch up with him before he could do too much damage. If he didn't possess something she needed, she would have aided the wolves. Or at the very least, given them a heads up on what he was doing.

She couldn't tell them what he was planning, because he wouldn't tell her everything. She had tried to find out what his plans were, but he kept them a closely guarded secret. Just like he was doing with the thing she wanted.

She still wasn't sure he actually had what she was looking for.

He assured her that he had it, but he refused to show her. So, she had nothing but his word to go on, and that wasn't exactly trustworthy.

As she dragged Anya's unconscious body the last few feet to her car, she let out a sigh of relief that nobody was around to see her. The last thing she wanted was to be caught dragging a body across a car park.

In hindsight, she should have parked closer to the cave. Even waiting until they were closer to the car before blowing the sleeping powered into Anya's face would have been a better idea, but she hadn't wanted to continue lying to her.

As soon as they reached the vehicle, Kassadi opened the boot and then unceremoniously dumped Anya inside before closing it again. She climbed into the driver's seat and started the engine. She didn't bother putting on a seatbelt before speeding off.

It was going to be a long drive, but Kassadi had no doubt the spell keeping Anya asleep, would continue to do so until they reached their final destination.

CHAPTER EIGHTEEN

Before he even opened his eyes the next morning, Connor knew something was wrong. He didn't know how, but he knew without a doubt that Anya wasn't in her bedroom.

Hoping he was wrong, he still checked her bedroom, but just as he'd known, she wasn't there. The bed was neatly made, and the bag of clothes Candi had dropped off was placed on the end of the bed next to a small pile of clothes.

"Fuck!"

How the hell had she managed to sneak out the house without him knowing? Yes, he'd probably been asleep when she left, but he wasn't a heavy sleeper, so he should have heard her. Especially since she would have needed to go past his bedroom to reach the stairs.

The bedroom window was still closed, so she hadn't gone out that way. It was a long way down for a human, and there was nothing for her to hold on to while she shut the window behind her, so it would still be open if she'd left that way.

Connor didn't hesitate in going after her. If he was fast enough, he might be able to catch up with her before she made it through the portal.

As soon as he stepped out onto the back porch, he shifted into a wolf. Using his heightened sense of smell, he easily picked up her scent.

He breathed a sigh of relief when she appeared to be heading away from the portal, but that relief was short lived. She hadn't made it far before suddenly changing direction and heading straight for the portal.

Connor picked up speed. He ran flat out towards the cave with the portal to the human realm. Now that he knew she was definitely heading to the cave, he didn't need to track her scent.

It didn't take him long to reach the cave entrance. He had hoped to catch up with her before she reached the cave, but he hadn't seen any sign of her.

It was easier to traverse the cave in human form. Plus, he didn't want her to see him shift. So, he quickly shifted back into his human form and then walked inside.

"What the hell?"

Connor didn't know how it was possible, but Anya's scent was gone. He knew she'd come through this way because her scent was right outside the cave entrance, but as soon as he entered, her scent vanished.

Frustration and worry replaced the shock of her scent vanishing when his search of the cave resulted in finding nothing. There was absolutely nothing in the cave to indicate she'd been there recently. But what was even more troubling, there wasn't even any hint that she'd been through the cave at all.

He knew it was where she'd been found, so there should have been some sign she'd been there. He should have been able to pick up her scent, at least, but there was nothing.

He was kicking himself for not making it to the cave in time to stop her from going through, but more than that, he was worried about her. And with every second that passed with no sign of her, he became even more concerned for her.

He still didn't know why he was dreaming of her, or what the dreams meant, but he couldn't shake the feeling she was in danger. Her sudden disappearance was not helping to ease those fears, either.

There was nothing else he could do in the cave, so he headed to Rush's house to give him the bad news. He knew Rush was going to be pissed with him for losing her, but it would be nothing compared to how pissed off he was with himself.

If he'd kept a closer eye on her, then she wouldn't have been able to sneak out of his house. Better yet, if he'd made her feel more welcome, or at the least, not treated her so badly after she'd give her body to him, then maybe she wouldn't have wanted to leave.

People were already milling around Rush's house by the time he got there. Connor didn't stop to speak with any of them, and thankfully, nobody tried to speak to him. He really wasn't in the mood to make small talk.

Connor let himself into the house and headed straight for Rush's office. The door was closed, so he knocked and waited to be invited in. As much as he wanted to barge in, he knew better than that, so he waited patiently for Rush to answer.

"Come in!" Rush shouted through the door a moment later.

Connor walked in and closed the door behind him. Rush sat at his desk. He indicated for Connor to take a seat as he leaned back in his chair. Connor was too agitated to sit, so he rested his hands on the back of the chair instead.

"What can I do for you, Connor," Rush asked casually.

"Anya's gone," he said without preamble.

With those two words, Connor had managed to piss Rush off. He watched as the casual, laid back Rush was replaced by an extremely pissed off and irritated Rush, and all in under thirty seconds as well. That had to be a world record for Connor.

"What do you mean, she's gone?" he demanded.

No matter how angry Rush was with him, it was nothing compared to how angry he was with himself.

"I mean she gone, as in, no longer in this realm."

Rush pinched the bridge of his nose between his thumb and forefinger. "Tell me what happened?"

"When I woke up this morning, I knew something wasn't right," he told Rush. "I had a feeling she wasn't in my house, so I went to check on her, but she wasn't in her room. I didn't bother checking the rest of the house because I knew she wasn't there. As soon as I stepped outside, I picked up her scent and followed it. At first, she was heading away from the portal, but then she suddenly changed course and headed straight for it."

"How would she know which way to go?" Rush asked. "Was there anyone else with her?"

"I didn't pick up anyone else's scent, so I assumed she was alone," Connor confessed. "But who would help her?"

"That's a good question," Rush said. "Another good question would be, why? It wasn't as if she was in any danger here, so why would someone help her run away?"

"I can't see it being anyone here," Connor said. "Everybody knew she was here, and that there was a reason you hadn't sent her back to the human realm."

"I agree," Rush said. "I can't see it being anyone here, either. But we're not the only ones that can access this realm."

"You think somebody came here to help her?" Connor asked.

Instead of answering, Rush asked, "Have you checked the cave?"

Connor stared at Rush for a moment before nodding his head.

"Yes, I followed her scent there, but then it disappeared." He still wasn't sure how that was even possible, but there was no denying the fact that her scent vanished as soon as she entered the cave.

"What do you mean?" Rush asked. "She's human, she can't hide her scent. Not many beings can."

"I don't know how she did it, but as soon as I stepped inside the cave, her scent was gone. It was as if she just vanished into thin air."

"What the hell is going on?"

Rush spoke more to himself than to Connor, but Connor answered anyway. "I don't know."

"I know you don't," Rush told him. "Otherwise, you wouldn't be here."

Connor wasn't looking forward to telling Rush the rest of it, but he knew he had to.

"There's more."

Rush's onyx eyes lifted to glare at Connor. "What else happened?"

Connor blew out a breath. "She might have seen Balzar last night."

"How?"

"He turned up at my house… in his dragon form."

"You've got to be fucking kidding me?" Rush said as he pushed to his feet and began to pace.

"Unfortunately, I'm not."

"Did she see him?"

"I don't know," Connor admitted. "She had already gone up to bed before he arrived, so it's possible she might have already been asleep."

"Anything else?" Rush asked as he stopped pacing and turned to look at him.

"Just one more thing."

"What?"

It was Connor's turn to start pacing. He had hoped that he wouldn't need to divulge this bit of information, but if it played any part in her running off, then he had to let Rush know.

He took a deep breath and blew it out before turning to Rush and answering. "I slept with her the night before last."

Rush didn't say a word as he let it all sink in.

Connor watched in silence as Rush retook his seat. He leaned his elbows on his desk and lowered his head into his hands. He massaged his temples for a moment before looking back up at Connor.

"I had a feeling that might happen," he said, finally breaking the silence.

Connor couldn't have been more shocked if Rush had got up and punched him in the face.

Connor frowned. "You... what?"

"After seeing you with her in medical the other day, and then dreams you've been having of her as well, it only made sense," Rush said cryptically.

"What made sense?" Connor was confused. None of what Rush had just said made any sense to him.

"That she's your mate."

Connor's mouth dropped open as he stared at Rush.

"She's not my mate," he said adamantly.

He would know if she was, wouldn't he? His parents had known they were mates from the moment they laid eyes on each other; he just assumed it would be the same for him. But maybe that wasn't the case for everyone.

"Are you sure about that?" Rush asked him.

"Of course, I'm sure."

"So, you would be fine never seeing her again? If that's the case, we might as well not bother looking for her."

Connor growled. Over his dead body would they not going looking for her. She was in danger, he just didn't know what from. But the longer she was out there on her own, the more chance she had of running into whatever... or whoever... was the cause of the danger stalking her in his dreams.

The rest of Rush's words finally registered in his mind. The thought of never seeing her again... no, that just wasn't an option. Connor didn't care what it took, he was going to find her and bring her back to his home where she would be safe. Where she would be with him. He didn't want another minute to pass without her in his life.

That's when it finally hit him. "She's my mate." Connor was stunned at his own revelation.

"I would say so, yes."

"I can't lose her."

"I know."

"What are we going to do?" he asked, frantic with worry for her.

Rush shook his head. "There's not a lot we can do at the moment."

"I can't just sit here and do nothing," Connor snapped.

"I didn't say we were going to do nothing," Rush said. "Just that there isn't much we can do at the moment."

"You're not making any fucking sense, Rush." Connor was losing his patience. He wanted to be out looking for Anya, not trying to decipher what Rush was babbling on about. "What aren't you telling me?"

"Quite a lot actually," Rush said. "But most of its shit you wouldn't be interested in, anyway."

"I mean about Anya. What aren't you telling me about Anya?"

If Rush didn't spill the beans soon, Connor was likely to punch him square in the face, and that would definitely be a bad idea. Rush was easy going the majority of the time, but if you pissed him off, you had better run for cover, and fast.

"Well, for starters, her friend Sasha paid me a visit," Rush told him.

That surprised Connor. "Really? How did she know Anya was here?"

"Because Sasha isn't human."

"What is she?"

"I'm not sure, yet," Rush said, frustration evident in his voice. "But trust me, I'm going to find out."

"What did she tell you about Anya? Does she know how Anya came to be here?"

"She didn't say a lot." Rush shook his head. "She was more interested in asking me questions than answering mine."

"How do you know she isn't human? She could have follow Anya here, for all we know."

"Because she appeared out of thin air, in the middle of my office, the day we found Anya in the cave."

"And you waited this long to say anything?"

"There wasn't anything to say," Rush told him. "She appeared, told me her and Anya's name, asked what happened to Anya, and wanted to know where we found her. Then she told me to look after Anya before disappearing again. So, tell me, Connor, what did you get from learning all of that?"

Rush was right. None of that information was useful to helping them figure out what was going on with Anya or the dreams he was having. The only thing they had learnt from her arrival was the fact Anya knew somebody who wasn't human. But even then, they didn't know what she was, only that she could appear out of thin air.

"So, we're back to square one," Connor said.

"I wouldn't say that," Rush told him. "I do have my own way of finding out information, or have you forgotten?"

Connor could have kicked himself. All that time trying to figure out who she was by getting to know her, and he could have just gone to the tech unit and got one of them to dig up everything they could find about her. He could have had the information he wanted days ago.

Rush raised an eyebrow as he looked at Connor. "I see you've finally clicked?"

"Yes."

"About bloody time."

"So, what did you find out?"

"Her current address, place of work, which doctors she's with, quite a bit about her past," Rush said. "Everything we need to know where she might have gone."

"That's great!" Connor said, eager to get going. "What are we waiting for? Let's go."

"Unfortunately, none of that is going to help us."

"Why the fuck not?"

"Because somebody has gone to great lengths to

conceal her scent," Rush said. "Why would they do that if they were planning on just letting her go home? We could easily find her there, so they wouldn't need to hide her scent from us, or theirs."

As much as he hated to admit it, Rush was right again. Whoever had helped her hadn't done it out of the goodness of their hearts, because if they did, they wouldn't have needed to cover their tracks.

"So," Rush continued. "Whoever is aiding her, knows who we are, and they know how to avoid being tracked by us. They are also more than likely the danger you've been dreaming about."

"Which means they intend on harming her, not helping her."

"Correct."

Connor didn't like the idea that Anya had willingly gone with the very people who wanted to cause her harm just to get away from him. He knew he hadn't treated her very well, and would spend the rest of his life making it up to her if she'd have him, but he would never forgive himself if he was the reason she'd run off and something bad happened to her.

"Don't worry, Connor," Rush said, reading his thoughts.

"You're not to blame. We're not giving up on her; we just need to figure out where we go from here."

He knew they weren't going to give up on her. He just hoped they reached her before anything bad could happen.

***

Sasha wasn't having any luck finding out what had happened to Anya. She knew something had gone down in the alley around the corner from where Anya lived, she just didn't know what.

She could feel the magic that was used in the area, and there was a faint smell of a wolf around one of the large bins, but she couldn't be sure if it was a shifter or a regular wolf. She was leaning more towards a shifter though, because regular wolves weren't native to this part of the world.

Other than that, there was absolutely nothing in the alley. So, she turned her attention to Anya's apartment.

She went through Anya's belonging with a fine-tooth comb. She didn't like invading her friend's privacy, but there wasn't another way. She needed to know what happened to Anya, if she was going to be able to help her.

Unfortunately, there was even less to find in her apartment. Sasha was running out of ideas. There was nowhere else for her to look to find out what happened to Anya.

With nothing left to do, Sasha decided to go back to the shifter realm to see Anya. Hopefully, Anya could shed some light on the situation.

Using her magic, Sasha tried to teleport straight to where Anya was staying. When she was unable to locate Anya in the shifter realm, she widened the search, thinking she might be on her way home already. But again, there was nothing.

"What the fuck is going on?"

Sasha hated being kept in the dark, and that's exactly where she was at that moment in time. Stuck in the dark, blindly searching for the light switch.

Veiling herself, she teleported back to Rush's home in the shifter realm.

CHAPTER NINETEEN

After they had finished talking, Rush called another emergency meeting, and within the hour, the living room was full to bursting again. Every inch of space was taken up by a hunter.

Connor watched as each person arrived and found a place to either sit or stand. They spoke quietly amongst themselves as they waited patiently for Rush to address them.

When he spotted Aidan and Kellen walk in with Myra, he wondered what she was doing with them, but then he realised she must have been helping out at Balzar's cave. No doubt she offered to help when she found out Misti and Caleb would be there. He was glad he'd spoken with his parents before bed, because it had been the last thing on his mind when he woke up.

As soon as they spotted him stood near the front where Rush stood, they walked over to join him.

"What's going on, Connor?" Myra asked him.

"Anya ran off," he told them.

Myra put a hand on her hip as she glared at him. "What did you do?"

"I didn't do anything," he frowned at her.

"I don't believe that for one second," she said as she continued to glare at him.

"Whether you believe it or not, it's the truth."

"She might be right, Connor." Kellen took Myra's side as usual. "You weren't exactly welcoming from what we saw last night."

"Yeah, you were acting like a complete dick," Aidan agreed.

"What did he do?" Myra asked.

"Just being an asshole," Aidan told her. "He kept snapping at her…"

"And Aidan," Kellen interrupted.

Aidan nodded. "Yep, he kept snapping at me as well."

"You deserved it," Connor told him. "You wouldn't stop hitting on her."

Myra rolled her eyes at him. "Aidan hits on everyone."

"Hey, no I don't," Aidan mocked being hurt by the statement.

"Yes, you do," Myra grinned at him. "I've even seen you hitting on my mum."

Connor growled at that news.

"Oh, shut up," Myra told him. "It was harmless. Plus, dad was there, he found it amusing."

"He made her feel so uncomfortable, she didn't stay downstairs with us for long," Aidan continued. "She looked ready to cry when she went to bed last night."

"So, it's all my fault then?" Connor asked. "Is that what you're saying?"

"Who else's fault would it be?" Myra asked him. "Everybody else has made her feel welcome, and they certainly haven't made her cry."

"I didn't make her cry," he said adamantly, but he knew it for the lie it was. Even he'd seen the tears she held back as she left the room. "And her leaving couldn't possibly have anything to do with Balzar, could it?"

"Why would Balzar have anything to do with it?" Myra asked, confused.

"Because he turned up at my house last night looking for Kellen, in dragon form," Connor told her.

Her eyes widened as she asked, "Really?"

Connor and Aidan nodded, while Kellen looked sheepish.

"Is that when you made the arrangements with him for today?" she asked.

"Yes," Kellen admitted.

"So, it's both your faults then," Myra said.

"How is it my fault?" Kellen asked her. "I didn't tell Balzar to go to Connor's house."

"Maybe not, but he was still there to see you."

"Yeah, because of Kayla, not me."

"Doesn't matter how you swing it, he was still there for you, whether it was about Kayla or not," Myra stated. "It doesn't matter, anyway. What's done is done."

"Have you told Balzar why you're not there?" Connor asked Kellen.

"Yeah, I spoke to him this morning and explained the situation."

"I take it he was fine with that," Connor said.

"Oh, hell no." Kellen shook his head. "He thinks this is just an excuse."

"He still wants you to go?" Connor frowned.

"Yep," Kellen grimaced. "As soon as we've finished here."

"Unbelievable." Connor understood why Balzar wanted them there as soon as possible, but under the circumstances, he could have at least given them a bit more time. After all, moving the rocks from the entrance to his home wasn't as life threatening as the situation Anya could possibly be in.

"You can't blame him," Myra said. "What Kayla has done is unacceptable. She should be made to clear up her mess."

"Yes, but Kellen doesn't need to be punished," Connor told her.

"He isn't," Myra said adamantly. "Balzar just wants Kellen to keep an eye on Kayla while she clears to the rocks. He's not asking Kellen to do the work himself."

"Why are you going?" he asked her.

"Because she won't be able to do it all by herself in one day, and I don't think she did it alone," Myra sighed.

Neither did Connor, but he couldn't prove his siblings were involved. Since Misti and Caleb weren't going to fess up to being involved, there wasn't anything he could do, but it didn't mean he couldn't make them help clear up the mess.

Before any of them could say another word, Rush addressed the room.

"Now that you're all here," he said, looking around the room. "I'll get straight to the point. Last night, Anya managed to slip past Connor while he slept and has now, as far as we know, gone through the portal to the human realm. As soon as Connor woke up, he realised she was gone and quickly went after her. He was able to pick up her scent and follow it to the cave where the portal to the human realm is located, but that's as far as he got before her scent disappeared."

Connor knew what they were all thinking, her scent should have been fresh enough for him to easily find her, but it wasn't in the cave, which frustrated the hell out of him.

"How long did he wait before looking for her?" Krystal asked.

She was one of the younger female hunters. Even though she hadn't been a hunter for long, she was good at her job, if a little reckless at times.

"As soon as he woke up, he went after her," Rush repeated.

"Then why couldn't he just track her down by her scent?" Krystal asked.

"Because, for reasons we don't yet know, her scent vanished after she stepped foot inside the cave," Rush told her.

"That's not possible," Markus said.

Connor looked over to see the shocked expression on Markus's face. It was the same expression most people in the room had on their faces, and no doubt Connor looked exactly the same when he realised her scent had vanished.

"You said she's a human," Ashleah, another female hunter, pointed out. "They don't have the ability to hide their scent from us."

"Plus," Krystal added. "Why would she feel the need to if she doesn't know about us being shifters?"

"Yes, as far as we know, she is only human," Rush said.

"Do you think she's getting help from someone?" Myra piped up next to him.

"It's the only explanation for how she disappeared without a trace," Rush said. "But we can't rule out the possibility that she isn't human."

"Who do you think is helping her?" Krystal asked.

"We don't know," Rush said. "But whoever it is, we don't think they're doing it out of the goodness of their heart."

"You think she's in trouble?" Markus asked.

"Yes."

"Why?"

Rush filled everyone in on the dreams Connor was having, and how they were trying to figure out what they meant. The room was silent as all the new information sank in.

When Rush was finished, everyone in the room turned to look at Connor expectantly. He didn't have anything else to add, so he stood silently, waiting for the barrage of questions to begin. It didn't take long.

Before long, he was drowning in a sea of noise. Connor could barely hear himself think, let alone make sense of all the questions flying around.

It was getting louder and louder by the second until Rush finally snapped.

"Shut up!!" he bellowed.

Instantly, the room went silent as everyone turned their attention back to Rush.

"Now that I've got your attention again," he said, staring daggers at everyone. "I'll continue. To answer some of your questions. Yes, it appears Anya is Connor's mate. No, she doesn't know about us or about being Connor's mate. No, as far as we know, she doesn't have a clue Connor has been dreaming of her. *If* somebody is helping Anya, or pretending to help her, then we will find them and deal with them accordingly. Whoever it is, they will probably be responsible for hiding her scent, as well. As soon as we know where she is, we'll be leaving. We don't think she will be at her home, but we will be checking it out, as well as other places she's likely to go. But at this moment in time, we're still trying to figure all that out."

"Maybe I can help you with that." Came a female voice Connor hadn't heard before. Everyone turned to look at the newcomer.

CHAPTER TWENTY

As soon as Sasha arrived at Rush's house, it became blatantly clear something was going on. The place was packed full of people.

She made her way inside and found a spot at the back of the room that was out of the way. It didn't take her long to realize they were all there because of Anya.

After telling Rush to keep Anya safe until she returned, it seemed they had done the complete opposite. Sasha didn't think she had asked much of them, but obviously she was wrong.

Staying veiled, she listened to Rush debriefed everyone on what had happened before answering a barrage of questions. She couldn't help grinning as she watched him try to keep up with all the questions.

She was surprised Anya hadn't been told about the shifters yet, especially since she was Connor's mate. Sasha had known Anya was Connor's mate, it was written all over his face the first moment he laid eyes on her.

Eventually, Rush gave up trying to answer each person individually. After silencing the room, he answered as many questions as he could, but it was clear he didn't know anything about Anya's current whereabouts.

"Maybe I can help you with that," she said, dropping her veil and stepping forward.

Rush's onyx eyes, as well as everyone else's in the room, instantly swung her way. She ignored everyone else as she walked to where Rush stood. She didn't take her eyes off him, but she could still see people staring at her out of the corner of her eye.

Sasha hadn't expected to cause quite a stir, but it seemed they weren't used to having visitors. Or maybe it was because she had appeared out of thin air? Either way, her arrival had caused quite the stir.

Rush glared at her as she strolled over to him. He didn't look too pleased to see her.

As if she gave a shit about his happiness, though. The one person she gave a shit about was now missing, thanks to him. She only gave him one job to do, and he still managed to completely fuck it up. How hard was it to keep an eye on one female?

"Who is she?" the shifters whispered to each other.

"I don't know. I've never seen her before."

"What is she? I can't pick up any scent from her." A couple of them said as she passed by them.

"Maybe she's the one concealing Anya's scent from us."

Nope, that one wasn't her, but it probably would have been a good idea if she'd done something like that before she left Anya there in the first place. It wouldn't have stopped Anya from running off, but it would've made it harder for someone else to find her.

A better idea would have been to put a tracking spell on Anya. That way, she would be able to find her now, and quickly. Instead, it was going to take her time to locate Anya. First, she had to break the spell that was concealing Anya from her, which was easier said than done.

"Hello again, little wolf," she greeted as she stopped in front of him.

Rush instantly growled at the nickname. Silly wolf, did he think that growl was going to scare her? If that was his intention, then he was sorely mistaken. If anything, it made her want to ruffle his fur even more.

She heard a few people chuckle at the nickname, but she had a feeling even more were hiding grins. It did make her smile.

"This is Anya's friend, Sasha." Rush announced to the room before turning his onyx eyes on her again. "What are you doing here?"

"What do you think I'm doing here?" Sasha asked. She put a hand on her hip and glared at him. "I told you I would be back. I also told you to keep Anya safe until I returned, which you haven't done."

"How were we supposed to know she would run off?" he asked in return.

"That's why you were supposed to keep an eye on her," Sasha told him. "Did you even attempt to go after her?"

Rush growled at her again. "Of course we did."

"Then you should have been able to catch up with her," she pointed out.

"I know." Rush raked a hand through his hair. "I honestly didn't think she would get very far because of her injuries, but somehow, she recovered a lot faster than she should have done."

That was an interesting tidbit she wasn't expecting. By rights, Anya shouldn't have recovered already. Could it be a result of whatever had happened to her? Sasha didn't know, but she was certainly going to find out.

"How long have you been here?" Rush asked her.

"Long enough."

"How much did you hear?" he asked.

"I know everything."

"So, you know where Anya is?" Connor asked.

She turned to look at Connor. "Except that."

"You don't know everything then, do you," he retorted.

"I'm not all seeing," she told him. "Unfortunately, someone is using magic to hide her from me."

"Not just you," Rush told her. "They've hidden her from us as well."

"That's not hard though, is it?" she said smugly.

There was that growl again. Sasha just smiled.

"So, if you can't locate her either, how the hell do you plan on helping us?" Connor asked.

The answer to that was she couldn't. At least, not at that moment in time, but she was working on it. And when the time came, they were going to need her help getting to Anya's location as quickly as possible.

She hadn't stopped looking for a way around the magic since she first realized she couldn't locate Anya.

"You can't do anything either, can you?" Connor asked.

"Sooner or later, I will find a way around the magic being used to conceal Anya," she told him. "And when that time comes, I can help transport everyone to her location in the blink of an eye."

"Is that it? You can get us from A to B?" Connor asked.

"I can do a lot more than that, pup." She winked at him. "You'll want me on your side if it comes to a fight."

"Why?" Aidan asked. "You don't look like you've ever been in a fight in your entire life. Do you even know how to fight?"

"Trust me," she told him. "I've been in more fights than you can imagine."

Which was true. For the majority of her very long life, she had been fighting for one reason or another. It wasn't something she enjoyed, but thankfully, she was good at it. She needed to be.

"Prove it," Aidan dared her.

Sasha raised her eyebrows as she stared at him. "I don't have to prove a damn thing to you."

She could see Aidan wanted to goad her into showing him her skills, but she wasn't easily manipulated into doing something she didn't want to. Plus, she would only fight when she absolutely had to. She certainly didn't do it for fun, or to show off.

"Enough, Aidan," Rush intervened when Aidan opened his mouth to say something else.

Aidan pouted, but he did as his alpha told him.

Rush then turned to her. "Thank you for the offer to help us, but we can manage on our own."

"The only offer I was giving," she told him. "Was for you to join me in rescuing Anya. I don't care whether you want me there or not, Anya is my best friend, so I *will* be helping in her rescue." Sasha held up her hand to silence him when he was about to interrupt her. "Not to mention, I already trusted you to keep an eye on her, and you couldn't even do that right. So, I'm certainly not going to leave her rescue down to you alone."

As the old saying goes, if you want something done right, do it yourself.

CHAPTER TWENTY-ONE

It was all coming together seamlessly. There may have been a slight hiccup when Anya was in the shifter realm, but she was finally back in the human realm and on her way to him. In fact, she was due to arrive any minute.

The witch had assured him no-one would be able to find or track Anya. She mentioned something about a magic bubble, or something along those lines, but he really didn't care. All that mattered; was that Anya was on her way to him, and that nobody would be able to find her.

But just in case the witch was wrong, he had a greeting party waiting to deal with the shifters, or anyone else that might come looking for Anya.

He was determined not to lose the opportunity to see through the experiment with Anya. So, he had prepared as best as he could for anything, or anyone, that might interfere with his plans.

There was a knock on his office door a moment

later.

"Come in," he ordered.

The door opened and one of the humans he employed walked in. He stopped in front of the desk and bowed his head.

"They're here, sir," he said when he looked back up.

It was about time they arrived. His impatience had been growing while waiting for them to get there.

"Good," he said. "Put the woman in her cell, and bring the witch to me."

"Yes, sir." The man bowed his head again and then turned and left, shutting the door behind him.

If everything turned out the way he had planned, then it was going to be the beginning of a very profitable operation. He just needed to be sure that the witch wasn't lying. But the only way he would know for sure, was to see if what they had done to Anya in London had worked as planned.

A couple of minutes later, his office door opened. He didn't need to see who it was to know who had entered. There was only one person who walked into his office without knocking first, and that was the witch.

"Have you got what you promised me?" she demanded as soon as she walked in.

"Please, take a seat," he told her calmly, even though he felt anything but calm.

"I don't want to take a seat," she said, placing a hand on her hip as she leaned to the side. "I want what you promised me, and then I'll be on my way. So, have you got it or not."

"Not."

"You promised me!" she said angrily.

"I promised I would have it when the time came," he reminded her. "And the time has not come yet."

He could see it wasn't the answer she was looking for, but it was the only answer she was going to get. He couldn't tell her that the item she was after had never been in his possession. Nor could he inform her that he didn't intend on acquiring it for her either.

No, if she knew any of that, she would walk away right there and then. He couldn't let that happen, because he still needed her for the time being. As soon as she was no longer needed, he would enjoy breaking the news to her, but until then, he would continue to dangle the item over her head.

"That's not good enough," she told him. "I've done everything you've asked me to do. Our deal is done, it's time for payment."

Her anger was growing by the second. Not that he cared if she was pissed off or not.

"I'll tell you when our deal is done," he said, showing his own anger. "Not the other way around. Until then, you better remember who you are talking to."

He didn't care how much magic she wielded; he could rip her head from her shoulders before she even knew what was happening.

"When will that be?" she asked.

"When I'm sure nothing has gone wrong with the spell."

"Nothing has gone wrong," she assured him. "It will

work just as I said it would. By the end of tomorrow night, Anya will be a wolf shifter, just like you wanted."

"Even if that's true, I want you here for her first time shifting, just in case something goes wrong then."

She crossed her arms over her chest as she finally relented. "Fine, but as soon as it's over, I want the item you promised me."

"Good," he said, ignoring her terms. "Now, go. I'll call you when you're needed."

***

Kassadi was fuming. She couldn't believe she had let herself be manipulated like a fool. She should have known he wouldn't keep his side of the deal. Evil sons of bitches couldn't be trusted, and he was definitely an evil son of a bitch.

Not wanting to be near him for a second more, she turned on her heel and stormed out of his office. She didn't even want to be in the same building as him. So, she hunted down a large mirror. Thankfully, it didn't take her long to find what she was looking for.

A full length, freestanding mirror stood in one corner of the master bedroom.

She grinned. "Perfect."

Closing the door behind her, she walked across the room and stopped in front of the mirror. Using magic, she drew runes onto the glass, turning it into a portal. Within seconds, the solid mirror was transformed into liquid silver that rippled from the centre outward.

As soon as she stepped through the portal, she was instantly transported to a secluded cabin in the middle of nowhere. Her muscle relaxed, and she let out a sigh of relief the moment the portal closed behind her.

The small cabin was her home for the time being. It wasn't exactly luxurious, but it would do her for the time being.

She didn't know the name of the area, and she didn't care either. It was isolated, but that was what she wanted. The only way for anyone to reach the cabin was either by foot, or by teleporting. It was a hell of a long walk from the nearest road, and most beings that could teleport, needed to at least know where they were going.

The cabin could do with a few more utilities, like indoor plumbing for one, but it was hers. Somewhere she could let her guard down for a little while.

Even knowing nobody knew where the cabin was, she still checked the wards around the cabin and surrounding area to make sure nobody had been there while she'd been gone. Thankfully, everything was as it should be.

She looked around at the meagre belongs she had managed to save from her last home just before it burned to the ground. She lost so much that day, more than just her belongings and her home that had been filled with so many happy memories.

Kassadi mentally shook her head. Nothing good would come of her dwelling on the past. What was done was done. All she could do was look to the future.

The small building only had two rooms. A living room with a small kitchen area to one side, and a bedroom. She stored a wooden bath under her bed when not in use, and dragged it into the living room when she needed to.

She didn't mind moving the bath around the place. It was filling it with a bucket and large cooking pot that she wasn't a fan of. In the summer when the weather was nice, she washed in the river that was near to the cabin, but it wasn't possible in the winter because of the thick snow and freezing water.

And the toilet? Well, that was in a little square shed set away from the cabin. Yep, the place definitely wasn't luxurious, but it was only temporary, so she could put up with it.

Kassadi's mind kept going back to Anya. It didn't matter how much she told herself she didn't care about the woman, she couldn't help but feel guilty about everything she had put the poor woman through.

Nobody deserved to have their life altered the way Anya had. Kassadi didn't know what he planned to do with Anya after she shifted for the first time, but it couldn't be anything good.

What Kassadi regretted the most however, was giving him the means to do the same thing to other people, as well. If she could get her hands on the scroll with the spell on it, she could prevent him from doing it again.

Hindsight was a bitch. It was only after she had given him the spell that she realized she had made a very big mistake. It was the evil glint in his eyes as he had looked over the spell that sent a shudder down her spine, warning her that she'd made a mistake.

But, she hadn't cared. She had given him the power to play with people's lives, all because he had something she wanted. Something she needed. What was worse was he probably didn't even have the item she wanted.

Kassadi may have been stupid, naive even, in believing he was doing it for a good reason. And even more naive to think he would hand over payment without a problem, but he had made a mistake as well.

He had dismissed her and her magic as something he could easily control, something he could easily manipulate. She had let him for a while, but no more.

Kassadi wasn't going to be a doormat for him to walk all over any more. She was going to take back control of her life, and take back possession of the spell she had given him. In the process, she could also start to make amends for what she had done to Anya as well.

With her mind made up, Kassadi collected everything she would need, and then she opened another portal.

CHAPTER TWENTY-TWO

Anya slowly woke up to a dripping sound. She inhaled deeply as she stretched her arms and legs, but instantly regretted it.

The rancid scent that invaded her lungs was enough to turn her stomach. It smelt worse than a sewer, the air just as damp as it would be in a sewer as well. But that wasn't what alarmed her.

What caused her blood to freeze in her veins and her eyes to snap open, were the chains wrapped tightly around her wrists and ankles. They prevented her from moving more than an inch.

Anya wracked her mind, trying to figure out where she was and why she was chained to a bed. Or what she assumed was a bed.

The metal springs dug into her wherever she touched the mattress. What padding had originally been there was long gone. The only thing that remained was the metal springs and the thin piece of fabric covering them.

She attempted to look around the room, hoping

something would jog her memory, but even that was easier said than done. She just about managed to lift her head off the mattress to peek over her arms, but there wasn't anything of interest to see, and there were definitely no clues as to where she was or how she got there.

The last thing Anya could remember, she had been leaving the cave with the woman who had been helping her get away from Connor. Or more precisely, the dragon.

At least, she had thought the woman had been there to help her. Turned out, Anya had been wrong. The woman hadn't been there to help her. Which was made blatantly obvious by her current situation.

In her attempt to get away from the dragon, she had managed to get herself into something she might not be able to get out of. Especially not on her own. Unfortunately, she doubted anyone would be coming to her rescue.

For the life of her, Anya couldn't remember what the woman's name was. It was right there, teetering on the edge of her mind, but every time she tried to reach for it, it would move further away.

Anya could kick herself for not listening to her intuition. She knew something was off about the woman, but because she had wanted to get away from the dragon...a dragon that shouldn't even exist...she had ignored her gut feeling and accepted the help.

There was nothing she could do about it now. As much as she wanted to, she couldn't turn back the clock. If she could turn back the clock, she definitely wouldn't go on a hike on her own. That's when all the trouble began.

Anya lifted her head again and looked around the room. She noted the small window above the bed, and the metal door behind her.

The window would be less than useless if she somehow managed to get out of the chains. It was way too small for her to fit through, not to mention the bars covering it. No doubt the door was locked, ruling that out as a possible escape route as well.

The bare brick walls made the room even more dark and gloomy than it was. She could see water seeping down the walls in places, but she could see where the dripping was coming from.

Apart from the bed, there was absolutely nothing else in the room. There wasn't even a toilet. Not that she could use one while chained to the bed anyway, but it would have been nice to have the option. Even a bucket would do.

Scurrying sounds caught her attention. Anya had never been squeamish about rodents, but she was glad she couldn't see them racing around the room. Bugs were a different matter. She shuddered at the thought of bugs crawling on her.

Anya definitely regretted her decision to leave Connor's house. In fact, she regretted leaving home and going on holiday with Sasha.

Never before had so much bad shit happened to her at once. What was supposed to be a nice, relaxing holiday had turned into her worst nightmare. The only good thing that had happened to her in weeks was her one night with Connor, even if he had regretted it the next day.

She took comfort in the memory of their time together, short as it may have been. She used it to keep her mind off her surroundings and current predicament.

Anya didn't know how long she had been lying there thinking about Connor, but she was beginning to go numb where the chains were holding her in place for so long.

"So, you're awake at last," a male voice came from the doorway.

She hadn't heard anybody enter the room, but when she lifted her head and looked towards the door, a man stood staring at her.

He was tall and muscular, with black hair and cold blue eyes. She would have considered him handsome if it wasn't for the evil glint in his eyes.

He wore a dark grey trouser suit with a white shirt and blood red tie. Even dressed as impeccably as he was, there was no denying the malice coming off him in waves.

She would have thought his smart attire would be at odds with the cold, dank cell, but it was the opposite. He seemed to fit right in even wearing the suit.

"Who are you?" she demanded. "And why am I chained to a bed?"

"You can call me Mr. Smith," he told her.

"Nope, that doesn't sound right," Anya said before she could think better of it. "You don't look like a Mr. Smith. Are you sure that's your name?"

He laughed. "Very intuitive. You are correct, it isn't my name, but it's the only one I'm giving you."

"Okay," she said. "But that doesn't answer my second question. Why am I chained up? And where am I?"

"It doesn't matter where you are," he said. "And the chains are there to prevent you from escaping."

"How the fuck do you expect me to escape?" she asked, genuinely wanting to know the answer. "Even without the chains, I wouldn't be able to get out of this room. I heard you unlock the door," she lied. "So there's no chance I can escape that way. There's bars on the window," she pointed out. "And even if there wasn't, it's not big enough for me to fit through. I can't magically make myself smaller… as much as I wish I could sometimes. So, please, tell me how the fuck I'm supposed to escape?"

"It doesn't matter what you say, the chains are staying," he told her. "At least, for the time being, anyway."

"Why am I here? What do you want with me?"

"Do you think I'm going to tell you all my plans? Is that it?" he asked. "Do you think because I have you chained up, I'm going to tell you everything?"

Anya could admit to herself that she had thought he would tell her everything, but now she knew differently. He had absolutely no intention of telling her anything.

He tutted when she remained silent. "You've been watching far too many movies, Anya. That's not what is going to happen. In fact, I'm not going to tell you anything at all."

"Why?" she couldn't stop the word from slipping from her lips.

She really was curious to know why he didn't plan on telling her. She thought it was what all bad guys did. Gloat about what they were going to do right before they did it. But more importantly, she wanted to know what he planned to do to her.

If the chains around her wrists and ankles were anything to go by, then she wasn't going to like the answer.

"Because, where is the fun in that?"

"I don't understand."

"Of course, you don't," he said smugly. "Because you've always been told through movies that bad guys act a certain way, when in reality, it is completely different. Not every bad guy wants let on what they're going to do. It ruins the suspense."

Anya knew he was right, but that didn't mean she had to like it. Not that she was going to tell him.

"And another thing, there isn't always a good guy that saves the day, either," he told her. "So, don't expect anyone to rescue you."

Anya didn't expect anyone to rescue her anyway, so it was no surprise to her, but she still would have liked to know what he planned to do with her.

"Fine," she said. "Just tell me one thing."

Anya almost burst out laughing when *he* eyed her suspiciously.

"How long do you plan on keeping me like this?" She rattled the chains attached to the cuffs around her wrists. "It's just; my arms are starting to go numb."

"Don't worry; you won't be staying in that position for too much longer."

Anya wasn't sure she wanted to know what position he was going to put her in next, but she couldn't prevent the question from leaving her mouth, anyway. "What position are you going to put me in next?"

He had an evil glint in his eyes as he said; "You will see."

Anya didn't want to wait and see. She just wanted to go home, but that wasn't going to happen any time soon, either.

"Well, as much as I've enjoyed our conversation," he said, clapping his hands together and making her jump. "There are other things that demand my attention."

"You're going already?"

"Would you rather I stayed?"

"Nope," she admitted. "I would rather you just let me go."

He laughed at her comment. "That's not going to happen, no matter how amusing you are."

Anya wasn't trying to be amusing, but if it was going to work in her favour, then she would give it her best shot. Unfortunately, before she could say another word, he walked out the room, shutting the door behind him.

Anya heard the bolts slide into place and the keys jingle as he locked the door.

Fuck!

How the hell had she managed to get herself into this

situation? But more importantly, how the hell was she going to get herself back out of it?

Anya hadn't lied when she told him her arms were going numb. She didn't know how long she had been chained for, but she had lost all feeling in her hands and wrists while they had been speaking, and now the numbness was slowly creeping up her arms.

Her legs and feet were in the same boat. She tried to wiggle her toes, but when she peered down at them, they didn't even twitch.

Just great!

Anya pulled against the chains, trying to get into a better position, but no matter what she tried, she was unable to move an inch.

How the fuck am I gonna get out of this one?

Anya would be amazed if she made it out alive, but that was looking less and less likely as the minutes ticked by. From what she could tell, there was absolutely no way for her to get herself out of this situation without help. And since it was highly unlikely that anyone was even looking for her, she didn't see any help arriving any time soon.

Sasha was more than likely back in London, and she didn't know where Connor was, but she couldn't see him searching for her. He was probably happy she was finally out of his life, and she couldn't blame him, either.

Every time she thought of Connor, she was reminded of their time together. Anya knew it meant nothing to him, just a bit of fun to pass the time, but it didn't stop her heart from wanting more. Like a drug, she was addicted to him after just one taste.

As much as she wanted another taste of him, she knew it was never going to happen. For starters, she was being held prisoner by a madman. There was no telling what he had in store for her.

Even if she did manage to make it out in one piece, there was no guarantee Connor would want anything more to do with her. Especially after she'd run away from him. She wouldn't blame him if he'd already forgotten about her and moved on.

The thought of him with another woman hurt more than she cared to admit. So, she refused to let it enter her mind. If this was going to be the end for her, then she wasn't going to spend what little time she had left with negative thoughts running through her mind.

Since she couldn't escape the chains or the madman, then she would at least fill her mind with the few happy memories she had.

CHAPTER TWENTY-THREE

Kassadi kept to the shadows as she made her way around the building. She didn't stop until she came to the room she was looking for.

When she peeked through the small window on the door, she spotted Anya lying on a bed. Her strawberry blonde hair was a stark contrast to her pale skin. She would have thought Anya was dead if she hadn't noticed her chest slowly rising and falling with each breath she took.

Thick metal cuffs wrapped around her wrists and ankles. Even from a distance, Kassadi could see the marks the cuffs were leaving on Anya's skin.

The cuffs were attached to heavy metal chains, which were pulled tight, making it impossible for Anya to move. Only her head was free to move, but even then, she could only lift it slightly because of the position she was in.

Kassadi swallowed as guilt ate at her for what she'd put Anya through. Even though she wasn't the one to chain Anya to the bed, she was the one responsible for handing her over to the evil bastard that would do such a thing.

She dragged her eyes away from Anya's prone form long enough to make sure the coast was clear before turning her attention back to Anya. She whispered the spell to unlock the cuffs from around her wrists and ankles. When she clicked her fingers at the end of spell, the chains instantly fell to the floor.

The heavy metal clanged as it hit the floor. The sound reverberated through the empty corridors.

Kassadi held her breath, hoping nobody heard the noise. When she didn't hear the sound of boots stomping in her direction, she breathed out a sigh of relief.

The chains were only part of the battle. Getting Anya out of the building without her being seen was going to be the hard part. All the while, Kassadi needed to avoid being seen as well, by Anya or anyone else.

Anya was a long way from being free yet, so they needed to be careful, but especially Kassadi. As much as she hated working for him, she still needed him for the time being. So, the last thing she needed, was to be caught helping Anya escape.

Thankfully, it didn't take Anya long to get to her feet. She rubbed at her wrists as she looked around the room in confusion.

Kassadi quickly stepped back when her eyes swung towards the door. If Anya knew she was helping her, she might not accept the help. Not that Kassadi could blame her.

Nonetheless, Kassadi was Anya's only hope of

getting out of there alive. Unfortunately, if Kassadi was right, then Anya didn't have time to wait for the wolf shifters to find her.

She moved further away from the room and hid in the shadows before unlocking the door for Anya. She watched as Anya gingerly opened the door and peeked outside.

Now that Anya knew the sound of Kassadi's voice, she couldn't give Anya directions on which way to go, so it was going to make her escape that much harder.

Other than unlocking the doors ahead of her, there was only one other thing Kassadi could do, and that was to drop the shield around Anya. At least then the shifters should be able to track her down.

As she watched Anya leave the room and head down the corridor, she dropped the spell surrounding Anya. Now, it was all down to Anya to find her way out.

To cover her tracks, Kassadi quickly left the area and entered a room occupied by a group of demons. She leaned against a wall, giving the appearance she was bored, and waited for the alarm to go off that a prisoner had escaped.

**

Connor couldn't have sat still even if he wanted to, so he paced from one side of Rush's living room to the other. He was too agitated to do anything else as he waited for the go-ahead to go after Anya.

He understood why Rush was making him wait, but it didn't make it any easier. Anything could be happening to her while he stood around doing nothing.

Most of the hunters had cleared out of Rush's home hours ago, leaving just a handful of people behind. It was those few people that were going with him to rescue Anya.

Connor would have preferred to have double the amount going, but Rush wanted to make sure there were plenty of hunters left in the shifter realm in case anything happened while they were gone. Rush was concerned it was all a ruse to get them to leave the pack unprotected.

At that moment in time, though, Connor didn't give a shit about anyone other than Anya. He knew he would feel differently once she was safe and sound, but at the moment, his only concern was Anya.

"I need to do something, anything." Connor threw up his hands in frustration. "I can't just sit here doing nothing."

"You need to sit the fuck down, that's what you need to do," Sasha told him. "I'm trying to concentrate here."

She hadn't stopped trying to break the spell hiding Anya from them since she arrived. He didn't have a clue what she was doing, but it just appeared as if she sat there with her eyes closed.

"And what is it you're going to do?" Myra asked him.

"Anything has got to be better than doing nothing."

"Not really. You could end up looking in the wrong place for starters. At least if we're here, we can get prepared while Sasha tries to locate Anya," Myra said.

"We're as prepared as we're going to be," he told her. "The only way we could be more prepared is if we bring more people with us."

"That's not going to happen," Rush told him.

No matter how much he wanted to argue, Connor knew it would be pointless.

"I know, but what if she can't find her?" he nodded towards Sasha. "We'll just be wasting valuable time sitting around waiting, when we could be searching the human realm."

"There is no point randomly searching different areas in the human realm in the hope of finding her," Rush said. "That would be a complete waste of time. Not to mention, there isn't enough of us to search that wide of an area."

Connor knew what Rush was saying was right, but that didn't stop the worry from building. Anything could be happening to Anya while they stood around doing sod all. If something did happen to her and he could have prevented it, then he would never forgive himself.

"Why don't you go outside and take a walk?" Rush suggested.

"No," he shook his head. "I want to be here ready when we get the information we need."

There was no way he was leaving the room. He wanted… needed… to be there when they got the information on Anya's whereabouts.

"I'll let you know the moment we know anything," Rush offered.

"Thanks, but no thanks," he reiterated. "I would

rather be here."

"Fine, but sit the fuck down," Rush snapped. "You're doing my head in with all the bloody pacing. Have a drink if you need one, but chill the fuck out. There's nothing we can do for the time being."

"Fine," Connor said, as he sat down on the sofa next to Myra. "What's got under his skin?" he asked her.

"I don't know," Myra said. "But he's right; your pacing was getting on my nerves, as well."

"Do you think it has anything to do with Sasha?" Aidan asked. "He didn't seem too happy to see her here."

"Could be," Myra said.

"What do you think she is?" Aidan Asked.

"I don't know, but she's definitely not human," Myra told him.

"Yeah, I got that when she appeared out of thin air," Aidan rolled his eyes dramatically. "Not to mention, I can't pick up her scent."

"Neither can I," Myra said. "I wonder how she met Anya."

Connor was curious about the same thing. He would bet that Anya didn't have a clue her friend wasn't human.

"If it wasn't for the fact she's here looking for Anya, I would have thought she was the one hiding her," Connor admitted.

"Yeah, from what you said about Anya's scent disappearing, and Sasha not having one, I would have thought the same thing," Myra agreed. "It's only the fact she seems to be just as concerned about Anya's whereabouts as us, that makes me think otherwise."

A moment later, Sasha's eyes snapped open, and she jumped up from her seat. "I know where she is."

Everyone in the room turned to look at her.

"Oh, and by the way," she said, turning to glare at him and Myra. "I may not have enhanced hearing like the rest of you, but I can still hear you talking about me."

Myra looked embarrassed as she apologised to Sasha, but Connor wasn't sorry for what he said, so he returned her glare.

"Where is she?" Rush asked.

"Well, I don't have an exact location," she hedged. "But I know which realm, and I have a rough idea of the area to search."

"About fucking time," Connor said as he got to his feet. "What are we waiting for? Let's go."

They already knew what they had to do when they arrived at the location, so there was no need to hang around any longer.

"Hold on a second," Rush said, halting him before turning his attention to Sasha. "How large is the area we need to search?"

"Roughly within a ten-mile radius."

"What's that got to do with anything?" Connor snapped.

"It matters because we don't want to spread out too thinly," Rush told him. "If it's too large an area, and likely to take our small group hours to search, then we need to bring more people with us."

"We should be taking more people with us anyway,"

he ground out.

Rush ignored Connor's comment, and instead said. "It shouldn't take long to search the area with the amount of people coming with us."

"It's a rural location as well," Sasha told him. "So, you should be able to cover most of the distance in your wolf forms."

"How are you going to keep up with our wolves?" Myra asked her.

Connor didn't give a shit how she was going to keep up; he just wanted to get going already.

"Don't worry about me," Sasha said with a wink. "I can keep up just fine."

"It might be best if you stay in one location," Rush told her. "As soon as we come across something, I'll send someone back for you."

"Good try, little wolf." She shook her head. "But that's not going to happen. I'm not stupid enough to believe that you would hold off on rescuing Anya while someone comes back to fetch me."

"Understand, if you slow us down, we will leave you behind," Rush told her bluntly.

"Understand," she repeated in the same tone as she raised an eyebrow at him. "It will be you who slows me down, not the other way around."

Rush growled at Sasha, but she just stuck her tongue out at him in reply.

"Yep, it's definitely something to do with Sasha," Aidan whispered to Myra.

"I thought as much," she replied.

"Can we please just get going already?" Connor

asked.

"I'm ready when you are," Sasha told him.

"Are you sure you can transport so many of us at once?" Rush asked Sasha.

"Yep, it's a piece of cake," she said confidently.

"Okay," Rush said, not sounding convinced. "Take Connor, Kellen, Aidan, Dominic, Autumn, and Myra first, then come back for the rest of us."

"No problem."

Rush turned to glare at Connor. "Don't fucking run off on your own. Wait until everyone is there, then we can pair off and search. We won't be far behind you."

Connor wasn't going to make a promise he knew he couldn't keep, so he kept quiet.

"I'm warning you," Rush told him. "Don't fucking run off."

This time Connor nodded his head, but he still wasn't promising anything. He didn't care how quickly they arrived after him; he wasn't hanging around waiting any longer. Anya needed him, and he was damn well going to be there for her, no matter what it took. Even if it meant going against Rush's order.

"Ready boys and girls?" Sasha asked the group. When they all nodded, she added, "Gather round in a circle, grab hold of the person next to you, and don't let go."

As soon as everybody was in position, Sasha grabbed hold of Connor's hand and then teleported them to the human realm.

CHAPTER TWENTY-FOUR

The numbness was just starting to reach her shoulders and thighs, when all of a sudden, the chains fell away.

Anya didn't know how it was possible, and she didn't really care. All that mattered was that she was now free. Well, kind of. She was still locked in the room, but at least she could move around.

She gingerly sat up on the bed and looked around the room. It was even more dingy than she first thought. The concrete floor was covered in a thick layer of dirt and God only knows what else, and the bed was the only item of furniture in the there.

As she looked at the discarded restraints hanging from the bed frame, her thoughts turned to how they had come undone when nobody was in the room with her. She didn't normally believe in ghosts or magic, but after seeing a real-life dragon, she found she was more open to the possibility of both being real. So, just in case it was Casper the Friendly Ghost, she whispered thank you.

Anya stood up and stretched her muscles. She absently rubbed her wrists where the metal cuffs had dug into her while she moved around the room, looking for anything she could use as a weapon.

Anya caught movement out of the corner of her eye. She turned towards the door and looked through the little window, but it was too dark on the other side for her to see anything. She heard the locks click in the door a moment before it creaked open.

Anya froze as she waited for someone to enter. Her heart was racing so fast, it felt like it was about to burst out of her chest.

After a moment's hesitation, Anya managed to pluck up the courage to walk over to the door and peek outside. Thankfully, the corridor appeared to be empty. She didn't know what she would have done if somebody had been out there.

Probably scream, her subconscious piped up.

The corridor was completely devoid of anything that would give her a clue as to her whereabouts, but it was just as empty and uninviting as the room. There were a few doors dotted on either side of the corridor. Some had little windows like hers did, but most were solid doors. There was also a door at either end of the corridor.

Since there wasn't any exit signs, she assumed one of the doors at either end of the corridor would be the exit. She just didn't know which one it might be. So, she did the only thing she could think of, and left it down to fate to decide.

Anya pointed, "Eeny, meeny, miney, mo, catch a

tiger by the toe, if he hollers, let him go, eeny, meeny, miney, mo."

Yeah, she knew it wasn't a mature way to decide, but she figured there was a 50/50 chance either way.

It was now or never. If she didn't make her move now, then she might not ever get the chance again. Since somebody had gone to all the trouble of helping her out by unlocking the cuffs and door, she didn't want to pass up the opportunity they had given her.

Taking a deep breath, Anya opened the door and stepped out into the corridor. She half expected an alarm to sound the second she crossed the threshold. When no alarms immediately rang out, letting everyone know she was escaping, she breathed a sigh of relief. She knew there was still a long way to go before she was in the clear, but she thanked her lucky stars all the same.

Staying as close to the wall as she could, she slowly made her way along the corridor to the door at the end. She didn't have a clue if she was going in the right direction, but she had to take a chance and hope that she was.

As soon as she reached the door, she pressed her ear against it and listened for any sounds coming from the other side. Not hearing anything, she tried the handle. The door wasn't locked, but it also didn't lead outside, either. It opened up in to a massive room.

The room looked like a massive warehouse. It wasn't as brightly lit as the corridor, but it was bright enough for her to see that there was nobody inside. Other than a couple of small boxes against one wall, there was nothing in the room. It was good because it meant there wasn't anywhere for the bad guys to hide, but it also meant that she didn't have anywhere to hide either.

Anya was about to close the door and head back in the other direction when she caught sight of a door on the other side of the room. It was close to the corner where the light didn't quite reach. If it hadn't been for the light glinting off the metal bar across it, she would never have noticed it.

She looked over her shoulder to check nobody was watching her before stepping into the room and quietly closing the door behind her. Anya didn't hang around. As soon as the door was closed, she ran as fast as she could to the other door.

Please be the right way.

It would be just her luck to make it all the way across the room without being seen, only to find out it wasn't the way out. It was a risk she had to take though, because if she didn't, she might as well turn around and go back to the room where she'd been held prisoner.

Anya didn't know what he had planned for her, but whatever it was, she didn't want any part of it.

As soon as she reached the door, she skidded to a stop. Breathing heavily, she quickly looked back across the room to make sure nobody had come in after her.

She didn't bother pressing her ear against the door this time.

She wouldn't have been able to hear anything over

the beating of her heart in her ears.

She pressed the metal bar and cracked the door open enough for her to peek outside. Cool air hit her, confirming she had chosen the right direction. She waited for her eyes to adjust to the darkness before looking around outside for any bad guys.

She couldn't see anyone, but that didn't mean the coast was clear. For all she knew, there could be cameras all over the place. Somebody could have been watching the entire time. She didn't think that was the case, since nobody has tried to stop her, but it was still a possibility.

Other than a couple of security lights hanging from the building, there were no street lights nearby. If it wasn't for the moon, she wouldn't have been able to see where she was going.

Anya had never paid much attention to the phases of the moon before. She enjoyed gazing up at it in all its phases, but she never knew the dates when it would be a new or full moon. Looking up at it now, she thanked her lucky stars that it was almost a full moon.

She stepped outside, shutting the door quietly behind her. After all, there was no point in giving herself away when she was so close to freedom.

From the outside, the building definitely appeared to be some sort of warehouse. There were a few windows around the top of the building, but they were too high up for anyone to look through. The room she had been kept in was on the other side of the building, so even if people were in the other rooms along the corridor, they wouldn't be able to see her where she was.

Unfortunately, she wasn't on a trading estate, so she couldn't go to the next building along to ask for help. Instead, she would have to navigate her way through thick woodlands until she found a road that she could follow.

A six foot fence with barbed wire around the top surrounded the perimeter of the building. Anya could only see one road leading away from the building. She couldn't tell how long the road was because it disappeared into the woodlands.

He certainly is paranoid, she thought, as she looked around for a way through the fence.

Luckily for her, he wasn't so paranoid that he had guards posted at the gate she came across a moment later. At least, there was none that she could see.

Anya continually looked around as she carefully made her way over to the gate. She expected it to be locked when she reached it, but again, she was surprised to find that it wasn't.

Once through the gate, Anya followed the road as it wound its way through the woodlands. She stayed as close to the road as she could, all the while staying hidden in the woodland. It took her longer to put some distance between her and the building, but at least she wasn't exposed like she would be if she walked on the road.

The trees and foliage hadn't completely gone dormant for the winter, so there was still plenty of greenery on them. There were also a lot of bushes for her to hide behind if anyone came looking for her.

Everything was eerily silent as she made her way

through the woods. The only sound she heard was her own breathing, and even that was mostly drowned out but the loud thumping of her heart in her ears.

Anya didn't know how long she had been walking, but when she finally looked back, she could no longer see the imposing building through the trees. She couldn't even see any light coming from that direction.

The further she made it away from the building without any sign that someone was coming after her, the more hope that filled her. But she should have known it wouldn't be so easy to get away.

Anya only made it a little further before she heard what sounded like a wolf howling. The haunting sound echoed through the dark woods, but she could have sworn it was coming from the direction of the building. She didn't know if the animal had anything to do with the building, but since it sounded as if it was coming from there, she wasn't going to hang around and find out.

Anya didn't look back as she picked up speed. She went from a steady walking pace to a full-out run in seconds, jumping over rocks and tree roots that were sticking out of the ground. She did her best to avoid getting hit by branches as she ran as fast as she could.

Anya could hear something barrelling through the woods behind her. Taking a risk, she quickly looked over her shoulder and instantly regretted it when she spotted a massive wolf hot on her heels. Just as she turned back around, her foot caught on a bit of tree root sticking out of the ground and went tumbling over.

She got to her feet as quickly as she could, but she knew that tumble had cost her dearly. She didn't bother looking back, there was no point. She knew what was behind her now, and she couldn't risk falling again. As it was, the animal was almost upon her.

Her lungs were burning as she tried to gulp in air as she pumped her arms and legs as fast as she could, trying to outrun the animal. But deep down, Anya knew it was impossible. She had known it was only a matter of time before the animal caught up to her, and her time had just run out.

Before she knew what was happening, the animal rammed into her from behind, knocking her face first into the dirt. She narrowly missed hitting her head on a large rock. It was sticking out the ground inches away from her face.

She didn't get a chance to catch her breath and scream for help before the animal was on her again. It pinned her to the ground as a vicious growl escaped its mouth.

The sound, as well as the weight of the animal on her back, sent her mind straight back to the alley in her nightmare. The two animals sounded exactly the same. She knew it wasn't possible for them to be the same animal, but that didn't stop the panic from rising.

Oh, god, no! Please don't let it be real.

But it was. And what was even worse, the animal wasn't alone this time. Something even more frightening accompanied the huge wolf.

When the animal finally stepped off her back, she was roughly pulled up by her hair and came face to face with an honest to God, demon. Its dark red skin looked like that of a snake as it glistened under the moonlight, and two sharp horns protruded on the top of its head.

Frozen from fear, Anya screamed in her head. But before any sound could make it past her lips, something was blown into her face. She instantly felt herself falling into a dark abyss.

Just before the darkness swallowed her whole, she heard Connor's voice in her head. *"Hold on Anya, I'm coming!"* And then there was nothing.

CHAPTER TWENTY-FIVE

It was pitch black by the time everyone arrived in the human realm. It only took seconds for Sasha to go back and grab the rest of the group, so Connor didn't have a chance to slip off before Rush arrived.

Rush nodded at him before turning his attention to the group. "I want everyone to split up and search in groups of two. We don't know who or what we're dealing with, so until then, I don't want anyone wandering off on their own." He looked pointedly at Connor as he said the last few words. "Sasha, I would like you to take half the group to the other side of the search area. Once everybody is in place, I want you all to fan out and begin searching. The plan is to meet somewhere in the middle. Unless, of course, one of the search parties come across any sign of Anya."

"What about the extra person?" Autumn asked. "Once we're all in pairs, there's going to be one person left on their own."

"That person is Sasha, and she can stay close to me,"

he stated.

Sasha put her hand on her heart as her head tilted to one side as she looked at him. "Aww, you want to keep me safe. How sweet of you, little wolf, but completely unnecessary. I can look after myself. Plus, we can cover more ground if I search on my own."

"Not happening," he told her. "I may not have a say in whether you're here or not, but am I fuck letting you wander off by yourself."

"You really care that much?" she asked sweetly.

"That's not the reason," he told her. "We're here to rescue Anya. I don't want to have to rescue you as well."

"Keep telling yourself that," she said and then winked at him. "But I know the truth."

A couple of people in the group chuckled while the rest tried to hide a grin. Sasha was definitely getting under Rush's skin, and it was rather amusing to watch. It would have been more amusing if they weren't wasting time when they should be searching for Anya.

Connor couldn't wait any longer. The fear that something bad was happening to Anya while they stood around talking, was growing stronger by the second.

He was about to turn on his heel and head off in search of her when he suddenly heard her screaming in his head. The fear and panic he heard in her voice sent his own fear skyrocketing.

He instantly reached out to her with his mind. *"Hold on Anya,*
I'm coming!"

Before he could take a step, Rush grabbed hold of his arm. Connor growled in return.

"Get the fuck off me," he demanded.

"Just wait a minute."

"For what?"

Surely, if everyone else heard her, they would have picked up on the fear in her voice, as well? He couldn't have been the only one to notice.

"What the fuck?" Aidan asked. "I thought she was human?"

It took a moment for Aidan's question to register in his mind. Rush raised an eyebrow at him when it did.

As he looked around at the group, he realised he wasn't the only one surprised by Anya's scream.

"How the hell did she do that?" Myra asked.

"Did Anya show any signs that she wasn't human?" Rush asked.

"No, none at all," Connor said adamantly. "As far as I'm aware, she is only human."

Connor thought back over their time together, trying to pick up anything that she might have said or done that would give any indication that she was more than just a human, but there was absolutely nothing.

"Something must have happened to her already," Rush said.

"What, though?" Kellen asked.

"And when?" Myra added.

All eyes turned to Sasha. She had remained quiet throughout the conversation. Connor had a feeling that she knew more than she was letting on. Otherwise, why would she appear to be so calm? Shouldn't she be concerned about her friend?

The more Connor thought about it, the more questions ran through his mind. None of which would help get Anya back, but knowing what she was, might help them understand why someone had taken her in the first place. It might also give them an idea of who they were up against.

Rush must have thought the same as Connor, because he turned to Sasha and said, "What aren't you telling us?"

"What do you mean?" Sasha said as she crossed her arms over her chest.

"You know exactly what I mean," Rush told her. "You already know that she isn't human, don't you? So, what is she?"

Sasha let her arms fall to her sides as she blew out a breath. "Fine. Anya isn't human anymore. I'm not a hundred per cent sure what she is now, but I think she's been turned into a wolf shifter."

Everyone was silent as Sasha's announcement sank in.

Myra was the first to break the silence. "That's impossible," she stated.

"Not impossible," Sasha countered. "Just very difficult."

"It is impossible," Aidan told her. "Humans can't be turned into a wolf shifter. We're not bloody werewolves, you know. You don't turn into one of us if we bite you."

"Aidan's correct," Rush confirmed. "We can't turn anyone with a bite."

"Not with a bite alone, no," Sasha said. "But, if someone were to use magic, it would be possible."

"So, you're saying someone with magic has teamed up with a wolf shifter to turn Anya into one of us?" Myra asked.

"Yes."

"But, why?"

That's what Connor couldn't understand. Why would anyone want to turn a human into a wolf shifter? What could they possibly think to gain by doing something like that? The only way they were going to get any answers, was to find Anya and the people who took her.

"How the fuck should I know," Sasha said, breaking into his thoughts.

"Is it possible then?" Aidan asked Rush.

Everyone waited with bated breath for Rush to answer, but he was silent for so long, Connor didn't think he was going to.

Finally, he said, "Yes, it's possible. But the person with the magic would have to be extremely powerful in their craft to be able to accomplish it."

"But it is extremely dangerous," Sasha added. "A human body isn't built to shift into an animal. There's no telling whether Anya will survive the transition or not."

Connor couldn't have been more shocked if he had just been punched in the face. Anya was a shifter? Did she know she was one? Question after question raced through his head. He didn't have an answer to any of them.

"Shit," Aidan said. "If that's true…"

"It means she's one of us," Autumn finished for him.

"Yes, she is," Rush agreed.

Myra turned to Sasha. "Does she know?"

Sasha shook her head. "As far as I know, she doesn't have a clue."

"When was this done to her?" Rush asked her.

"A few days before she stumbled across your realm."

"That explains how she saw the cave," Connor said. "It's only hidden from humans. If she's no longer human, she would be able to see it without a problem."

"Do you know who's behind it all?" Aidan asked.

"Unfortunately, no, I don't." She let out a frustrated sigh. "At least, not yet."

"Assuming the same people who turned her are the ones who have her now, we'll find out soon enough," Rush said.

Connor hoped Rush was right, but either way, he would hunt down those responsible. He didn't care who was involved, he would kill them for what they had done, and what they were still doing, to Anya.

"If she doesn't know, how do you think she's going to take the news?" Myra asked.

"I honestly don't know," Sasha said. "I don't think she even knows shifters exist. Or anything else, for that matter. If she does, she's never mentioned anything to me."

"But you're her friend," Autumn pointed out. "Surely you should know if she'll be able to handle the news or not?"

"Finding out your life has been turned upside down and inside out, effects people differently," Sasha said. "If you're asking if I think she's strong enough to handle the news, then my answer is, yes. But that doesn't mean she's going to accept it willingly, or easily. However she takes the news, it's going to take her some time to adjust."

Connor had to agree with Sasha. There was no telling how Anya was going to take the news, but he had no doubt she would adjust once she was given time. And he would be there to help her every step of the way. That's if she will let him.

Connor thought about Anya and how scared she had sounded when she screamed in his head. He couldn't wait around any longer. He needed to find her, to make sure she was okay. Because if anything happened to her, he would never forgive himself.

While everyone else was distracted as they discussed what to do about Anya, he slipped off unseen into the dark woodland. If he stood any chance in reaching her before something even worse happened to her, then he needed to get moving, and fast.

CHAPTER TWENTY-SIX

Anya didn't want to wake up. But no matter how much she tried, she couldn't stay asleep.

"It's about time you woke up," came a voice she remembered all too well. It filled her with dread. "I told you I wasn't finished with you."

Any hope she might have had of it all being just a nightmare, were quickly dashed with those two sentences. Just the sound of his voice sent shivers down her spine, and not the good kind either.

Anya groaned as she opened her eyes and looked to where the voice came from. "Fuck. Not you again."

He was the last person in the world she wanted to see. She would have much preferred to wake up to the sound of Connor's voice next to her. Just thinking of him filled her with sadness.

She wished things had been different between them. Even if he wanted nothing more from her, she wished she'd at least said goodbye to him. Anya knew why she hadn't. If she had done, he would have tried to stop her from leaving.

Well, at least if he had done, you wouldn't be in this situation now, her subconscious pointed out.

"Afraid so, my dear," he said, breaking into her thoughts. "And if all goes well tonight, you will be seeing a lot more of me."

Fear so deep that it penetrated her bones shot through her at the look in his eyes as he spoke. Whatever he had planned for her, she wanted no part of it. Not that she had a choice. Her one and only chance of escape had been a complete and utter failure. She wasn't likely to get a second chance, and certainly not before tonight.

"Why? What's happening tonight?" she asked, hoping to find out what he was going to do to her.

He tutted at her. "If I told you that, it would give away the surprise."

"Good, I don't like surprises," she lied. "So, you might as well tell me."

"I think not," he said. "Did nobody ever tell you that patience is a virtue?"

"Nope," she shook her head. "And even if they did, I would have told them to shove their virtue up their asses."

Anya knew she was playing with fire, but she couldn't seem to stop herself. After everything she'd been through, it seemed she had finally lost the plot. She didn't care if she pissed him off anymore. He wasn't going to release her, no matter what she said or how she spoke to him.

All she wanted to do was go home. Back to her normal, mundane life. She would give anything to be sat on her balcony watching the world go by with a nice hot cup of coffee in her hands. But that wasn't going to happen any time soon, if at all.

Her mind brought up images of Connor. If she were truly honest with herself, it wasn't her home she wanted to go back to, it was Connor's. She missed him more than she'd ever missed anyone in her life, and she longed for nothing more than to be in his arms again, even if it was just one more time. But she doubted that would happen again, especially after the way he acted the following morning.

It was blatantly obvious he regretted what they had done. She tried not to let it hurt, but it did.

"Well, you don't have much longer to wait," he said, dragging her back to the present.

Anya blinked back the tears that threatened to fall. She would not show any weakness in front of Him.

"I thought you said I would be chained differently?" she said, thankful her voice didn't give away her emotions.

"You will be," he said slyly. "When the time comes."

"Wouldn't it have been easier to do it while I was asleep?"

"Who's to say you won't be asleep when we do?"

"How do you do that?"

Anya didn't like how easily they were able to put her to sleep. First, it was Kass, and now him. If she found out how they were able to do it, maybe she would be able to prevent anyone from doing it to her again.

"What?" he asked, tilting his head slightly.

"How do you make me go to sleep like that?"

"Magic." He said the word as if it should answer her question, but instead, it just gave her more.

"Fine, don't tell me then," she sighed.

He tutted at her again. "Poor thing. You don't believe in magic, do you?"

"There's no such thing as magic." But even as she said the words, she knew they weren't true.

Magic was the only explanation to how a man had turned into a dragon. Not to mention, how the chains holding her prisoner had unlocked and fallen to the ground when nobody was in the room with her.

So, as much as she wanted to deny its existence, she knew magic was real.

"Ah, so you do believe," he said after a moment. "What have you seen, Anya? What was it that opened your eyes and mind to magic?"

"Nothing," she lied. "I stand by my statement, there's no such thing as magic."

She didn't know why she felt the need to protect the knowledge she had about the man-dragon, but she wasn't going to ignore her intuition. So, she kept that information to herself.

"Keep your secrets," he told her. "It doesn't matter if you believe in it or not, because soon you will have no choice but to accept that magic is real, as well as many other things you thought were just stories."

Anya didn't like the glint in his eyes, or the grin on his face, as he finished speaking. It sent a shiver of dread down her spine.

She swallowed the lump in her throat as she looked

up at him. There was no doubt in her mind that he was planning on hurting her. It was right there in his eyes as he stared down at her.

As if he knew what was going through her mind, the grin spread across his face before he turned on his heel and walked away, leaving her alone with her thoughts once again.

As soon as the door slammed shut behind him, she thought about everything she'd seen and done since stumbling across that cave.

She couldn't deny magic existed, the same as she couldn't deny the existence of dragons or demons. She'd seen them with her own two eyes. And even though she hadn't seen or felt magic, she knew deep down that it was somehow responsible for releasing her from the chains.

Anya wondered if that was how the door had been unlocked as well. At the time, she thought somebody on the other side had unlocked it, but now she wasn't so sure.

Then her mind drifted to Connor once again. She thought back to when she'd seen him and Kellen in the garden, looking up at the dragon. Neither of them had seemed fazed that a dragon the size of the house stood in the garden. Which made her think that they had seen one before.

What if they're dragons as well?

If they were, then they would be even less likely to be looking for her, especially if they knew that was the reason why she'd run away from them. But for some reason, she didn't think Connor was a dragon. She wasn't so sure he was human, either. She didn't know what he was, and she would probably never find out.

After coming face to face with a demon, the dragon didn't frighten her as much as it had. It could be because Connor and Kellen hadn't been scared of the dragon, but it was more likely because of how terrifying the demon was.

Its glowing red eyes were going to haunt her for the rest of her life. Just knowing creatures like that existed was enough to make her want to run for the hills. The memory of them alone was enough to send a shiver down her spine.

Then there was Kass. Anya didn't know what she was, but there was no denying she'd used magic. First when she'd spoken to Anya through her mind, and then when she'd blown something into Anya's face, knocking her out cold in a heartbeat.

Anya suddenly remembered hearing Connor's voice in her mind when she'd been caught escaping. It had been faint, but she'd definitely heard his voice calling to her. Since she heard him speaking in her mind, did it mean he was like Kass?

It was possible she had imagined his voice. After all, she had just come face to face with her worst nightmare. Anya didn't know the answer, but that didn't stop her from clinging to the small shred of hope that he was coming for her.

CHAPTER TWENTY-SEVEN

Connor had spent the entire day searching for any sign of Anya. He had gone over the search area twice, but there was still no sign of her.

He hadn't heard from Rush or anyone else, either. Connor knew Rush was going to be pissed with him for running off, but he also knew Rush would have informed him if there was any news on Anya's whereabouts. The silence meant that he wasn't the only one who hadn't found anything.

The fear and worry for her safety hadn't lessened any. If anything, it was getting worse the longer he went without finding her. He was glad he'd run off on his own. There was no way he would be able to make small talk with anybody, not even Kellen and Aidan. And certainly not Myra.

He didn't need his little sister asking questions about him and Anya, and he knew she would want to know, everything. No, it was better that he was on his own.

Thankfully, the majority of the search area was dense woodland. So, he'd been able to cover most of the ground in wolf form.

There were a few villages dotted around, but Anya wasn't in any of them. He'd made sure to shift back into human form before going anywhere near the villages. Mainly because wolves weren't native to the area, but also so he could question the villagers as well. If anything shady was going on in the area, they would be the first to know.

It wasn't long after Connor left one of the villages that he realised he was heading in the wrong direction. It was his own fault. He'd let his mind wonder back to the night he'd spent with Anya. It was a safer train of thought than the alternative.

Connor didn't turn back straight away. Going over the same ground was getting him nowhere. For all he knew, Sasha could be wrong about where to look for Anya. She hadn't been able to locate her at first, and even when she did pick up on where Anya was, she couldn't pinpoint the location. So, it couldn't harm to expand the search area a little bit.

He couldn't let himself think about what was happening to Anya. If he did, he would go insane. He couldn't think about the way he'd treated her the morning after, either. So, instead, he thought about the pleasure they had shared.

He'd wanted nothing more than to stay in bed with her that morning, to see her beautiful light blue eyes open sleepily. But he'd been an idiot. Instead of showing her how much their night had meant to him, he'd disappeared into the basement and ignored her. And then he'd made her cry when Aidan and Kellen had visited.

He couldn't blame her for running off, and he wouldn't blame her if she never wanted to see him again. He just hoped she could forgive him. It would break his heart if she couldn't, but he would understand.

That didn't mean he wouldn't try to win her heart. He would do anything to have her by his side. She was his mate. The only female he would ever give his heart to, the one female he would ever love.

As darkness descended around him again, Connor began to lose hope of finding Anya. He wasn't about to give up, and he knew the other shifters searching wouldn't give up either. But that didn't stop him from worrying that they would never find her. Or that they wouldn't get to her in time.

Connor mentally shook his head. He wasn't going to think like that. He would find her, even if it was the last thing he did. And he would be in time to save her from whatever the people holding her had in store for her.

He was about to open a telepathic link with Rush, when he suddenly stood dead in his tracks. The wind had changed direction briefly, but it was long enough for him to catch a whiff of Anya.

Without thinking, Connor shifted into his wolf and lifted his muzzle into the air. He breathed in deeply through his nose, taking in all the scents around him. Anya's scent was faint, but there all the same. And more importantly, it was enough for him to follow.

Connor didn't hesitate. He quickly followed her

scent before it could disappear again.

Instead of it disappearing, her scent got stronger with every step he took. Unfortunately, so did the fear he picked up on her scent. Whoever had Anya, she was scared to death of them.

He came to a patch of earth that had been disturbed. He didn't need to sniff the ground to know Anya had been there. But she also hadn't been alone. There was a bunch of other scents mixed in with Anya's, one of which was a wolf shifter.

Connor didn't know who the scents belonged to, not even the wolf shifters scent, but they were definitely the cause of Anya's fear.

He continued following her scent until he came to a warehouse surrounded by a six foot fence. The barbed wire around the top of the fence would do little to keep him out, but he resisted jumping over just yet. First, he needed to make sure nobody would see him.

Walking the perimeter, he made sure to keep to the shadows as he took note of everything within the compound. By the time he was finished, he knew every inch of the place on the outside.

He hadn't seen anybody standing around or wandering about the grounds on his reconnaissance, but he wasn't stupid, he knew there would be people inside the large building. The question was, were they expecting someone to come for her? If so, did they know it would be him and the rest of the wolf shifters?

If Sasha was to be believed, then somebody had turned Anya into a wolf shifter. Which meant, whoever had her, knew about the rest of them. In that case, they were probably expecting the wolf shifters to come after her.

Even knowing it could possibly be a trap, he was still going in after her.

Connor opened a telepathic link with Rush as he shifted back into human form. *"I know where Anya is. I picked up her scent and followed it to an abandoned warehouse in the middle of the woods. It appears to be the only building in the area."*

Rush replied instantly. *"Good. Where is it?"*

Connor not only explained where it was, he also told Rush what he'd found so far. Which wasn't much.

"Wait there for us," Rush said when he was finished. *"We won't be long. Do* not *go in there on your own, Connor."*

"Okay."

"I mean it, Connor. Don't disobey me on this."

Instead of answering, Connor severed the link. He wasn't about to make a promise he couldn't keep.

It didn't matter how much trouble he was going to get in for ignoring Rush again, but there was no way in hell he was going to hang around outside waiting on the others to arrive.

Anya was in there somewhere, and she was petrified of whoever was in there with her. Just the thought of something happening to her while he stood outside, was enough to spur him into action.

Connor double checked the area around the building from within the fence before making his way inside. He hadn't spotted any cameras, but he wouldn't be surprised if there was some dotted around the place, just hidden from view.

There was only one way in or out of the building that he could see. He was dubious about using it because it would be the perfect place to set a trap. But unless he wanted to break a window and alert the people inside that he was there, he had no choice but to go through the only door.

With no other options, Connor made his way over to the door. He turned the handle slowly and then opened the door just a crack. He stood still, listening for any sounds coming from within. When he heard nothing, he opened the door wider and peeked inside to see a large room.

The room was completely empty bar a couple of small boxes off to one side. He released the breath he'd been holding and stepped inside, closing the door quietly behind him.

There was only one other door in the room, so he headed straight for it. He made it half way across the large room before he was surrounded by Imfera demons.

Shit!

He'd walked straight into a trap.

Connor didn't see the metal pole coming his way until it was too late. His knees gave out as pain exploded in his head, and white dots clouded his vision.

***

"How did they find us?" he demanded.

"How the hell should I know?" Kassadi said.

She made sure to sound just as pissed off as him about the wolf shifters finding their location. It was hard to keep up the pretence, but she didn't want him to find out that she'd turned against him.

Until he handed over what he'd promised her, she had to make him think that she was working with him, even though she had changed her mind long ago. She just wished she'd come to that decision before she'd helped him destroy Anya's life.

"It's your magic!" he shouted.

She put a hand on her hip as she leaned to one side. "And?"

"You assured me nothing would go wrong," he growled.

"I also told you my magic is unpredictable," she reminded him. "But you didn't believe me."

It was a lie, a massive one, but she wasn't about to tell him the truth. Her magic had never been unpredictable, and hopefully, it would never be. But she'd told him it was when they'd first met.

At the time, Kassadi hadn't known why she'd kept it a secret, only that her intuition had told her to. It didn't take long for her to understand why she hadn't wanted him to know. It was also the reason she hadn't told him how strong her magic was.

If he'd known, he would have tried to control her even more than he already was. That was something Kassadi wouldn't allow, which was why she hadn't told him in the time since then.

"It's a good job I had the demons here as a backup

plan, isn't it?"

Well, no, not really. Kassadi kept that thought to herself.

In fact, having the demons there only made it harder for her to secretly help Anya and the shifters.

In hindsight, Kassadi realized it was her fault Anya hadn't managed to escape last time. She should have used the spell to conceal Anya from him, just like she had done to hide her from the wolf shifters. But she hadn't done it because he would have become suspicious of her.

Not that there weren't plenty of other witches around that would be more than willing to aid the wolf shifters in a fight against him. Especially if they knew what he'd done to Anya.

"What are you going to do now?" she asked him.

"The same thing I was going to do all along."

Kassadi shouldn't have been surprised, but she was. "You're still going through with it?"

"Of course." He frowned at her. "The demons can hold them back long enough for what I need."

"Then what?" she asked, hoping he would tell her more of his plans.

Unfortunately, he wasn't falling for the bait.

"Then nothing," he told her.

Kassadi didn't believe that for one minute. She knew he had other plans, she just didn't know what they were.

CHAPTER TWENTY-EIGHT

Rush knew he should have kept an eye on Connor. He had hoped that Connor would obey orders, but he should have known he wouldn't. Especially since it was obvious Anya was his mate.

Admittedly, Rush hadn't thought Connor would put his own life, as well as Anya's, in danger. But that's exactly what he'd done by going in to the warehouse on his own. For all they knew, that's what the bad guys wanted.

Until they knew more about the people they were up against, they needed to be careful. There was no telling who or what was inside the building, so they couldn't rule out the possibility that it was a trap.

"So, what's happening?" Sasha asked, as she appeared next to him with Myra.

In hindsight, he should have paired up with Sasha. He might have made it to Connor before he did something stupid. But in all honesty, he'd been more than happy to let her pair up with Myra.

Rush growled. "Your fucking brother has run off

again."

Myra gaped at him, but it was Sasha who answered.

"I don't have a brother," she told him.

Rush inhaled deeply before releasing it. "Not yours. Myra's."

"Oh, I didn't know Connor was your brother," she said, as she turned to Myra.

"Yep," she sighed. "As you can probably tell, I got all the brains."

Sasha laughed. Whatever she was going to say after that was interrupted by the rest of their group arriving.

"Where's Connor?" Krystal asked as she walked up with Dominic.

"He's in there." Myra nodded to the warehouse.

"Fuck," Dominic said. "He could have walked right into a trap."

Rush had a feeling that was exactly what had happened. It was the only explanation as to why Connor hadn't replied when he'd reached out telepathically. Rush had been trying to reach Connor that way since he'd arrived and found no sign of him.

"Precisely," Rush said. "This is why I didn't want him running off on his own. It's why I didn't want anyone running off on their own." Rush shook his head. "I knew I should have made Connor stay at home. At least then, we wouldn't be in this situation now."

"He wouldn't have listened," Kellen said as he and Aidan joined them. "At least this way we know where he is, even if it is with whoever is waiting for us in there."

"I can't believe the idiot managed to get himself caught," Aidan said.

"I'm never going to let him live this one down," Kellen laughed. "After all the shit he gives me about my little sister, and then he pulls a stunt like this? Now that is priceless! At least my sister is only a pup."

"He's in a shit load of trouble, that's for sure," Rush sighed.

He didn't see the funny side. It was bad enough they had to rescue Anya, but now, because of Connor's rash behaviour, they had to rescue him as well. Yep, Rush was well and truly pissed off.

"I picked up the scent of another wolf in the area," Dominic said. "But I don't know who it belongs to."

"A witch as well," Sasha said. "That's how they were blocking me from locating Anya."

If Sasha was right about Anya being a wolf shifter, then it would explain how they were able to do it. The right mixture of magic and a wolf shifter's bite would be more than enough to turn her into one of them.

He just didn't understand why anybody would want to do it. There must be a reason behind it. But no matter how much he racked his brain trying to figure it out, he couldn't come up with an answer.

"I'm just glad you were able to find a way around the magic,"
Rush told her.

"Oh, I didn't," she announced. "They dropped the spell." When he stared at her, she added, "Did I forget to mention that?"

"Yes, you did," he growled. "You could have led us

right into a fucking trap. If you'd said something sooner, we could have come prepared."

"I thought you were prepared," she said. "Isn't that what you were doing while I was trying to break the spell? Plus, I don't think it is a trap."

"And how would you know?" he asked.

"Just a feeling."

"Well, your feeling," he said, emphasising the last word. "Might well have just got Connor killed, and possibly Anya as well."

"Don't be so melodramatic," she told him. "I'm sure everything will be fine."

Considering it was her friend in there, Sasha was being incredibly laid back about the situation. It made him wonder if she was actually involved in it and had been all along.

"What's the plan, boss man," Krystal said as she clapped her hands together cheerfully.

"From what I've seen, there's only one way in and out of this place." He pointed to the door in question. "Nobody seems to be home, but that could be a ruse to get us to let our guard down."

"Krystal and I had a quick look around the perimeter before joining Rush here, and I agree, there's no other way in the building," Dominic confirmed. "Most of the windows are either too small, or too high up. Not to mention, most of them have bars on them."

"Jumping sounds fun." Krystal grinned. "We could have a competition to see who can jump the highest. Whoever wins gets to be the boss of Rush for the day."

"Don't start tonight, Krystal," Rush told her. "I'm not in the mood."

Rush liked Krystal. She was good hunter, but she was also like the annoying little sister he never had. Normally, he could put up with her sass, but with everything that was going on right now, he really didn't need her being a pain in the arse.

"I surrender." She had a cheesy grin on her face as she held her hands up in the air. "I'll behave, so no need to get your knickers in a twist."

"So, what's the plan?" Kellen asked.

Bringing his mind back to the task at hand; he turned to face all of them. "Krystal, Cipher, Bliss, and Ashleah, I want the four of you to stay out here and keep an eye out for anyone joining the party. But be ready just in case we need you as backup. The rest of us are going in to rescue Anya and Connor."

"Boring," Krystal complained.

Rush knew she liked to be in on the action, which was one of the reasons she became a hunter. But somebody had to stay outside to watch their backs, and this time she was it.

"It may be boring," he said. "But we don't know what we're going to be up against yet. If it is a trap, I would rather not have everyone else caught up in it with Connor." Rush looked around at each of them as he spoke, making sure they were all paying attention to him. "As it is, we're going to have our work cut out for us. We don't know the layout of the building, and we don't know how many people are in there. The last thing I need is for more of you to disobey or argue about my orders. We need to get in and out as quickly and hassle free as possible, is that clear?"

Everybody except Krystal and Sasha voiced their agreement. Krystal nodded reluctantly, while Sasha remained silent.

"If I must," Krystal finally huffed when he glared at her. "But what if it turns out that you guys are having fun in there, can we disobey then?"

"No!" Rush snapped.

"Okay, okay, keep your panties on," she told him. "Geesh, I was only having a bit of fun."

Rush shook his head before turning to Sasha. "I would like you to stay out here as well."

"I don't think so." Sasha glared at him as she placed her hands on her hips. "I'm not part of your pack, so you can't order me to stay put as well."

"I know you're not," he told her. "But I would still like it if you stayed out here."

"Tuff, I'm going in whether you like it or not."

They didn't have time to argue about it, so he relented. "Fine, but stay back so you don't get hurt if a fight breaks out."

"Yeah, okay." She rolled her eyes dramatically. "I'll do just that."

Rush knew he was going to regret the decision to let her join them, but there wasn't much he could do to stop her. After all, she could just teleport herself inside the building any time she wanted.

"Why doesn't Sasha just teleport inside to check out the place?" Ashleah asked. "That way, you'll at least know what you're walking into."

"No." He shook his head. "It's not worth the risk. If she's caught, then that's three people we'll have to rescue."

"Awe, aren't you sweet," Sasha said. "But I don't need you to look out for me. I think you're wasting a good opportunity to scout the building out before going in."

"The answer is still no," he said. "Who's to say that you won't end up teleporting right into the middle of a trap?"

"So little faith in my abilities." She shook her head. "That's likely to come back and bite you on the ass, you know."

She was probably right, but he still wasn't willing to risk it. Saving two people was going to be hard enough; he didn't want it turning into three.

"Considering I don't know what abilities you have, other than being able to teleport," he told her. "You should think yourself lucky I'm letting you come along at all. It's only the fact that Anya is your friend that you're here to begin with." When she went to speak, he held up a hand, silencing her. "So, unless you're going to divulge more about what you're capable of, or I see it for myself, I won't have any faith in your abilities."

She folded her arms over her chest. "Fair enough. But just so you know, I can do a hell of a lot more than just teleport. Trust me; you'll be grateful I've stuck around to help."

"We'll see," he said sceptically.

"Yes, we will see," she said smugly.

"Can you two stop bickering?" Kellen asked them.

"Yeah, grow up you two," Aidan added. "And get a room already."

"Shut up, Aidan!" The three of them said in unison.

"Fine." He held his hands up in surrender. "I know when my advice isn't wanted."

Rush glared at Aidan. Out of the corner of his eye, he noticed Kellen smack his forehead with the palm of his hand. Sasha seemed to find Aidan's comment amusing, and she wasn't the only one. Everybody except Kellen was staring at him with massive grins on the faces.

Rush ignored them all as he turned towards the building. "Right, lets go," he said, keeping his expression and voice devoid of emotion.

CHAPTER TWENTY-NINE

Connor was about to warn Rush that it was a trap when the door leading outside opened and he walked in. All but four of the other shifters walked in after him.

He could only watch as Rush and the others filed in the room. While he'd been on the ground after they'd hit him over the head with a metal pole, the demons had taken the opportunity to jump him.

Rush grimaced when he spotted the two demons holding Connor between them. Their sharp claws dug painfully into his arms and shoulders as they forced him to remain on his knees, but he refused to show any sign of discomfort.

Sasha was the last to enter. As she crossed the threshold, her hair and clothing changed. The long white strands of her hair were pulled up into an intricate braid away from her face, and black tight fitting clothing encased her body. Black leather vambraces covered in silver studs wrapped around her forearms, and black knee-high boots with silver buckles completed the look.

A couple of the other wolf shifters did a double take when they noticed she'd changed her hair and clothing. Even some of the demons looked twice at her.

Rush was the only one not to look at her. He kept his eyes on Connor and the demons the entire time.

"Okay, I stand corrected," Sasha said as she came to a stop with the rest of them. "It is a trap."

Even from a distance, Connor could hear Rush growl at her.

"Fuck's sake," she continued. "Why does it have to be these bastards? I just had my hair done."

Imfera demons were notorious for setting things on fire. Their skin was made up of thick red scales, and they had horns protruding from the tops of their heads.

Even though the creatures had razor sharp claws, the main weapon in their arsenal was the fireballs they created with their hands. Connor's fur had been singed by their fireballs many times, which was why he didn't like fighting them, especially in wolf form.

"By all means," Rush said to Sasha. "Sit this one out."

"Oh, hell, no." She crossed her arms over her chest as she shook her head at him. "I'm not letting you lot have all the fun."

Connor didn't know what Sasha was, but he hoped she was as good at fighting. Imfera demons preferred to use fireballs, but they weren't afraid to get their hands dirty, either.

Rush opened his mouth to reply, but before he got a

word out, Sasha threw her arms out, flicking her hands towards the demons holding Connor. He caught a glint of something metal as it flew past his head, and then the demons hold on him loosened enough for him to scamper free.

Connor didn't waste any time in joining Rush and the others as they faced off against the demons. As he reached them, he heard two loud thuds. When he turned around, he noticed the two demons that had been holding him were now dead. Their lifeless bodies slumped on the floor.

His gaze snapped to Sasha, who had a massive grin on her face.

"One down, one to go," she said, winking at him.

"Holy, shit! Did you see that?" Aidan asked.

"How the fuck?" Kellen said.

Connor turned to look at Rush. He seemed just as surprised as everyone else that Sasha had taken the demons down so easily.

The demons looked dumbfounded as they stared at their fallen comrades. When they turned the gazes to Sasha, Connor could see the confusion on the faces. Sasha smirked at them in return.

In any other situation, Connor would have found it comical. But as it was, he couldn't stop the worry from building inside of him for Anya. Connor was grateful for Sasha's aid, because without her, he might still be held prisoner between the demons.

"Wow," Myra said as she looked Sasha up and down. "You really don't hang around, do you?"

"What's the point in hanging around?" Sasha asked.

"We all know these bastards have to die, so why drag it out?"

"True," Myra agreed.

"Well, I'm glad you're on our side," Aidan said.

The demons face's quickly contorted from one of bewilderment, to one of anger and hatred.

"You're going to be the first to die!" one of the demons spat at Sasha.

"Oh, I'm sorry," she replied sweetly. "Was that you wife?"

"I think you pissed them off," he heard Myra whisper to Sasha.

Sasha shrugged. "And?"

With a battle cry that grated on Connor brain, the demon that spoke suddenly broke away from the rest of them and rushed towards Sasha. Without batting an eye, she swung her arm up in an arch. As she did so, a sword appeared in her hand, slicing through the demon's neck before it made it within two feet from her.

Everyone watched in silence as the demon's body slumped to the floor like the first two. Its head rolled across the room, stopping in front of the other demons.

It took the demons a moment to register what had just happened and then all hell broke loose. The rest of the demons all rushed forward at once. They threw fireball after fireball until they were in reaching distance.

Connor ducked as a fireball was thrown at his head. He rolled to the side before leaping up and grabbing hold of the demon's head who had thrown it. Ripping the head off, he launched it towards another demon that was about to throw a fireball at Myra. She nodded her head in thanks before leaping into the fray.

While most remained in human form, he noticed a couple of shifters had taken on wolf form. He wasn't willing to risk his fur being singed, so he remained in human form.

He kicked back his leg as a demon attempted to jump him from behind. It grunted when his foot made contact with its abdomen, and doubled over. Connor quickly spun around and grabbed the demon by the head, snapping its neck before it could do anything.

The next demon that came at him, he punched through the ribcage and ripped out its heart. He stuffed the still beating heart into the demons gaping mouth before pushing it aside and reaching for the next demon.

Connor didn't see the fireball coming at him until it was too late. He attempted to sidestep, but the fireball hit his arm. He quickly lunged forward and grabbed the demon by the neck.

"That fucking hurt," he growled at the demon right before he ripped out its windpipe.

He ripped the head off a demon and threw it at another one that was about to jump on Kellen while he was distracted. Kellen didn't have time to thank Connor before he was dodging fireballs. Several demons threw them at Kellen at once. Thankfully, Aidan and Dominic were on hand to help him.

As Connor turned away from Kellen and the others, he caught sight of Sasha. She cut down demon after demon as they continuously attacked her. She was mesmerizing to watch, her movements were as graceful as a dancer.

A fireball narrowly missed him. It would have been his own fault; he should be paying attention to the fight, not watching Sasha. There was no doubt the female could hold her own against the demons. She moved fluidly from one opponent to the next, cutting down anyone that got in her way.

A bit further away, he could see some of the other shifters fighting against the demons as well. Only one of them remained in wolf form, the others had shifted. He wouldn't be surprised to see bits of missing fur when they were next in wolf form.

No matter how many demons they killed, they couldn't make headway. They seemed to be coming out of the woodwork. For every one they cut down, another two seemed to take its place.

Moving from one to the next, Connor didn't slow down as he fought his way through the crowd. One way or another, he was going to reach Anya. He knew she was on the other side of the door; he just had to keep fighting. Sooner or later, he was going to get through that door.

He didn't care how many demons he had to rip apart or decapitate, he wasn't going to stop. Not when he knew Anya needed him. Connor had already let her down once; he wasn't going to do it again.

If she would let him, Connor planned on spending the rest of his life making up to Anya for the way he'd treated her. But first, he had to reach her.

"Keep a look out for an unknown wolf shifter and a witch,"

Rush said through the telepathic link.

Connor hadn't forgotten about the unknown wolf shifter's scent he'd picked up outside with Anya's, but the witch was news to him. He wondered how Rush knew a witch was in the area. He assumed Rush probably found out because of Sasha.

Connor couldn't stop the unease that crept into him at their absence. He didn't know what was preventing them from showing their faces, but it couldn't be good. Either that or they were too cowardly to show themselves.

He didn't think it was because they were cowardly. He had a feeling it had something to do with Anya. The thought of her alone with them made him even more determined to get past the demons.

Connor doubled his efforts. He ignored the rest of the room as he concentrated solely on the demons standing between him and Anya. He brutally ripped apart any who dared step in his way. Nothing was going to stop him from reaching the door, and Anya.

***

Kassadi managed to get one of the demons to help her move Anya before he ran off to join his comrades in the fight against the wolf shifters.

The demon didn't stand a chance against the shifters, but she wasn't about to warn him. The only reason she hadn't killed him was because they were supposed to be on the same side. She'd worked too hard, come too far, to blow it all by killing one of the demons.

She looked at Anya's sleeping form and couldn't help but feel envious of the woman. There were a lot of people who cared about her, and she didn't even know it. Even now, she was oblivious to what was going on; to the fight that was happening as the people who loved her tried to get to her.

Yes, Kassadi couldn't help but be envious. There had only ever been one person who cared enough about Kassadi to fight for her, but they were now gone. Kassadi had let them down when they needed her most.

Kassadi mentally shook her head. She refused to think about her past at the best of times, but she certainly couldn't let her mind go there now.

Anya would be awake soon. Kassadi had only blown a small amount of sleeping powered into Anya's face, it was just enough for her to stay asleep so she could be moved from one room to another.

When she'd entered Anya's cell, she'd hidden behind the demon until the sleeping powered had taken effect. She knew it was cowardly of her to hide, but she had already put Anya through enough. She didn't want to be the cause of more distress. If that meant she had to hide behind a demon so she wasn't seen, then so be it.

While Anya was still asleep, Kassadi removed the chains from around her wrists and ankles. She wasn't going to need them anymore.

She didn't think it was possible to feel even worse,

but seeing the marks where the chains had rubbed against Anya's skin, made Kassadi feel even guiltier about her part in it all. Even knowing she was doing it for a good reason, didn't make it any easier.

It wasn't as if she could explain her situation to Anya, either. She would never understand, so there was no point in trying to explain.

Kassadi hadn't been expecting to see a camcorder set up in the room she had moved Anya into. She didn't have a clue why he would want to record Anya. It might be because he wanted to review the footage when he didn't have the wolf shifters howling at his door, but it could also be for another reason altogether.

Whatever the reason, Kassadi had a bad feeling about it.

CHAPTER THIRTY

Anya had barely woken up when a wave of nausea washed over her. She swallowed several times, hoping the feeling would pass, but it didn't. Her stomach decided to cramp instead.

She cracked her eyes open slightly and was instantly blinded. It took her eyes a moment to adjust to the bright light. When they did, she opened her eyes to find that she was in a different room. It was vastly different from the bare brick walls in the previous room.

Bright white walls reflected the overhead light, blinding her. The old, rickety bed that smelt awful had been replaced by a padded bed similar to those used in hospitals. And the chains around her wrists and ankles had been replaced by thick straps that pinned her on her side to the bed.

Anya was seriously getting fed up of being made to sleep every two minutes. Every time they put her to sleep, they moved her to a different location. She didn't have a clue where she was, or even how much time had passed since she'd left Connor's house.

How the hell were they even putting her to sleep? He said it was magic, and she was seriously inclined to believe him. After everything she'd seen, the idea of magic being real wasn't as far-fetched as it used to be.

For all Anya knew, she could be in a totally different country. She didn't think that was the case, but still, it would be nice to know where they had taken her.

Even when she'd escaped... or attempted to anyway... there hadn't been any clue as to where she was. All she'd seen was one road leading through the woodland. There had been no sign posts or recognisable landmarks of any kind.

If she had taken the time to check the other rooms along the corridor when she tried to escape, then she might know if she was still in the same building. But that had been the last thing on her mind at the time.

After all, what idiot went looking around when they were trying to escape? Not her, that's for sure. She was the type of person who always screamed at the idiot on TV who went looking for where the bad guys were hiding.

The building wasn't as quiet as it had been when she tried to escape. She didn't know what was going on, but it sounded like there was fighting going on somewhere in the building.

She screamed for help, hoping somebody might hear her and come to her rescue, but nobody came. They either couldn't hear her, or they were too wrapped up in whatever they were doing.

Anya attempted to wiggle out of the straps holding her down, but no matter how hard she tried, she couldn't move an inch. She was barely about to breathe in the position they had her in. Not to mention, the straps dug painfully into her.

When they had her chained to the bed before, her arms had been outstretched above her head and her legs had been pulled tight towards the foot of the bed. Now she was lying on her side with her arms and legs outstretched in front of her.

She didn't know what the new position was all about, and she didn't want to know. Whatever he had in store for her couldn't be good.

The voice she was coming to hate most in the world broke into her thoughts. A moment later, he stepped into view.

"Are you comfortable?" he asked.

The deep timbre of his voice sent shivers down her spine. Even though he didn't sound much different from Connor, his voice had the polar opposite effect on her. Where Connor's voice gave her a warm and fuzzy feeling... along with other feelings... the man standing in front of her made her blood turn to ice.

"Not really," she said, rolling her eyes. "Was I supposed to be?"

"Trust me, it will be more accommodating in the long run," he grinned.

"If you say so."

Anya didn't like the words he spoke, or the tone he used. But the evil glint in his eyes was even more worrisome.

Another wave of nausea hit, only stronger this time. As the cramp in her stomach intensified, she could feel beads of sweat break out on her forehead. She tried to breathe through the pain and sickness, but it was taking a lot longer to pass than it had before.

He disappeared from view, but he didn't leave the room. She could hear him rummaging around behind her for a moment before taking up his spot in front of her again. When he returned, he was carrying a camcorder.

Anya didn't want to know what the camcorder was for, but the words slipped out, anyway. "What's with the camcorder?"

He looked down at the item in question before replying. "So I can record you, of course."

"Of course," Anya said as she rolled her eyes. "Why didn't I think of that?"

"If you really must know…"

"I must," she interrupted.

"You are going to do something soon, and I would like to record it."

A chill raced down her spine at the ominous tone he used.

"Yeah? What am I going to do?"

He wiggled his index finger from side to side as he shook his head. "Now that would be telling."

"Of course, it would," she said. "That's why I asked."

He laughed at her. "You are amusing."

"That's what I was aiming for," she said sarcastically.

"It will be a shame if this doesn't work."

"Why's that?"

"Because you'll be dead," he said casually.

Anya's mouth dropped open as she stared at him in disbelief. It boggled her mind how he made it sound as if they were discussing nothing more than the weather. When in fact, he was talking about her death. She couldn't think of a retort, so she closed her mouth and remained silent.

"Don't worry," he told her. "The witch has assured me that won't happen."

"Oh, what wonderful news," she said in mock excitement. She would have clapped her hands together as well, but she was unable to move.

The entire time they had been speaking, the cramp in Anya stomach had gradually gotten worse. It was now at the point where she was finding it difficult to keep track of the conversation. She put it down to lack of food and water at first, but now she was second guessing herself.

With the way he was speaking and acting, she wouldn't be surprised if it was the result of something he'd done to her. The question was what?

Had he poisoned her? If so, how? He hadn't given her anything to eat or drink, and she would have remembered if he'd injected her with something, so she couldn't see how he would have poisoned her. Unless, he'd done it one of the times she'd been knocked out?

He would've had the perfect opportunity, so she couldn't rule it out. But there was something niggling at the back of her mind that told her whatever he'd done to her, hadn't been done while she was asleep.

Anya thought she was winning the battle over her body when the strongest spike of pain hit her. Even with the straps holding her tight, she double over as the pain radiated outward from her abdomen. It consumed every inch of her body.

"Ah, it looks like it's time to begin," he grinned.

"What... the fuck... have you... done... to me?" she managed to ask between shock waves of pain that left her fighting for breath.

"I've given you a new life," he said cryptically.

He stepped back and positioned the camcorder before pressing a button. The flashing red light let her know everything that happened from here on out, was going to be recorded.

Her skin crawled, and it had nothing to do with the man stood in front of her. Something was under her skin, and it was trying to get out.

Anya tried her hardest not to make a sound or show any sign that she was in pain, but it became too much for her to bear. The scream she'd been holding back ripped from her throat as her body convulsed.

Her blood felt like lava as it flowed through her veins, burning her from the inside out. Bones crunched and cracked as they reshaped themselves into something new.

Anya begged for the pain to stop, but it just kept getting worse. She even begged him to kill her, just to put a stop to the excruciating pain, but he ignored her plea.

There wasn't an inch of her that didn't feel like it was being ripped apart. At the same time, it felt as if she'd been set on fire.

Her body convulsed uncontrollably as ripples ran along her skin. When the convulsions finally eased off a bit, she began violently throwing up what little food and water she had in her stomach.

Red and white dots floated around her vision, making it harder to see anything, but she could have sworn she'd seen thick fur covering her arms. The noise in her ears was deafening. She didn't have a clue what was causing the noise, but it was hurting her ears and head. But that was the least of her worries.

The pain quickly intensified to the point where she couldn't take it anymore. The last thing she saw before darkness enveloped her, was him smirking at her.

CHAPTER THIRTY-ONE

It took longer than he would have liked, but with help from Rush and Kellen, Connor eventually made it past the demons and over to the door leading into the rest of the building.

As soon as he stepped through, he closed the door behind him. The corridor he found himself in wasn't as dark and dingy as the warehouse had been, but it wasn't exactly inviting, either.

He could still hear the fighting in the other room, but he paid no attention to it as he began searching for Anya. He knew she was in the building somewhere. He just had to find her. Thankfully, he picked up her scent straight away and followed it.

Nobody was around to try to stop him as he made his way along the corridor. He knew the demons were being kept busy by the rest of the shifters, but he had expected to find some resistance.

Connor checked room after room, but each one was empty. He was halfway along the corridor before he came across the room they had kept Anya in. It was a dank room with nothing except a metal bed with a mattress that had seen better days.

The smell coming from inside the room was horrendous, but that wasn't what made his blood boil. No, the metal chains and cuffs attached to the bed frame was the cause of that. Connor was ready to kill the person responsible for holding Anya captive. Whether they placed the chains on her or not, just putting her in a room with them was bad enough.

The small amount of light that filtered through the dingy window made the place seem like a dungeon. Even if it was daylight outside, Connor couldn't image that much more light would make it inside.

Anya wouldn't have stood a chance of using the window as a means of escape. Not only was it too high up and too small for her to fit through, it also had thick metal bars covering it.

The next room he came to was empty, but the one after that appeared to be an office. He knew Rush would want to check it out before he left, so Connor took a mental note of which room it was in.

If nothing else, there might be something in the office that would give them an indication of who had taken Anya and why. Connor didn't plan on letting the culprit get away, but since there was still no sign of those responsible, he didn't hold out much hope of them being dealt with straight away.

The demons were involved, but they weren't in charge. They were just following orders from somebody else.

His heart sank when he opened the next door. He

didn't need to look inside to know Anya was in there. Her scent hit him as soon as he opened the door, but so did the metallic scent of blood.

He took a deep breath to prepare himself for what he might find when he entered the room, and then he rushed in. If he'd hoped to find those responsible inside, he was sorely mistaken. The room was completely empty, except for a single wolf that was lying motionless on a gurney.

He knew instantly that the wolf was Anya. The animal's fur was exactly the same strawberry blonde as her hair.

Sasha was right, Anya had been turned into a wolf shifter, but the question was, had she survived the transformation?

He gingerly walked over to her, but she didn't move. Didn't even twitch. He knew she was alive because he could see her chest rising and falling gently with her breathing, but he didn't know what state she was going to be in physically or mentally.

The last thing he wanted to do was cause her anymore distress. She had already been through enough already.

There were several straps holding Anya in place. He quickly set to work undoing each one. As he did, he spoke softly to her, trying to coax her awake, but she didn't show any sign that she heard him.

The longer Anya went without moving, the more concerned

Connor became. Had something gone wrong? Was that why she wasn't waking up?

Rush walked in as he was undoing the last strap. Connor didn't take his eyes off Anya, but he nodded his head in greeting.

"Is she okay?" Rush asked after a moment.

Connor let out a long sigh. "I honestly don't know. Other than a couple of cuts and bruises from where she's been restrained, I can't see anything wrong with her, but she won't wake up."

"Did you see who took her?" Rush asked.

"No," Connor shook his head. "They were long gone by the time I got here."

Which was a shame. Connor was looking forward to getting his hands on them, but that will have to wait for another day. His main priority now was getting Anya home, back to his home. She would be safe there as long as she didn't run off again.

He didn't think she would be safe if he returned her to her home. But not only that, he wanted her to be with him. To be his mate.

If she wanted to return to her home, he would go with her. He would do anything she wanted, go anywhere she desired, because she was his mate. He would lay down his life for her.

Connor realised he'd been silent while stroking her fur. He needed to touch her, no matter what form she was in, just to assure himself she was there and she was alive.

Without taking his hands off Anya, he stood up and looked at Rush. "I take it the demons are no more."

Rush raised an eyebrow. "I wouldn't be in here with you if they were."

"Are they all dead?"

He may not have been able to get his hands on those responsible, but they could interrogate one of the demons, if any were still alive.

"Unfortunately, not," Rush said. "But we also can't interrogate one of them."

Connor frowned. "Why not?"

It was Rush's turn to sigh as he raked his fingers through his hair. "Because the rest of them teleported away a few minutes ago."

"Shit. I was hoping they could give us some answers."

"So were the rest of us," Rush said. "Hopefully, we'll find something when we search the office."

"I was going to tell you about the office after I'd found Anya," Connor confessed.

Before Connor could say more, Rush held up a hand to stop him. "I know you would have done, but you were preoccupied with Anya. She needs you now." Rush looked down at Anya's sleeping form before he continued. "You need to take her back to the shifter realm. Don't worry about anything here, we've got it covered."

"Thank you," Connor said.

Connor had a feeling he needed her a lot more than she needed him, but he would be there for her no matter what. He would help her in whatever way she needed him, and he would be with her every step of the way as she learnt about their kind.

He still couldn't get over the fact she was now a wolf shifter.

Even looking at her in wolf form, it didn't quite feel real. He was amazed it was even possible, but grateful at the same time.

He wouldn't have to watch her grow old and die while he stayed the same. Now that she was a wolf shifter, she would live just as long as him.

"She'll be okay," Rush assured him.

"I hope so."

"She will be, you just have to give her time."

"I just wish she would wake up," Connor admitted.

"There's something else worrying you as well, isn't there?" Rush asked.

"Yes."

"I'm sure whatever it is, you can work it out."

Connor closed his eyes as he thought about the way he'd treated her. He wouldn't blame her if she never wanted to speak to him again. But if she would give him a chance, he would spend the rest of his life making it up to her.

"Come on," Rush said, breaking into his thoughts. "The others are waiting for us."

Sliding his arms under her body, Connor lifted her up. He held her tight against him as he followed Rush out of the room and along the corridor.

When they entered the large store room, he looked around at the dead bodies carpeting the floor. Connor was grateful somebody had cleared a space for him to walk through. He didn't fancy stepping on dead bodies as he carried Anya across the room.

As soon as Myra spotted him, she raced over and put her hand on Anya. "Is she okay?"

He shook his head. "I don't know."

"Where's Sasha?" Rush asked.

"I don't know," Myra said. "Nobody has seen her since the demons disappeared."

"She's probably gone home," Aidan said.

"Yeah, maybe," Rush agreed, but he didn't sound convinced.

Connor wasn't either. After all the fuss she'd kick up about being a part of the search and rescue, there was no way Sasha would have gone anywhere without making sure Anya was safe first.

He hoped Sasha was okay, and that nothing happened to her, but he wasn't about to go looking for her. His only priority at that moment in time was Anya. He would help find Sasha later, if she didn't turn up in the meantime. But right now, he wanted to get Anya back home and checked over by Candi.

***

Kassadi had left the building long before the fight was over between the wolf shifters and the demons, but she hadn't gone far.

She made sure to stand downwind as she watched Connor carrying Anya out of the warehouse. He held her like she was the most precious cargo he'd ever held in his hands. Even from a distance, she could see the love in his eyes as he gazed down at Anya's sleeping form.

Kassadi couldn't tear her eyes away from them. She longed for a man to look at her the way Connor was looking at Anya. But love wasn't in her cards. Someone like her didn't get to have a happy ending. She knew that, had accepted it years ago, but it didn't stop her heart from yearning for it.

Kassadi shook her head to clear her thoughts. She needed to keep her mind on the task at hand.

As soon as the last person left the warehouse, she snuck back inside. There was only one thing on her mind, and that was the item he had promised her.

She had come through on her promise, but just as she had assumed, he hadn't. She wouldn't be surprised if he never had the item. She certainly wouldn't put it past him to lie about it just to get her to help him.

Well, that was over now. No matter what he promised her, she was never going to help him again.

Kassadi didn't waste any time in searching his office. Even if the item was in his possession, there was no guarantee it would be in his office, but she had to look, anyway. It was too important not to.

After searching every inch of the office and coming up empty, Kassadi let out a frustrated scream. One way or another, she was going to make him pay for deceiving her.

CHAPTER THIRTY-TWO

Anya rolled over, wrapping the thick duvet tightly around her at the same time. She didn't want to wake up. For the first time in God only knows how long, she was warm and comfortable. She snuggled deeper into the duvet, pulling it up over her head.

Unfortunately, her bladder wouldn't let her sleep for much longer, and neither would her stomach. She didn't know how long it had been since she'd last eaten anything. By the sound of her stomach, it had been days at least.

"You can't sleep all day," Connor said. She could hear the smile in his deep, sexy voice as he continued. "At some point, you need to feed that stomach of yours. It's been growling for the last hour."

Her heart skipped a beat as she peeked her head out of the duvet and saw him sat in a chair facing the bed. But the joy she felt at seeing him soon faded when she remembered how things had ended between them.

If she hadn't run off after seeing the dragon in his

garden, then things might have been different. After everything she'd been through, the thought of coming face to face with a dragon didn't seem as scary as it once had.

"How long have I been out?" she asked.

The smile left his face as he said, "Two days."

Anya groaned. How much time had she lost in total? One week? Two? Anya didn't think she wanted to know the answer.

Reading her mind, Connor said, "It's been twelve days since you first arrived here."

Her boss was not going to be happy with her. She would be lucky if she even had a job to go back to. Hopefully, Sasha had told her boss that she'd gone missing on a hike. If so, they would understand why she hadn't at least phoned in sick.

"Oh, God, Sasha," she said as she sat up. "I bet she's worried sick about me."

Anya got a bad feeling in her stomach when Connor began fidgeting in his seat.

"Tell me," she said.

Connor didn't bother to ask her what she was referring to. He cleared his throat and leaned forward in his chair before telling her everything that had happened.

Anya didn't know what surprised her more. The fact her best friend wasn't human, or the news that she was now a wolf shifter. Either one was mind boggling on its own, but both was just... wow! What else was real that she didn't know about?

"So, I hadn't imagined the man turning into a dragon

in your garden?"

"No, you didn't imagine it," he said. "That was Balzar. He had come to speak with Kellen about his younger sister, Kayla. He shouldn't have been here, but he was so angry, he hadn't cared that you were here and might see him."

"Do you know what Sasha is? Did she tell you?"

Connor shook his head. "I'm sorry, I don't know, and she didn't say anything either."

"Where is she?" Anya looked around the room even though she knew Sasha wasn't there. "I'd like to thank her for helping to rescue me."

Connor looked at the floor for a moment. He released a breath before his gaze lifted to her once again. "I'm sorry, Anya, we don't know where she is. She had already gone by the time the fighting was over. We're not sure if she left of her own accord, or if she was taken. Either way, we won't stop looking until we find her, I promise."

Anya believed him. She didn't know if it was the determined look on his face, or the tone of his voice, but she knew he wouldn't stop looking for Sasha.

A pang of jealously shot through her at the thought of Connor being with Sasha. She didn't get the impression anything had happened between the two of them, but that didn't stop her from feeling jealous.

"Are you okay? Are you in any pain?" Concern laced his words.

"I'm okay," she lied.

It wasn't as if she could tell him the truth. That just the thought of him being with Sasha, filled her with jealousy and made her heart hurt. He would probably laugh at her.

"You can tell me anything, Anya," he told her. "I'm here for you, no matter what."

It warmed her heart at the sincere look in his eyes as he spoke, but she still wasn't going to admit to being jealous.

"Apart from the fact I've probably lost my job, and most likely my home as well, everything is great," she said, trying not to sound sarcastic.

Anya wasn't as upset about the thought of being jobless and homeless as she should have been. She was more concerned with never seeing Connor again after she returned to home.

She didn't want things to end between them, but he'd made it blatantly obvious he didn't want anything to do with her. Yes, he had come to her rescue when she needed him, but that didn't mean he wanted a relationship with her.

"You're not homeless," he said out of the blue.

"How would you know? Have you spoken to my landlord?" she asked.

"No," he shook his head. "But I was hoping you would stay here, with me."

Anya stared at him, unsure she'd heard him right. "You... what?"

He moved from the chair to sit on the bed close to her. "I'm sorry for the way I treated you before. I have no excuse for my behaviour, but if you'll let me, I'll spend the rest of our lives making it up to you." He swallowed nervously before continuing. "I love you,

Anya, and I want you to be my mate."

Anya's heart swelled at his declaration. "Connor…"

"You don't have to answer now," he interrupted. "Take some time to think about it first. I'll wait for as long as you need."

"I don't need any time to think about it," she told him.

She wanted nothing more than to spend the rest of her life with Connor. Hearing him say that he wanted her to live with him was a dream come true.

Before she'd gone to Scotland, she might have needed time to think about moving in with someone. But if the last couple of weeks had taught her anything, it was that life was too short.

She loved Connor with all of her heart. It had taken some time for her to admit it to herself, but now that she knew Connor felt the same way, there was no denying it any longer.

She certainly wasn't going to let what her ex had done to her get in the way of her future happiness. She had let her ex's actions rule her life for long enough, but no more.

Taking her words as a bad sign, Connor lowered his head. "I understand. You can stay as long as you need…"

"I don't think you do understand," she interrupted. "I don't need time because I already know what the answer is."

Anya didn't say anything more until he was looking at her. The mix of hope and despair in his eyes made her want to pull him into her arms, but somehow, she managed to stay seated.

She couldn't stop her lips from tilting up in a smile. "Yes, Connor. A thousand times, yes."

"You'll stay?" he asked.

Anya pushed the duvet away, and then leapt into his arms. "Yes," she nodded. "I want nothing more than to spend the rest of my life with you.

He was beaming as he wrapped his arms around her and pulled her tight against him. "I promise, you won't regret it."

Before she could reply, he leaned forward, claiming her mouth with a searing kiss that made her toes curl.

***

Connor's heart felt like it was going to burst, he was so happy.

He couldn't believe Anya had agreed to stay with him, let alone to be his mate. But he was over the moon she had. He hadn't lied; he would spend the rest of his life making up for the way he'd treated her.

Anya pulled at his shirt, trying to take it off him. He broke the kiss long enough to remove both of their clothes, and then he was right back where he wanted to be. In her arms.

He shifted position so he could lower her to the bed. Anya instantly opened her legs, making room for him.

Connor hadn't even touched her yet, but he could already feel how wet she was for him. If he had any thoughts of going slow, they were dashed the moment he felt the heat of her against his cock.

He had to adjust his position. Otherwise, he was going to lose all control and enter her in one swift thrust.

Anya moaned when he pulled away from her lips to trail kisses down her neck and chest. It soon turned into a gasp as he sucked one of her nipples into his mouth.

She writhed beneath him as he paid each breast the same amount of attention before moving on. She tried to reach between them to grab his cock, but he moved out of the way. If she touched him now, he was going to lose what little control he still had. As it was, he was holding on by a thread.

Connor shuffled down the bed until his face was level with her sex. He inhaled deeply, filling his lungs with her heady scent before leaning forward and sliding his tongue between her moist folds.

Anya's gasp quickly turned into a moan of pleasure as he devoured her. She ran her fingers through his head as she held his head against her.

Normally, he would be happy to spend hours between her legs, but not this time. He needed to be buried deep inside her, and now.

With one last lick, Connor climbed back up the bed. He positioned his cock at her entrance and then held still. Anya's beautiful blue eyes gazed up at him through a desire filled haze.

"Don't look away," he told her.

He waited for her to nod in agreement before finally breaching her walls. She was so hot and wet, there was no way he was going to last.

He bit back a groan as he slowly entered her. Her head tilted back, exposing her neck to him. His fangs lengthened as his mouth watered in anticipation of piercing her skin. His cock twitched inside her at the thought of tasting her blood on his lips, marking her as his mate.

When he was buried all the way to the hilt inside her, he held still, giving her time to adjust to his size.

Anya looked up at him in confusion as her tongue slid across her teeth.

"Your fangs have extended in anticipation of you biting me," he managed to ground out. "It's how wolf shifters mate."

The smile that pulled at her lips was slow and seductive.

"Are you sure this is what you want?" he asked. "Because once we've mated, there's no going back."

The smile disappeared from Anya's face to be replaced by a serious expression. He hated to be the cause of her smile disappearing, but he had to make sure she it was what she wanted as well.

As much as it would pain him, he would stop if she'd had a change of heart.

Ha! It would fucking kill you, his subconscious pointed out.

She lifted one of her hands and gently placed it on the side of his face. "I want this more than anything in the world. I want you, all of you."

"Good answer," he grinned. "Before I start moving… because I won't be able to stop once I've started… I have to tell you something."

"Okay," she dragged out the word questioningly.

"It's about the mating," he said.

"Ah, okay," she nodded.

Connor really wished he'd told her everything *before* he buried his cock inside her, but it was better late than never.

"Wolf shifters communicate telepathically." He couldn't miss the surprise in her eyes at his announcement. "It's how we talk to in wolf form, but it's also how we start the mating ceremony. During sex, we open a telepathic link with each other, and hold that link until we've climax together. After that, but before I pull out of you, we mark each other by sinking our teeth into each-others neck."

"Oh."

"It won't hurt, I promise," he told her when he saw the uncertainty in her eyes. "You'll only feel pleasure."

Her seductive grin returned. "I can certainly cope with that."

"Good," he grinned and then leaned down to take her mouth in another searing kiss.

Connor couldn't hold still for another second. He broke the kiss and locked eyes with Anya as he began to move. He tried to go slowly, but he couldn't.

He quickly picked up the pace, and before long, he was pounding in and out of her.

Thankfully, he didn't need to try to explain how or when to open a link. He was overjoyed to feel 'her reaching out to him with her mind. He didn't think twice about reaching back and opening the link with her.

He was instantly flooded with her emotions. Lust, desire, pleasure, he felt it all coming from her. He could feel how close she was to tipping over the edge into ecstasy. But the one that stood out the most was love. She was so filled with love for him, and she didn't try to hide it.

He knew the moment she realised she was feeling his emotions as well. Her eyes widened in surprise as she stared at him.

"I love you, Anya, now and forever."

She pulled him down for a kiss. Her lips gently brushed against his. *"I love you too."*

Connor didn't stand a chance against the tidal wave of pleasure that raced through Anya. Mind, body, and soul, they were joined together. As she tipped over the edge, she took him with her.

CHAPTER THIRTY-THREE

"It's good to see you up and about," Myra said. "I thought Connor was going to keep you locked in the bedroom for the rest of your life."

Anya couldn't stop the blush that crept up her cheeks. It had been two days since she'd woken up, and Connor had confessed his love for her. They had mated straight away, and then spent the days following in bed together. She still couldn't quite believe Connor was hers, but she was glad he was, because she loved him as well.

Neither one of them had wanted to get up and face the world, but they both knew they couldn't stay in bed forever. Not when there was a madman running amok in the human realm.

Anya wasn't sure she would ever get used to there being more than one realm. It was weird just thinking of the planet as a realm.

"If I had my way, we would still be in bed," Connor said, breaking into her thoughts.

"I don't blame you," Aidan grinned, as he winked at her mischievously. "I would want to keep Anya in bed as well."

Connor didn't rise to the bait. Instead, he returned Aidan's grin. "Don't worry, it'll be your turn soon enough."

"No, thanks," Aidan shook his head. "I'm happy being single, thank you very much."

"One day it will happen," Myra told him. "And when it does, I'm going to remind you that you said that."

"Go ahead," he told her. "You'll be waiting a long time."

"I don't think she'll be waiting as long as you think," Kellen told him. "I wouldn't be surprised if you're the next one to find your mate."

"So, do we know what Rush plans to do about the guy Anya told us about?" Aidan said.

Everybody burst out laughing at his attempt to change the subject, but it quickly died down.

"I'm not sure," Connor said. "He hasn't said anything to me, but I'm sure he's coming up with a plan of action."

"I know he's sent a couple of people to the human realm to see if they can find out anything about the male," Myra told them. "But so far, nothing."

Anya was glad somebody was looking for him. She'd felt guilty about spending time alone with Connor, but she had needed that time. Between their bouts of lovemaking, Connor had taught her about the shifter realm and what it was to be a wolf shifter.

She couldn't wait to explore all the places he'd told her about, and to meet new people, but it would have to wait. She needed to be involved in tracking down the bad guy. Not to mention, the witch that had helped him. Both of them needed to be stopped before they could do any more damage.

She wouldn't change her new life with Connor for anything, but that didn't mean she wanted other people to go through what she'd gone through.

Connor pulled her into his arms and kissed her on the top of her head. "Don't worry, my love, we'll find them."

"I know we will," she said, as she snuggled into his arms.

She had no doubt they would find the culprits. She just wished it was sooner rather than later.

And then there was Sasha. There still hadn't been any word from her. Anya was beginning to worry that something bad had happened to her friend, but she didn't know what.

Anya didn't even know where to start looking for Sasha. From what Connor and the rest of them had told her about what Sasha could do, she was definitely not human.

She thought it was going to be difficult finding her before she found out about the other realms. Now that she knew there were thousands of different realms, it seemed impossible.

Connor assured her they wouldn't stop looking for Sasha, but there was only so much he could do as well. Especially since they still didn't know if she'd left the warehouse willingly, or if she'd been taken. Until they found her, they wouldn't know the answer.

The conversation in the room quickly turned to happier topics. Anya looked around the room at all the smiling faces as everybody talked and laughed.

She couldn't believe how quickly she'd been accepted as one of them. Anya had always dreamed of having a family. Now she had one. And the best part, was Connor.

She turned her face up to him and smiled. "I love you."

He instantly returned her smile. "I love you too."

With her heart full of love, for the first time in her life, she looked forward to the future. A future with the man of her dreams by her side.

Epilogue

He was fuming with the witch. If he ever laid eyes on her again, he was going to rip her to pieces. He knew she had something to do with the shifters finding them, he just couldn't prove it. Not yet, anyway.

If it wasn't for his backup plan, they probably would have caught him. The demons had held them back long enough for him to get the evidence of his success on camera. Unfortunately, it also meant he could no longer use the warehouse and office space because it had been compromised.

Thankfully, he wasn't stupid enough to keep all his eggs in one basket. So, he may have lost Anya and everything at the warehouse, but he wasn't defeated.

It didn't matter if Anya told the shifter about him. Even if she gave a detailed description of him, it didn't matter. There wasn't anything they could do to stop him. Not now. Not ever.

Nobody was going to interfere with his plans. Especially not the wolf shifters.

***

Sasha paced the small cage. She didn't know where she was, or who had taken her, but she was going to find out.

The last thing she remembered before waking up in the cage was fighting alongside the wolf shifters. She didn't know if they had won the fight, or even if Connor had rescued Anya.

She hoped Anya was okay. After what she'd been dealt with in life, she deserved happiness. And Connor would do anything to make her happy. Any male wolf shifter would want to do that for their mate, and Anya was definitely Connor's mate.

It had been in his eyes the moment he'd seen her lying in the bed at the medical centre.

Sasha didn't doubt the wolf shifters could have defeated the demons in her absence, but she would have like to be there when they found Anya. She had been a good friend. One of Sasha's only friends.

She wanted to know if Anya had been turned into a wolf shifter, as she suspected. Sasha bet she was a beautiful wolf. But she would have to wait to find out.

First, she needed to get out of the cage she was being held in. Which was going to be easier said than done.

Whoever had taken her, knew how to hold her. And that meant, they knew who she was.

Midnight Unchained

Prologue

Three days she waited, plotting her escape. Now the time was here, Nessa didn't know if she was strong enough to make it out on her own. Lack of food and water made her weak. But she had to try, she couldn't stay here. It wasn't safe.

When she first woke up in this dark dank cell three days ago, she thought she must be stuck in a nightmare. It wasn't unusual for her to have this nightmare, but normally she woke up when the bad guys came for her. This time she hadn't.

When the bad guys came for her, she had gone to sleep instead. Minding her own business as she made her way home from work late one night, two men and a woman had appeared out of nowhere. The men had grabbed hold of her arms so she couldn't get away.

If Nessa had expected the woman to help her, then she had been sorely mistaken. Instead of helping, the woman blew some powder into her face that knocked her out cold within seconds. Later on, when she finally woke up, she found herself locked in this god-awful place.

The stench of rotting meat permeated the air. Scurrying sounds were constant as rodents ran rampant, not only around the building but the room she was occupying as well.

Every time her captors had brought her food it had been crawling with cockroaches. Nessa knew she needed the sustenance if she stood any chance in escaping, but no matter how hungry she was, she couldn't bring herself to eat any of it.

It was bad enough drinking what passed for water around here. She was sure it was more mud than water, and the smell alone was enough to make anyone want to vomit. Pinching her nose whenever she had to drink any of it so she didn't have to smell it at the same time, then fighting to keep it down when it wanted to come straight back up again.

There wasn't much in the room she could use to aid her in escaping this place, but she would not let that stop her either. One way or another, she was getting out of here today.

The few items in the room she could choose from were a metal bed with a mattress that had seen far better days, a paper-thin pillow and a rough blanket. Plus, there was her personal favourite... a bucket in the corner of the room for her to use as a toilet. Yeah, it was definitely no five-star hotel.

When she had spotted the screws holding the bedposts in place, she could've jumped for joy. It was the perfect size and shape to use as a bat. And that's exactly what she would use it as. Not wasting any time, she had set to work on one of the posts.

Choosing the post that was wedged in the corner so it wasn't visible to the guards, she carefully pulled the bed out a little so she would have better access. Using her fingers and nails until they bled, she coaxed the screws loose with no one being the wiser about what she was doing.

Whenever she heard movement in the hallway, she quickly returned the bed to its original position as quietly as she could. The last thing she needed was for them to figure out what she planned before she had a chance to carry it through.

Finally, after days of trying, the last of the screws were out and the post was free. Now all she had to do was wait for the guards to return. All the hairs on her body stood on end as she listened to them walking past her door.

It was the same every day. Like clockwork, two guards walked along the corridor. Starting from the far end, they stopped at each room, handing out food and water to the occupants. Hers was somewhere around the middle. She didn't know if every room had someone inside, and she didn't know how many rooms there were, but she assumed that most did.

Ready to pounce the moment they opened the door, holding the metal post above her head, she didn't hesitate when the first guard stepped inside. Swinging the metal post in a downward arch with all her strength, she whacked him on the top of his head. As he doubled over, she lifted her knee, connecting it with his face.

Ignoring the throbbing pain radiating from her knee where it made an impact with the guard's face, she turned her attention to the other guard. It took the second guard a moment for it to sink in what had happened to his comrade, which gave her the advantage she was counting on.

Before he could react, she pulled back her arms and then swung the metal post straight into his face. Blood instantly squirted from his nose as the post made contact. When he lifted his hands to his face, she kneed him between the legs, dropping him instantly to the ground.

Nessa hit him over the head for good measure before grabbing the keys from where they landed on the floor and made her escape. Using the door to push the second guard further into the room, she quickly locked it behind her so they couldn't follow her straight away.

She didn't bother stopping at any of the other rooms. If she was going to get away before the others noticed she was missing, then she couldn't stop to help anyone else. The best thing she could do for them now was to escape and get help.

With a rough idea of the layout of the building, she was as prepared as she was going to be. Sending up a silent prayer, she took a deep breath and crept along the corridor to the door at the far end.

There was a stairwell on the other side of the door. She knew what was downstairs, it led further into the building and that was the last place she wanted to go. They had taken her down there not long after she arrived here.

Nessa shuddered at the memories of what they did to her while she was down there, she definitely didn't want a repeat of that experience.

No, she wanted to go up. That was the only way she hadn't been, at least not that she could remember, so she assumed that it was the way out. She didn't even care if it took her to the roof, as long as she wasn't in this building anymore. Nessa would shout for help from the rooftop if it came to it.

The door at the end of the corridor creaked as she opened it. Nessa froze, listening for any sounds. Only when she was certain no one heard it did she open the door further, just enough for her to squeeze through, then she closed it again as quietly as she could.

Making her way up the stairs, she listened intently for any sounds coming from either direction. Nessa didn't bother stopping to look through each door on her way up the stairwell; she didn't care what was behind them. It was only when she reached the top that she finally went through a door.

The bright sunlight blinded her momentarily. When her eyes adjusted to the light, she looked around at an empty rooftop.

Typical, she thought, *but at least I'm finally outside.*

It may be a small victory, but she was going to take it as a good sign that nobody else was up here. Now she just needed to find a fire escape to climb down.

Taking a deep breath of fresh air, she stepped outside, closing the door behind her. Nessa walked the perimeter of the building as she looked for the fire escape.

She sighed in relief when she found it. Even though it was only a few metal bars sticking out of the wall, it was still a way off this roof, and she was going to take anything she could to get away from this place.

Without a second thought, Nessa carefully maneuvered over the side of the building and climbed down the ladder. The cold metal bars, rusted with age, froze her bare hands and feet. Wishing she had more clothing on than just a pair of shorts and a vest top, she tried not to let the cold slow her down.

Reaching the bottom of the ladder, Nessa looked around to see which direction to go. All she could see was woodland. She couldn't even see a road leading through the woods from where she stood.

Not letting that stop her, Nessa picked what she hoped was north, then raced off into the woods. Sooner or later she was bound to come across civilization. Nessa just hoped it was sooner rather than later.

With what little energy she had left in her, she didn't think she would make it very far on foot.

Howling came from the building behind her, along with the sound of people shouting. They were trying to find her. She knew that it wouldn't take them long to realize she had escaped and to send out a search party to find her, but she hadn't thought it would be that quick.

Digging deep, Nessa pulled up the last of her energy reserves and ran as fast as she could. Not expecting it to have much effect, she was surprised with the speed and agility she could pull off with what little energy she had left.

Before she knew it, she broke through the tree line and was next to a busy dual carriageway. She risked looking back to see if anyone was following her. She could just about make out movement in the woods as they headed in her direction.

With no time to spare, Nessa started waving down cars and shouting "Help!" as she walked backward along the side of the road. All the while she kept trying to gain more distance between her and the bad guys.

It seemed like forever before one car finally pulled over. She raced over to it, praying it wasn't one of the bad guys. Luck was on her side for once as she looked through the open window and saw it was a little old lady behind the wheel.

"Are you okay?" she asked.

"No, nowhere close to being okay, but I'm hoping you can help remedy that," she said honestly. "Could you please give me a lift?"

"Of course," the lady said with a smile.

"Thank you so much. You don't know how much this means to me," Nessa said as she climbed in the car.

"Where would you like me to take you, dear?" the lady asked. "Do you need to go to the hospital?"

"No, could you drop me off at the closest police station please?" Nessa asked.

"Are you sure you don't want a hospital?"

"I'm positive. Please, just the police station, as soon

as possible."

Nessa knew they were getting closer, and the longer she sat here talking, the more chance they had of catching her before she could truly get away.

The little old lady looked her over, concern showing on her face, but without another word, she put her foot down and they sped off.

Nessa looked back just in time to see the bad guys break through the tree line. She hoped they hadn't seen her getting into the car.

***

Dear reader

I hope you enjoyed reading this book as much as I
enjoyed writing it.
Please could you take a moment to leave a review,
even if it's only a line or two, about what you thought
of the book.
Also, if you'd like to know about upcoming new
releases, sneak-peeks, and special offers you can sign
up to my newsletter. You can also find me on
Facebook, Bookbub, and Goodreads.

Thank you and much love.

Georgina.

www.georginastancer.co.uk
www.facebook.com/AuthorGeorginaStancer
www.bookbub.com/profile/georgina-stancer
www.goodreads.com/author/show/18724439.Georgina_Stancer

Guarded by Night series

Connor's New Wolf
Midnight Unchained
Darkest Bane

Infernal Hearts series

Heart of the Hunted
Heart of the Damned
Heart of the Cursed (coming soon)

Printed in Great Britain
by Amazon